AN EXCELLENT MYSTERY

D0037370

Other Brother Cadfael novels by the same author:

A MORBID TASTE FOR BONES
ONE CORPSE TOO MANY
MONK'S-HOOD
SAINT PETER'S FAIR
THE LEPER OF SAINT GILES
THE VIRGIN IN THE ICE
THE SANCTUARY SPARROW
THE DEVIL'S NOVICE
DEAD MAN'S RANSOM
THE PILGRIM OF HATE
THE RAVEN IN THE FOREGATE

Ellis Peters

AN EXCELLENT MYSTERY

Futura

A Futura Book

First published in Great Britain in 1985
by Macmillan London Limited

This Futura edition published in 1986
Reprinted 1986, 1987, 1989

ISBN 0 7088 2867 1

Printed and bound in Great Britain by
Hazell Watson & Viney Limited
Member of BPCC Limited
Aylesbury, Bucks, England

Futura Publications
A Division of
Macdonald & Co (Publishers) Ltd
66–73 Shoe Lane
London EC4P 4AB
A member of Maxwell Pergamon Publishing Corporation plc

ONE

August came in, that summer of 1141, tawny as a lion and somnolent and purring as a hearthside cat. After the plenteous rains of the spring the weather had settled into angelic calm and sunlight for the feast of Saint Winifred, and preserved the same benign countenance throughout the corn harvest. Lammas came for once strict to its day, the wheat-fields were already gleaned and white, ready for the flocks and herds that would be turned into them to make use of what aftermath the season brought. The loaf-Mass had been celebrated with great contentment, and the early plums in the orchard along the riverside were darkening into ripeness. The abbey barns were full, the well-dried straw bound and stacked, and if there was still no rain to bring on fresh green fodder in the reaped fields for the sheep, there were heavy morning dews. When this golden weather broke at last, it might well break in violent storms, but as yet the skies remained bleached and clear, the palest imaginable blue.

'Fat smiles on the faces of the husbandmen,' said Hugh Beringar, fresh from his own harvest in the north of the shire, and burned nut-brown from his work in the fields, 'and chaos among the kings. If they had to grow their own corn, mill their own flour and bake their own bread they might have no time left for all the squabbling and killing. Well, thank God for present mercies, and God keep the killing well away from us here. Not that I rate it the less ill-fortune for being there in the south, but this shire is my field, and my people, mine to keep. I have enough to do to mind my own, and when I see them brown and rosy and fat, with full byres and barns, and a high wool tally in good quality fleeces, I'm content.'

They had met by chance at the corner of the abbey wall,

5

where the Foregate turned right towards Saint Giles, and beside it the great grassy triangle of the horse-fair ground opened, pallid and pockmarked in the sun. The three-day annual fair of Saint Peter was more than a week past, the stalls taken down, the merchants departed. Hugh sat aloft on his raw-boned and cross-grained grey horse, tall enough to carry a heavyweight instead of this light, lean young man whose mastery he tolerated, though he had precious little love for any other human creature. It was no responsibility of the sheriff of Shropshire to see that the fairground was properly vacated and cleared after its three-day occupation, but for all that Hugh liked to view the ground for himself. It was his officers who had to keep order there, and make sure the abbey stewards were neither cheated of their fees nor robbed or otherwise abused in collecting them. That was over now for another year. And here were the signs of it, the dappling of post-holes, the pallid oblongs of the stalls, the green fringes, and the trampled, bald paths between the booths. From sun-starved bleach to lush green, and back to the pallor again, with patches of tough, flat clover surviving in the trodden paths like round green footprints of some strange beast.

'One good shower would put all right,' said Brother Cadfael, eyeing the curious chessboard of blanched and bright with a gardener's eye. 'There's nothing in the world so strong as grass.'

He was on his way from the abbey of Saint Peter and Saint Paul to its chapel and hospital of Saint Giles, half a mile away at the very rim of the town. It was one of his duties to keep the medicine cupboard there well supplied with all the remedies the inmates might require, and he made this journey every couple of weeks, more often in times of increased habitation and need. On this particular early morning in August he had with him young Brother Oswin, who had worked with him among the herbs for more than a year, and was now on his way to put his skills into practice among the most needy. Oswin was sturdy, well-grown, glowing with enthusiasm. Time had been when he had cost plenty in breakages, in pots burned beyond recovery, and deceptive herbs gathered by mistake for others only too like them. Those times were over. All he needed now to be a treasure to the hospital was a cool-headed superior who would know when to curb his zeal. The abbey had the right of appointment, and the lay head they had installed would be more than proof against Brother Oswin's too exuberant energy.

'You had a good fair, after all,' said Hugh.

'Better than ever I expected, with half the south cut off by the trouble in Winchester. They got here from Flanders,' said Cadfael appreciatively. East Anglia was no very peaceful ground just now, but the wool merchants were a tough breed, and would not let a little bloodshed and danger bar them off from a good profit.

'It was a fine wool clip.' Hugh had flocks of his own on his manor of Maesbury, in the north, he knew about the quality of the year's fleeces. There had been good buying in from Wales, too, all along this border. Shrewsbury had ties of blood, sympathy and mutual gain with the Welsh of both Powys and Gwynedd, whatever occasional explosions of racial exuberance might break the guarded peace. In this summer the peace with Gwynedd held firm, under the capable hand of Owain Gwynedd, since they had a shared interest in containing the ambitions of Earl Ranulf of Chester. Powys was less predictable, but had drawn in its horns of late after several times blunting them painfully on Hugh's precautions.

'And the corn harvest the best for years. As for the fruit . . . It *looks* well,' said Cadfael cautiously, 'if we get some good rains soon to swell it, and no thunderstorms before it's gathered. Well, the corn's in and the straw stacked, and as good a hay crop as we've had since my memory holds. You'll not hear me complain.'

But for all that, he thought, looking back in mild surprise, it had been an unchancy sort of year, overturning the fortunes of kings and empresses not once, but twice, while benignly smiling upon the festivities of the church and the hopeful labours of ordinary men, at least here in the midlands. February had seen King Stephen made prisoner at the disastrous battle of Lincoln, and swept away into close confinement in Bristol castle by his arch-enemy, cousin and rival claimant to the throne of England, the Empress Maud. A good many coats had been changed in haste after that reversal, not least that of Stephen's brother and Maud's cousin, Henry

7

of Blois, Bishop of Winchester and papal legate, who had delicately hedged his wager and come round to the winning side, only to find that he would have done well to drag his feet a little longer. For the fool woman, with the table spread for her at Westminster and the crown all but touching her hair, had seen fit to conduct herself in so arrogant and overbearing a manner towards the citizens of London that they had risen in fury to drive her out in ignominious flight, and let King Stephen's valiant queen into the city in her place.

Not that this last spin of the wheel could set King Stephen free. On the contrary, report said it had caused him to be loaded with chains by way of extra security, he being the one formidable weapon the empress still had in her hand. But it had certainly snatched the crown from Maud's head, most probably for ever, and it had cost her the not inconsiderable support of Bishop Henry, who was not the man to be over-hasty in his alliances twice in one year. Rumour said the lady had sent her half-brother and best champion, Earl Robert of Gloucester, to Winchester to set things right with the bishop and lure him back to her side, but without getting a straight answer. Rumour said also, and probably on good grounds, that Stephen's queen had already forestalled her, at a private meeting with Henry at Guildford, and got rather more sympathy from him than the empress had succeeded in getting. And doubtless Maud had heard of it. For the latest news, brought by latecomers from the south to the abbey fair, was that the empress with a hastily gathered army had marched to Winchester and taken up residence in the royal castle there. What her next move was to be must be a matter of anxious speculation to the bishop, even in his own city.

And meantime, here in Shrewsbury the sun shone, the abbey celebrated its maiden saint with joyous solemnity, the flocks flourished, the harvest whitened and was gathered in exemplary weather, the annual fair took its serene course through the first three days of August, and traders came from far and wide, conducted their brisk business, took their profits, made their shrewd purchases, and scattered again in peace to return to their own homes, as though neither king nor empress existed, or had any power to hamper the movements or threaten the lives of ordinary, sensible men.

'You'll have heard nothing new since the merchants left?' Cadfael asked, scanning the blanched traces their stalls had left behind.

'Nothing yet. It seems they're eyeing each other across the city, each waiting for the other to make a move. Winchester must be holding its breath. The last word is that the empress sent for Bishop Henry to come to her at the castle, and he has sent a soft answer that he is preparing himself for the meeting. But stirred not a foot, so far, to move within reach of her. But for all that,' said Hugh thoughtfully, 'I dare wager he's preparing, sure enough. She has mustered her forces, he'll be calling up his before ever he goes near her – *if* he does!'

'And while they hold their breath, you may breathe more freely,' said Cadfael shrewdly.

Hugh laughed. 'While my enemies fall out, at least it keeps their minds off me and mine. Even if they come to terms again, and she wins him back, there's at least a few weeks' delay gained for the king's party. If not – why, better they should tear each other than save their arrows for us.'

'Do you think he'll stand out against her?'

'She has treated him as haughtily as she does every man, when he did her good menial service. Now he has half-defied her he may well be reflecting that she takes very unkindly to being thwarted, and that a bishop can be clapped in chains as easily as a king, once she lays hands on him. No, I fancy his lordship is stocking his own castle of Wolvesey to withstand a siege, if it comes to that, and calling up his men in haste. Who bargains with the empress had better bargain from behind an army.'

'The queen's army?' demanded Cadfael, sharp-eyed.

Hugh had begun to wheel his horse back towards the town, but he looked round over a bare brown shoulder with a flashing glint of black eyes. 'That we shall see! I would guess the first courier ever he sent out for aid went to Queen Matilda.'

'Brother Cadfael . . . ' began Oswin, trotting jauntily beside him as they walked on towards the rim of the town, where the hospital and its chapel rose plain and grey within their long wattle fence.

'Yes, son?'

'Would even the empress really dare lay hands on the Bishop of Winchester? The Holy Father's legate here?'

'Who can tell? But there's not much she will not dare.'

'But . . . That there could be fighting between them . . .'

Oswin puffed out his round young cheeks in a great breath of wonder and deprecation. Such a thing seemed to him unimaginable. 'Brother, you have been in the world and have experience of wars and battles. And I know that there were bishops and great churchmen went to do battle for the Holy Sepulchre, as you did, but should they be found in arms for any lesser cause?'

Whether they should, thought Cadfael, is for them to take up with their judge in the judgement, but that they are so found, have been aforetime and will be hereafter, is beyond doubt. 'To be charitable,' he said cautiously, 'in this case his lordship may consider his own freedom, safety and life to be a very worthy cause. Some have been called to accept martyrdom meekly, but that should surely be for nothing less than their faith. And a dead bishop could be of little service to his church, and a legate mouldering in prison little profit to the Holy Father.'

Brother Oswin strode beside for some moments judicially mute, digesting that plea and apparently finding it somewhat dubious, or else suspecting that he had not fully comprehended the argument. Then he asked ingenuously: 'Brother, would *you* take arms again? Once having renounced them? For *any* cause?'

'Son,' said Cadfael, 'you have the knack of asking questions which cannot be answered. How do I know what I would do, in extreme need? As a brother of the Order I would wish to keep my hands from violence against any, but for all that, I hope I would not turn my back if I saw innocence or helplessness being abused. Bear in mind even the bishops carry a crook, meant to protect the flock as well as guide it. Let princes and empresses and warriors mind their own duties, you give all your mind to yours, and you'll do well.'

They were nearing the trodden path that led up a grassy slope to the open gate in the wattle fence. The modest turret of the chapel eyed them over the roof of the hospice. Brother

Oswin bounded up the slope eagerly, his cherubic face bright with confidence, bound for a new field of endeavour, and certain of mastering it. There was probably no pitfall here he would evade, but none of them would hold him for long, or damp his unquenchable ardour.

'Now remember all I've taught you,' said Cadfael. 'Be obedient to Brother Simon. You will work for a time under him, as he did under Brother Mark. The superior is a layman from the Foregate, but you'll see little of him between his occasional visitations and inspections, and he's a good soul and listens to counsel. And I shall be in attendance every now and again, should you ever need me. Come, and I'll show you where everything is.'

Brother Simon was a comfortable, round man in his forties. He came out to meet them at the porch, with a gangling boy of about twelve by the hand. The child's eyes were white with the caul of blindness, but otherwise he was whole and comely, by no means the saddest sight to be found here, where the infected and diseased might find at once a refuge and a prison for their contagion, since they were not permitted to carry it into the streets of the town, among the uncorrupted. There were cripples sunning themselves in the little orchard behind the hospice, old, pox-riddled men, and faded women in the barn plaiting bands for the straw stooks as they were stacked. Those who could work a little were glad to do so for their keep, those who could not were passive in the sun, unless they had skin rashes which the heat only aggravated. These kept under the shade of the fruit-trees, or those most fevered in the chill of the chapel.

'As at present,' said Brother Simon, 'we have eighteen, which is not so ill, for so hot a season. Three are able-bodied, and mending of their sickness, which was not contagious, and they'll be on their way within days now. But there'll be others, young man, there'll always be others. They come and go. Some by the roads, some out of this world's bane. None the worse, I hope, for passing through that door in this place.'

He had a slightly preaching style which caused Cadfael to smile inwardly, remembering Mark's lovely simplicity, but he was a good man, hard-working, compassionate, and very deft with those big hands of his. Oswin would drink in his solemn homilies with reverence and wonder, and go about his work refreshed and unquestioning.

'I'll see the lad round myself, if you'll let me,' said Cadfael, hitching forward the laden scrip at his girdle. 'I've brought you all the medicaments you asked for, and some I thought might be needed, besides. We'll find you when we're done.'

'And the news of Brother Mark?' asked Simon.

'Mark is already deacon. I have but to save my most fearful confession a few more years, then, if need be, I'll depart in peace.'

'According to Mark's word?' wondered Simon, revealing unsuspected depths, and smiling to gloss them over. It was not often he spoke at such a venture.

'Well,' said Cadfael very thoughtfully, 'I've always found Mark's word good enough for me. You may well be right.' And he turned to Oswin, who had followed this exchange with a face dutifully attentive and bewilderedly smiling, earnest to understand what evaded him like thistledown. 'Come on, lad, let's unload these and be rid of the weight first, and then I'll show you all that goes on here at Saint Giles.'

They passed through the hall, which was for eating and for sleeping, except for those too sick to be left among their healthier fellows. There was a large locked cupboard, to which Cadfael had his own key, and its shelves within were full of jars, flasks, bottles, wooden boxes for tablets, ointments, syrups, lotions, all the products of Cadfael's workshop. They unloaded their scrips and filled the gaps along the shelves. Oswin enlarged with the importance of this mystery into which he had been initiated, and which he was now to practise in earnest.

There was a small kitchen garden behind the hospice, and an orchard, and barns for storage. Cadfael conducted his charge round the entire enclave, and by the end of the circuit they had three of the inmates in close and curious attendance, the old man who tended the cabbages and showed off his produce with pride, a lame youth herpling along nimbly enough on two crutches, and the blind child, who had forsaken Brother Simon to attach himself to Cadfael's girdle, knowing the familiar voice.

'This is Warin,' said Cadfael, taking the boy by the hand as they made their way back to Brother Simon's little desk in the porch. 'He sings well in chapel, and knows the office by heart. But you'll soon know them all by name.'

Brother Simon rose from his accounts at sight of them returning. 'He's shown you everything? It's no great household, ours, but it does a great work. You'll soon get used to us.'

Oswin beamed and blushed, and said that he would do his best. It was likely that he was waiting impatiently for his mentor to depart, so that he could begin to exercise his new responsibility without the uneasiness of a pupil performing before his teacher. Cadfael clouted him cheerfully on the shoulder, bade him be good, in the tones of one having no doubts on that score, and turned towards the gate. They had moved out into the sunlight from the dimness of the porch.

'You've heard no fresh news from the south?' The denizens of Saint Giles, being encountered at the very edge of the town, were usually beforehand with news.

'Nothing to signify. And yet a man must wonder and speculate. There was a beggar, able-bodied but getting old, who came in three days ago, and stayed only overnight to rest. He was from the Staceys, near Andover, a queer one, perhaps a mite touched in his wits, who can tell? He gets notions, it seems, that move him on into fresh pastures, and when they come to him he must go. He said he got word in his head that he had best get away northwards while there was time.'

'A man of those parts who had no property to tie him might very well get the same notion now,' said Cadfael ruefully, 'without being in want of his wits. Indeed, it might be his wits that advised him to move on.'

'So it might. But this fellow said – if he did not dream it – that the day he set out he looked back from a hilltop, and saw smoke in clouds over Winchester, and in the night following there was a red glow all above the city, that flickered as if with still quick flames.'

'It could be true,' said Cadfael, and gnawed a considering lip. 'It would come as no great surprise. The last firm news we had was that empress and bishop were holding off cautiously from each other, and shifting for position. A little patience . . . But she was never, it seems, a patient woman. I wonder, now, I wonder if she has laid him under siege. How long would your man have been on the road?'

'I fancy he made what haste he could,' said Simon, 'but four days at least, surely. That sets his story a week back, and no word yet to confirm it.'

'There will be, if it's true,' said Cadfael grimly, 'there will be! Of all the reports that fly about the world, ill news is the surest of all to arrive!'

He was still pondering this ominous shadow as he set off back along the Foregate, and his preoccupation was such that his greetings to acquaintances along the way were apt to be belated and absent-minded. It was mid-morning, and the dusty road brisk with traffic, and there were few inhabitants of this parish of Holy Cross outside the town walls that he did not know. He had treated many of them, or their children, at some time in these his cloistered years; even, sometimes, their beasts, for he who learns about the sicknesses of men cannot but pick up, here and there, some knowledge of the sicknesses of their animals, creatures with as great a capacity for suffering as their masters, and much less means of complaining, together with far less inclination to complain. Cadfael had often wished that men would use their beasts better, and tried to show them that it would be good husbandry. The horses of war had been part of that curious, slow process within him that had turned him at length from the trade of arms into the cloister.

Not that all abbots and priors used their mules and stock beasts well, either. But at least the best and wisest of them recognised it for good policy, as well as good Christianity.

But now, what could really be happening in Winchester, to turn the sky over it black by day and red by night? Like the pillars of cloud and fire that marked the passage of the elect through the wilderness, these had signalled and guided the beggar's flight from danger. He saw no reason to doubt the report. The same foreboding must have been on many loftier minds these last weeks, while the hot, dry summer, close cousin of fire, waited with a torch ready. But what a fool that woman must be, to attempt to besiege the bishop in his own castle in his own city, with the queen, every inch her match, no great distance away at the head of a strong army, and the

Londoners implacably hostile. And how adamant against her, now, the bishop must be, to venture all by defying her. And both these high personages would remain strongly protected, and survive. But what of the lesser creatures they put in peril? Poor little traders and craftsmen and labourers who had no such fortresses to shelter them!

He had meditated his way from the care of horses and cattle to the tribulations of men, and was startled to hear at his back, at a moment when the traffic of the Foregate was light, the crisp, neat hooves of mules catching up on him at a steady clip. He halted at the corner of the horse-fair ground and looked back, and had not far to look, for they were close.

Two of them, a fine, tall beast almost pure white, fit for an abbot, and a smaller, lighter, fawn-brown creature stepping decorously a pace or two to the rear. But what caused Cadfael to pull up and turn fully towards them, waiting in surprised welcome for them to draw alongside, was the fact that both riders wore the Benedictine black, brothers to each other and to him. Plainly they had noted his own habit trudging before them, and made haste to overtake him, for as soon as he halted and recognised them for his like they eased to a walk, and so came gently alongside him.

'God be with you, brothers!' said Cadfael, eyeing them with interest. 'Do you come to our house here in Shrewsbury?'

'And with you, brother,' said the foremost rider, in a rich voice which yet had a slight, harsh crepitation in it, as though the cave of his breast created a grating echo. Cadfael's ears pricked at the sound. He had heard the breath of many old men, long exposed to harsh outdoor living, rasp and echo in the same way, but this man was not old. 'You belong to this house of Saint Peter and Saint Paul? Yes, we are bound there with letters for the lord abbot. I take this to be his boundary wall beside us? Then it is not far to go now.'

'Very close,' said Cadfael. 'I'll walk beside you, for I'm homeward bound to that same house. Have you come far?'

He was looking up into a face gaunt and drawn, but fine-featured and commanding, with deep-set eyes very dark and tranquil. The cowl was flung back on the stranger's shoulders, and the long, fleshless head wore its rondel of straight black hair like a crown. A tall man, sinewy but emaciated. There was the fading sunburn of hotter lands than England on him, a bronze acquired over more years than one, but turned somewhat dull and sickly now, and though he held himself in the saddle like one born there, there was also a languor upon his movements, and an uncomplaining weariness in his face, a serene resignation which would better have fitted an old man. This man might have been somewhere in his mid-forties, surely not much more.

'Far enough,' he said with a thin, dark smile, 'but today only from Brigge.'

'And bound further? Or will you stay with us for a while? You'll be heartily welcome visitors, you and the young brother here.'

The younger rider hovered silently, a little apart, as a servant might have done in dutiful attendance on his master. He was surely scarcely past twenty, lissome and tall, though his companion would top him by a head if they stood together. He had the oval, smooth, boy's face of his years, but formed and firm for all its suave planes. His cowl was drawn forward over his face, perhaps against the sun's glare. Large, shadowed eyes gazed out from the hood, fixed steadily upon his elder. The one glance they flashed at Cadfael was as quickly averted.

'We look to stay here for some time, if the lord abbot will give us refuge,' said the older man, 'for we have lost one roof, and must beg admittance under another.'

They had begun to move on at a leisurely walk, the dust of the Foregate powder-fine under the hooves of the mules. The young man fell in meekly behind, and let them lead. To the civil greetings that saluted them along the way, where Cadfael was well known, and these his companions matter for friendly curiosity, the older man made quiet, courteous response. The younger said never a word.

The gatehouse and the church loomed, ahead on their left, the high wall beside them reflected heat from its stones. The rider let the reins hang loose on his mule's neck, folded veined hands, long-fingered and brown, and fetched a long sigh. Cadfael held his peace.

'Forgive me that I answer almost churlishly, brother, it is not meant so. After the habit and the daily company of silence, speech comes laboriously. And after a holocaust, and the fires

16

of destruction, the throat is too dry to manage many words. You asked if we had come far. We have been some days on the road, for I cannot ride hard these days. We are come like beggars from the south . . . '

'From Winchester!' said Cadfael with certainty, recalling the foreboding, the cloud and the fire.

'From what is left of Winchester.' The worn but muscular hands were quite still, leaving it to Cadfael to lead the mule round the west end of the church and in at the arch of the gatehouse. It was not grief or passion that made it hard for the man to speak, he had surely seen worse in his time than he was now recalling. The chords of his voice creaked from under-use, and slowed upon the grating echo. A beautiful voice it must have been in its heyday, before the velvet frayed. 'Is it possible,' he said wonderingly, 'that we come the first? I had thought word would have flown thus far north almost a week ago, but true, escape this way would have been no simple matter. Have we to bring the news, then? The great ones fell out over us. Who am I to complain, who have had my part in the like, elsewhere? The empress laid siege to the bishop in his castle of Wolvesey, in the city, and the bishop rained fire-arrows down upon the roofs rather than upon his enemies. The town is laid waste. A nunnery burned to the ground, churches razed, and my priory of Hyde Mead, that Bishop Henry so desired to take into his own hands, is gone for ever, brought down in flames. We are here, we two, homeless and asking shelter. The brothers are scattered through all the Benedictine houses of the land, wherever they have ties of blood or friendship. There will never be any going home to Hyde.'

So it was true. The finger of God had pointed one poor devil out of the trap, and let him look back from a hill to see the scarlet and the black of fire and smoke devour a city. Bishop Henry's own city, to which his own hand had set light.

'God sort all!' said Cadfael.

'Doubtless he will!' The voice with its honeyed warmth and abrasive echo rang under the archway of the gatehouse. Brother Porter came out, smiling welcome, and a groom came running for the horses, sighting fraternal visitors. The great court opened serene in sunshine, crossed and re-crossed by

17

busy, preoccupied people, brothers, lay brothers, stewards, all about their normal, mastered affairs. The child oblates and schoolboys, let loose from their studies, were tossing a ball, their shrill voices gay and piercing in the still half-hour before noon. Life here made itself heard, felt and seen, as regular as the seasons.

They halted within the gate. Cadfael held the stirrup for the stranger, though there was no need, for he lighted down as naturally as a bird settling and folding its wings; but slowly, with languid grace, and stood to unfold a long, graceful but enfeebled body, well above six feet tall, and lance-straight as it was lance-lean. The young one had leaped from the saddle in an instant, and stood baulked, circling uneasily, jealous of Cadfael's ministering hand. And still made no sound, neither of gratitude nor protest.

'I'll be your herald to Abbot Radulfus,' said Cadfael, 'if you'll permit. What shall I say to him?'

'Say that Brother Humilis and Brother Fidelis, of the sometime priory of Hyde Mead, which is laid waste, ask audience and protection of his goodness, in all submission, and in the name of the Rule.'

This man had surely known little in the past of humility, and little of submission, though he had embraced both now with a whole heart.

'I will say so,' said Cadfael, and turned for a moment to the young brother, expecting his amen. The cowled head inclined modestly, the oval face was hidden in shadow, but there was no voice.

'Hold my young friend excused,' said Brother Humilis, erect by his mule's milky head, 'if he cannot speak his greeting. Brother Fidelis is dumb.'

TWO

'Bring our brothers in to me,' said Abbot Radulfus, rising from his desk in surprise and concern when Cadfael had reported to him the arrivals, and the bare bones of their story. He pushed aside parchment and pen and stood erect, dark and tall against the brilliant sunlight through the parlour window. 'That this should ever be! City and church laid waste together! Certainly they are welcome here lifelong, if need be. Bring them hither, Cadfael. And remain with us. You may be their guide afterwards, and bring them to Prior Robert. We must make appropriate places for them in the dortoir.'

Cadfael went on his errand well content not to be dismissed, and led the newcomers down the length of the great court to the corner where the abbot's lodging lay sheltered in its small garden. What there was to be learned from the travellers of affairs in the south he was eager to learn, and so would Hugh be, when he knew of their coming. For this time news had been unwontedly slow on the road, and matters might have been moving with considerably greater speed down in Winchester since the unlucky brothers of Hyde dispersed to seek refuge elsewhere.

'Father Abbot, here are Brother Humilis and Brother Fidelis.'

It seemed dark in the little wood-panelled parlour after the radiance without, and the two tall, masterful men stood studying each other intently in the warm, shadowy stillness. Radulfus himself had drawn forward stools for the newcomers, and with a motion of a long hand invited them to be seated, but the young one drew back deferentially into deeper shadow and remained standing. He could never be the spokesman; that might well be the reason for his self-effacement. But

19

Radulfus, who had yet to learn of the young man's disability, certainly noted the act, and observed it without either approval or disapproval.

'Brothers, you are very welcome in our house, and all we can provide is yours. I hear you have had a long ride, and a sad loss that has driven you forth. I grieve for our brothers of Hyde. But here at least we hope to offer you tranquillity of mind, and a secure shelter. In these lamentable wars we have been fortunate. You, the elder, are Brother Humilis?'

'Yes, Father. Here I present you our prior's letter, commending us both to your kindness.' He had carried it in the breast of his habit, and now drew it forth and laid it on the abbot's desk. 'You will know, Father, that the abbey of Hyde has been an abbey without an abbot for two years now. They say commonly that Bishop Henry had it in mind to bring it into his own hands as an episcopal convent, which the brothers strongly resisted, and denying us a head may well have been a move designed to weaken us and reduce our voice. Now that is of no consequence, for the house of Hyde is gone, razed to the ground and blackened by fire.'

'Is it such entire destruction?' asked Radulfus, frowning over his linked hands.

'Utter destruction. In time to come a new house may be raised there, who knows? But of the old nothing remains.'

'You had best tell me all that you can,' said Radulfus heavily. 'Here we live far from these events, almost in peace. How did this holocaust come about?'

Brother Humilis – what could his proud name have been before he thus calmly claimed for himself humility? – folded his hands in the lap of his habit, and fixed his hollow dark eyes upon the abbot's face. There was a creased scar, long ago healed and pale, marking the left side of his tonsure, Cadfael noted, and knew, the crescent shape of a glancing stroke from a right-handed swordsman. It did not surprise him. No straight western sword, but a Seljuk scimitar. So that was where he had got the bronze that had now faded and sickened into dun.

'The empress entered Winchester towards the end of July, I do not recall the date, and took up her residence in the royal castle by the west gate. She sent to Bishop Henry in his palace to come to her, but they say he sent back word that he would come, but must a little delay, by what excuse I never heard. He delayed too long, but by what followed he made good use of such days of grace as he had, for by the time the empress lost patience and moved up her forces against him he was safely shut up in his new castle of Wolvesey, in the south-east corner of the city, backed into the wall. And the queen, or so they said in the town, was moving her Flemings up in haste to his aid. Whether or no, he had a great garrison within there, and well supplied. I ask pardon of God and of you, Father,' said Brother Humilis gently, 'that I took such pains to follow these warlike reports, but my training was in arms, and a man cannot altogether forget.'

'God forbid,' said Radulfus, 'that a man should feel he need forget anything that was done in good faith and loyal service. In arms or in the cloister, we have all a score to pay to this country and this people. Closed eyes are of little use to either. Go on! Who struck the first blow?'

For they had been allies only a matter of weeks earlier!

'The empress. She moved to surround Wolvesey as soon as she knew he had shut himself in. Everything they had they used against the castle, even such engines as they were able to raise. And they pulled down any buildings, shops, houses, all that lay too close, to clear the ground. But the bishop had a strong garrison, and his walls are new. He began to build, as I hear, only ten years or so ago. It was his men who first used firebrands. Much of the city within the wall has burned, churches, a nunnery, shops – it might not have been so terrible if the season had not been high summer, and so dry.'

'And Hyde Mead?'

'There's no knowing from which side came the arrows that set us alight. The fighting had spilled outside the city walls by then, and there was looting, as always,' said Brother Humilis. 'We fought the fire as long as we could, but there was none besides to help us, and it was too fierce, we could not bring it under. Our prior ordered that we withdraw into the country-side, and so we did. Somewhat short of our number,' he said. 'There were deaths.'

Always there were deaths, and usually of the innocent and helpless. Radulfus stared with locked brows into the chalice of his linked hands, and thought.

'The prior lived to write letters. Where is he now?'

'Safe, in a manor of a kinsman, some miles from the city. He has ordered our withdrawal, dispersing the brothers wherever they might best find shelter. I asked if I might come to beg asylum here in Shrewsbury, and Brother Fidelis with me. And we are come, and are in your hands.'

'Why?' asked the abbot. 'Welcome indeed you are, I ask only, why here?'

'Father, some mile or two up-river from here, on a manor called Salton, I was born. I had a fancy to see the place again, or at least be near it, before I die.' He smiled, meeting the penetrating eyes beneath the knotted brows. 'It was the only property my father held in this shire. There I was born, as it so happened. A man displaced from his last home may well turn back to his first.'

'You say well. So far as is in us, we will supply that home. And your young brother?' Fidelis put back the cowl from his neck, bent his head reverently, and made a small outward sweep of submissive hands, but no sound.

'Father, he cannot speak for himself, I offer thanks from us both. I have not been altogether in my best health in Hyde, and Brother Fidelis, out of pure kindness, has become my faithful friend and attendant. He has no kinsfolk to whom he can go, he elects to be with me and tend me as before. If you will permit.' He waited for the acknowledging nod and smile before he added: 'Brother Fidelis will serve God here with every faculty he has. I know him, and I answer for him. But one, his voice, he cannot employ. Brother Fidelis is mute.'

'He is no less welcome,' said Radulfus, 'because his prayers must be silent. His silence may be more eloquent than our spoken words.' If he had been taken aback he had mastered the check so quickly as to give no sign. It would not be so often that Abbot Radulfus would be disconcerted. 'After this journey,' he said, 'you must both be weary, and still in some distress of mind until you have again a bed, a place, and work to do. Go now with Brother Cadfael, he will take you to Prior Robert, and show you everything within the enclave, dortoir and frater and gardens and herbarium, where he rules. He will find you refreshment and rest, your first need. And at Vespers you shall join us in worship.'

Word of the arrivals from the south brought Hugh Beringar down hotfoot from the town to confer first with the abbot, and then with Brother Humilis, who repeated freely what he had already once related. When he had gleaned all he could, Hugh went to find Cadfael in the herb-garden, where he was busy watering. There was an hour yet before Vespers, the time of day when all the necessary work had been done, and even a gardener could relax and sit for a while in the shade. Cadfael put away his watering-can, leaving the open, sunlit beds until the cool of the evening, and sat down beside his friend on the bench against the high south wall.

'Well, you have a breathing-space, at least,' he said. 'They are at each other's throats, not reaching for yours. Great pity, though, that townsmen and monastics and poor nuns should be the sufferers. But so it goes in this world. And the queen and her Flemings must be in the town by now, or very near. What happens next? The besiegers may very well find themselves besieged.'

'It has happened before,' agreed Hugh. 'And the bishop had fair warning he might have need of a well-stocked larder, but she may have taken her supplies for granted. If I were the queen's general, I would take time to cut all the roads into Winchester first, and make certain no food can get in. Well, we shall see. And I hear you were the first to have speech with these two brothers from Hyde.'

'They overtook me in the Foregate. And what do you make of them, now you've been closeted with them so long?'

'What should I make of them, thus at first sight? A sick man and a dumb man. More to the purpose, what do your brothers make of them?' Hugh had a sharp eye on his old friend's face, which was blunt and sleepy and private in the late afternoon heat, but was never quite closed against him. 'The elder is noble, clearly. Also he is ill. I guess at a martial past, for I think he has old wounds. Did you see he goes a little sidewise, favouring his left flank? Something has never quite healed. And the young one . . . I well understand he has fallen under the spell of such a man, and idolises him. Lucky for both! He has a powerful protector, his lord has a devoted nurse. Well?' said Hugh, challenging judgement with a confident smile.

'You haven't yet divined who our new elder brother is? They

may not have told you all,' admitted Cadfael tolerantly, 'for it came out almost by chance. A martial past, yes, he avowed it, though you could have guessed it no less surely. The man is past forty-five, I judge, and has visible scars. He has said, also, that he was born here at Salton, then a manor of his father's. And he has a scar on his head, bared by the tonsure, that was made by a Seljuk scimitar, some years back. A mere slice, readily healed, but left its mark. Salton was held formerly by the Bishop of Chester, and granted to the church of Saint Chad, here within the walls. They let it go many years since to a noble family, the Marescots. There's a local tenant holds it under them.' He opened a levelled brown eye, beneath a bushy brow russet as autumn. 'Brother Humilis is a Marescot. I know of only one Marescot of this man's age who went to the Crusade. Sixteen or seventeen years ago it must be. I was newly monk, then, part of me still hankered, and I had one eye always on the tale of those who took the Cross. As raw and eager as I was, surely, and bound for as bitter a fall, but pure enough in their going. There was a certain Godfrid Marescot who took three score with him from his own lands. He made a notable name for valour.'

'And you think this is he? Thus fallen?'

'Why not? The great ones are open to wounds no less than the simple. All the more,' said Cadfael, 'if they lead from before, and not from behind. They say this one was never later than first.'

He had still the crusader blood quick within him, he could not choose but awake and respond, however the truth had sunk below his dreams and hopes, all those years ago. Others, no less, had believed and trusted, no less to shudder and turn aside from much of what was done in the name of the Faith.

'Prior Robert will be running through the tale of the lords of Salton this moment,' said Cadfael, 'and will not fail to find his man. He knows the pedigree of every lord of a manor in this shire and beyond, for thirty years back and more. Brother Humilis will have no trouble in establishing himself, he sheds lustre upon us by being here, he need do nothing more.'

'As well,' said Hugh wryly, 'for I think there is no more he can do, unless it be to die here, and here be buried. Come, you have a better eye than mine for mortal sickness. The man is on

24

his way out of this world. No haste, but the end is assured.'

'So it is for you and for me,' said Cadfael sharply. 'And as for haste, it's neither you nor I that hold the measure. It will come when it will come. Until then, every day is of consequence, the last no less than the first.'

'So be it!' said Hugh, and smiled, unchidden. 'But he'll come into your hands before many days are out. And what of his youngling – the dumb boy?'

'Nothing of him! Nothing but silence and shrinking into the shadows. Give us time,' said Cadfael, 'and we shall learn to know him better.'

A man who has renounced possessions may move freely from one asylum to another, and be no less at home, make do with nothing as well in Shrewsbury as in Hyde Mead. A man who wears what every other man under the same discipline wears need not be noticeable for more than a day. Brother Humilis and Brother Fidelis resumed here in the midlands the same routine they had kept in the south, and the hours of the day enfolded them no less firmly and serenely. Yet Prior Robert had made a satisfactory end of his cogitations concerning the feudal holdings and family genealogies in the shire, and it was very soon made known to all, through his reliable echo, Brother Jerome, that the abbey had acquired a most distinguished son, a crusader of acknowledged valour, who had made a name for himself in the recent contention against the rising Atabeg Zenghi of Mosul, the latest threat to the Kingdom of Jerusalem. Prior Robert's personal ambitions lay all within the cloister, but for all that he missed never a turn of the fortunes of the world without. Four years since, Jerusalem had been shaken to its foundations by the king's defeat at this Zenghi's hands, but the kingdom had survived through its alliance with the emirate of Damascus. In that unhappy battle, so Robert made known discreetly, Godfrid Marescot had played a heroic part.

'He has observed every office, and worked steadily every hour set aside for work,' said Brother Edmund the infirmarer, eyeing the new brother across the court as he trod slowly towards the church for Compline, in the radiant stillness and lingering warmth of evening. 'And he has not asked for any help of yours or mine. But I wish he had a better colour, and a morsel of flesh more on those long bones. That bronze gone dull, with no blood behind it . . .'

And there went the faithful shadow after him, young, lissome, with strong, flowing pace, and hand ever advanced a little to prop an elbow, should it flag, or encircle a lean body, should it stagger or fall.

'There goes one who knows it all,' said Cadfael, 'and cannot speak. Nor would if he could, without his lord's permission. A son of one of his tenants, would you say? Something of that kind, surely. The boy is well born and taught. He knows Latin, almost as well as his master.'

On reflection it seemed a liberty to speak of a man as anyone's master who called himself Humilis, and had renounced the world.

'I had in mind,' said Edmund, but hesitantly, and with reverence, 'a natural son. I may be far astray, but it is what came to mind. I take him for a man who would love and protect his seed, and the young one might well love and admire him, for that as for all else.'

And it could well be true. The tall man and the tall youth, a certain likeness, even, in the clear features – insofar, thought Cadfael, as anyone had yet looked directly at the features of young Brother Fidelis, who passed so silently and unobtrusively about the enclave, patiently finding his way in this unfamiliar place. He suffered, perhaps, more than his elder companion in the change, having less confidence and experience, and all the anxiety of youth. He clung to his lodestar, and every motion he made was oriented by its light. They had a shared carrel in the scriptorium, for Brother Humilis had need, only too clearly, of a sedentary occupation, and had proved to have a delicate hand with copying, and artistry in illumination. And since he had limited control after a period of work, and his hand was liable to shake in fine detail, Abbot Radulfus had decreed that Brother Fidelis should be present with him to assist whenever he needed relief. The one hand matched the other as if the one had taught the other, though it might have been only emulation and love. Together, they did slow but admirable work.

'I had never considered,' said Edmund, musing aloud, 'how

remote and strange a man could be who has no voice, and how hard it is to reach and touch him. I have caught myself talking of him to Brother Humilis, over the lad's head, and been ashamed — as if he had neither hearing nor wits. I blushed before him. Yet how do you touch hands with such a one? I never had practice in it till now, and I am altogether astray.'

'Who is not?' said Cadfael.

It was truth, he had noted it. The silence, or rather the moderation of speech enjoined by the Rule had one quality, the hush that hung about Brother Fidelis quite another. Those who must communicate with him tended to use much gesture and few words, or none, reflecting his silence. As though, truly, he had neither hearing nor wits. But manifestly he had both, quick and delicate senses and sharp hearing, tuned to the least sound. And that was also strange. So often the dumb were dumb because they had never learned of sounds, and therefore made none. And this young man had been well taught in his letters, and knew some Latin, which argued a mind far more agile than most. Unless, thought Cadfael doubtfully, his muteness was a new-come thing in recent years, from some constriction of the cords of the tongue or the sinews of the throat? Or even if he had it from birth, might it not be caused by some strings too tightly drawn under his tongue, that could be eased by exercise or loosed by the knife?

'I meddle too much,' said Cadfael to himself crossly, shaking off the speculation that could lead nowhere. And he went to Compline in an unwontedly penitent mood, and by way of discipline observed silence himself for the rest of the evening.

They gathered the purple-black Lammas plums next day, for they were just on the right edge of ripeness. Some would be eaten at once, fresh as they were, some Brother Petrus would boil down into a preserve thick and dark as cakes of poppy-seed, and some would be laid out on racks in the drying house to wrinkle and crystallise into gummy sweetness. Cadfael had a few trees in a small orchard within the enclave, though most of the fruit-trees were in the main garden of the Gaye, the lush meadow-land along the riverside. The novices and younger brothers picked the fruit, and the oblates and schoolboys were allowed to help; and if everyone knew that a few handfuls went into the breasts of tunics rather than into the baskets, provided the depredations were reasonable Cadfael turned a blind eye.

It was too much to expect silence in such fine weather and such a holiday occupation. The voices of the boys rang merrily in Cadfael's ears as he decanted wine in his workshop, and went back and forth among his plants along the shadowed wall, weeding and watering. A pleasant sound! He could pick out known voices, the children's shrill and light, their elders in a whole range of tones. That warm, clear call, that was Brother Rhun, the youngest of the novices, sixteen years old, only two months since received into probation, and not yet tonsured, lest he should think better of his impulsive resolve to quit a world he had scarcely seen. But Rhun would not repent of his choice. He had come to the abbey for Saint Winifred's festival, a cripple and in pain, and by her grace now he went straight and tall and agile, radiating delight upon everyone who came near him. As now, surely, on whoever was his partner at the nearest of the plum-trees. Cadfael went to the edge of the orchard to see, and there was the sometime lame boy up among the branches, secure and joyous, his slim, deft hands nursing the fruit so lightly his fingers scarcely blurred the bloom, and leaning down to lay them in the basket held up to him by a tall brother whose back was turned, and whose figure was not immediately recognisable, until he moved round, the better to follow Rhun's movements, and showed the face of Brother Fidelis.

It was the first time Cadfael had seen that face so clearly, in sunlight, the cowl slung back. Rhun, it seemed, was one creature at least who found no difficulty in drawing near to the mute brother, but spoke out to him merrily and found no strangeness in his silence. Rhun leaned down laughing, and Fidelis looked up, smiling, one face reflecting the other. Their hands touched on the handle of the basket as Rhun dangled it at the full stretch of his arm while Fidelis plucked a cluster of low-growing fruit pointed out to him from above.

After all, thought Cadfael, it was to be expected that valiant innocence would stride in boldly where most of us hesitate to set foot. And besides, Rhun has gone most of his life with a cruel flaw that set him apart, and taken no bitterness from it,

28

naturally he would advance without fear into another man's isolation. And thank God for him, and for the valour of the children!

He went back to his weeding very thoughtfully, recalling that eased and sunlit glimpse of one who habitually withdrew into shadow. An oval face, firm-featured and by nature grave, with a lofty forehead and strong cheekbones, and clear ivory skin, smooth and youthful. There in the orchard he looked scarcely older than Rhun, though there must surely be a few years between them. The halo of curling hair round his tonsure was an autumn brown, almost fiery-bright, yet not red, and his wide-set eyes, under strong, level brows, were of a luminous grey, at least in that full light. A very comely young man, like a veiled reflection of Rhun's sunlit beauty. Noonday and twilight met together.

The fruit-pickers were still at work, though with most of their harvest already gleaned, when Cadfael put away his hoe and watering-can and went to prepare for Vespers. In the great court there was the usual late-afternoon bustle, brothers returning from their work along the Gaye, the stir of arrival in guest-hall and stable-yard, and in the cloister the sound of Brother Anselm's little portative organ testing out a new chant. The illuminators and copiers would be putting the finishing touches to their afternoon's work, and cleaning their pens and brushes. Brother Humilis must be alone in his carrel, having sent Fidelis out to the joyous labour in the garden, for nothing less would have induced the boy to leave him. Cadfael had intended crossing the open garth to the precentor's workshop, to sit down comfortably with Anselm for a quarter of an hour, until the Vesper bell, and talk and perhaps argue about music. But the memory of the dumb youth, so kindly sent out to his brief pleasure in the orchard among his peers, stirred in him as he entered the cloister, and the gaunt visage of Brother Humilis rose before him, self-contained, uncomplaining, proudly solitary. Or should it be, rather, humbly solitary? That was the quality he had claimed for himself and by which he desired to be accepted. A large claim, for one so celebrated. There was not a soul within here now who did not know his reputation. If he longed to escape it, and be as mute as his servitor, he had been cruelly thwarted.

Cadfael veered from his intent, and turned instead along the north walk of the cloister, where the carrels of the scriptorium basked in the sun, even at this hour. Humilis had been given a study midway, where the light would fall earliest and linger longest. It was quiet there, the soft tones of Anselm's organetto seemed very distant and hushed. The grass of the open garth was blanched and dry, in spite of daily watering.

'Brother Humilis . . . . ' said Cadfael softly, at the opening of the carrel.

The leaf of parchment was pushed askew on the desk, a small pot of gold had spilled drops along the paving as it rolled. Brother Humilis lay forward over his desk with his right arm flung up to hold by the wood, and his left hand gripped hard into his groin, the wrist braced to press hard into his side. His head lay with the left cheek on his work, smeared with the blue and the scarlet, and his eyes were shut, but clenched shut, upon the controlled awareness of pain. He had not uttered a sound. If he had, those close by would have heard him. What he had, he had contained. So he would still.

Cadfael took him gently about the body, pinning the sustaining arm where it rested. The blue-veined eyelids lifted in their high vaults, and eyes brilliant and intelligent behind their veils of pain peered up into his face. 'Brother Cadfael . . . ?'

'Lie still a moment yet,' said Cadfael. 'I'll fetch Edmund – Brother Infirmarer . . . .'

'No! Brother, get me hence . . . to my bed . . . This will pass . . . it is not new. Only softly, softly help me away! I would not be a show . . . . '

It was quicker and more private to help him up the night stairs from the church to his own cell in the dortoir, rather than across the great court to the infirmary, and that was what he earnestly desired, that there might be no general alarm and fuss about him. He rose more by strength of will than any physical force, and with Cadfael's sturdy arm about him, and his own arm leaning heavily round Cadfael's shoulders, they passed unnoticed into the cool gloom of the church and slowly climbed the staircase. Stretched on his own bed, Humilis submitted himself with a bleakly patient smile to Cadfael's care, and made no ado when Cadfael stripped him of his habit, and uncovered the oblique stain of mingled blood and pus that slanted across the left hip of his linen drawers and down into the groin.

'It breaks,' said the calm thread of a voice from the pillow. 'Now and then it suppurates – I know. The long ride . . . Pardon brother! I know the stench offends . . . . '

'I must bring Edmund,' said Cadfael, unloosing the drawstring and freeing the shirt. He did not yet uncover what lay beneath. 'Brother Infirmarer must know.'

'Yes . . . But no other! What need for more?'

'Except Brother Fidelis? Does he know all?'

'Yes, all!' said Humilis, and faintly and fondly smiled. 'We need not fear him, even if he could speak he would not, but there's nothing of what ails me he does not know. Let him rest until Vespers is over.'

Cadfael left him lying with closed eyes, a little eased, for the lines of his face had relaxed from their tight grimace of pain, and went down to find Brother Edmund, just in time to draw him away from Vespers. The filled baskets of plums lay by the garden hedge, awaiting disposal after the office, and the gatherers were surely already within the church, after hasty ablutions. Just as well! Brother Fidelis might at first be disposed to resent any other undertaking the care of his master. Let him find him recovered and well doctored, and he would accept what had been done. As good a way to his confidence as any.

'I knew we should be needed before long,' said Edmund, leading the way vigorously up the day stairs. 'Old wounds, you think? Your skills will avail more than mine, you have ploughed that field yourself.'

The bell had fallen silent. They heard the first notes of the evening office raised faintly from within the church as they entered the sick man's cell. He opened slow, heavy lids and smiled at them.

'Brothers, I grieve to be a trouble to you . . . '

The deep eyes were hooded again, but he was aware of all, and submitted meekly to all.

They drew down the linen that hid him from the waist, and uncovered the ruin of his body. A great misshapen map of scar tissue stretched from the left hip, where the bone had survived

31

by miracle, slantwise across his belly and deep, deep into the groin. Its colouration was of limestone pallor and striation below, where he was half disembowelled but stonily healed. But towards the upper part it was reddened and empurpled, the inflamed belly burst into a wet-lipped wound that oozed a foul jelly and a faint smear of blood.

Godfrid Marsecot's crusade had left him maimed beyond repair, yet not beyond survival. The faceless, fingerless lepers who crawl into Saint Giles, thought Cadfael, have not worse to bear. Here ends his line, in a noble plant incapable of seed. But what worth is manhood, if this is not a man?

THREE

Edmund ran for soft cloths and warm water, Cadfael for draughts and ointments and decoctions from his workshop. Tomorrow he would pick the fresh, juicy water betony, and wintergreen and woundwort, more effective than the creams and waxes he made from them to keep in store. But for tonight these must do. Sanicle, ragwort, moneywort, adder's tongue, all cleansing and astringent, good for old, ulcerated wounds, were all to be found around the hedgerows and the meadows close by, and along the banks of the Meole Brook.

They cleaned the broken wound of its exudations with a lotion of woundwort and sanicle, and dressed it with a paste of the same herbs with betony and the chickweed wintergreen, covered it with clean linen, and swathed the patient's wasted trunk with bandages to keep the dressing in place. Cadfael had brought also a draught to soothe the pain, a syrup of woundwort and Saint John's wort in wine, with a little of the poppy syrup added. Brother Humilis lay passive under their hands, and let them do with him what they would.

'Tomorrow,' said Cadfael, 'I'll gather the same herbs fresh, and bruise them for a green plaster, it works more strongly, it will draw out the evil. This has happened many times since you got the injury?'

'Not many times. But if I'm overworn, yes – it happens,' said the bluish lips, without complaint.

'Then you must not be allowed to overwear. But it has also healed before, and will again. This woundwort got its name by good right. Be ruled now, and lie still here for two days, or three, until it closes clean, for if you stand and go it will be longer in healing.'

'He should by rights be in the infirmary,' said Edmund

33

anxiously, 'where he could be undisturbed as long as is needful.'

'So he should,' agreed Cadfael, 'but that he's now well bedded here, and the less he stirs the better. How do you feel yourself now, Brother?'

'At ease,' said Brother Humilis, and faintly smiled.

'In less pain?'

'Scarcely any. Vespers will be over,' said the faint voice, and the high-arched lids rolled back from fixed eyes. 'Don't let Fidelis fret for me . . . He has seen worse – let him come.'

'I'll fetch him to you,' said Cadfael, and went at once to do it, for in this concession to the stoic mind there was more value than in anything further he could do here for the ravaged body. Brother Edmund followed him down the stair, anxious at his shoulder.

'Will it heal? Marvel he ever lived for it to heal at all. Did you ever see a man so torn apart, and live?'

'It happens,' said Cadfael, 'though seldom. Yes, it will close again. And open again at the least strain.' Not a word was said between them to enjoin or promise secrecy. The covering Godfrid Marescot had chosen for his ruin was sacred, and would be respected.

Fidelis was standing in the archway of the cloister, watching the brothers as they emerged, and looking with increasing concern for one who did not come.

Late from the orchard, the fruit-gatherers had been in haste for the evening office, and he had not looked then for Humilis, supposing him to be already in the church. But he was looking for him now. The straight, strong brows were drawn together, the long lips taut in anxiety. Cadfael approached him as the last of the brothers passed by, and the young man was turning to watch them go, almost in disbelief.

'Fidelis . . . . ' The boy's cowled head swung round to him in quick hope and understanding. It was not good news he was expecting, but any was better than none. It was to be seen in the set of his face. He had experienced all this more than once before.

'Fidelis, Brother Humilis is in his own bed in the dortoir. No call for alarm now, he's resting, his trouble is tended. He's asking for you. Go to him.'

34

The boy looked quickly from Cadfael to Edmund, and back again, uncertain where authority lay, and already braced to go striding away. If he could ask nothing with his tongue, his eyes were eloquent enough, and Edmund understood them.

'He's easy, and he'll mend. You may go and come as you will in his service, and I will see that you are excused other duties until we're satisfied he does well, and can be left. I will make that good with Prior Robert. Fetch, carry, ask, according to need – if he has a wish, write it and it shall be fulfilled. But as for his dressings, Brother Cadfael will attend to them.'

There was yet a question, more truly a demand, in the ardent eyes. Cadfael answered it in quick reassurance. 'No one else has been witness. No one else need be, but for Father Abbot, who has a right to know what ails all his sons. You may be content with that as Brother Humilis is content.'

Fidelis flushed and brightened for an instant, bowed his head, made that small open gesture of his hands in submission and acceptance, and went from them swift and silent, to climb the day stairs. How many times had he done quiet service at the same sick-bed, alone and unaided? For if he had not grudged them being the first on the scene this time, he had surely lamented it, and been uncertain at first of their discretion.

'I'll go back before Compline,' said Cadfael 'and see if he sleeps, or if he needs another draught. And whether the young one has remembered to take food for himself as well as for Humilis! Now I wonder where that boy can have learned his medicine, if he's been caring for Brother Humilis alone, down there in Hyde?' It was plain the responsibility had not daunted him, nor could he have failed in his endeavours. To have kept any life at all in that valiant wreck was achievement enough.

If the boy had studied in the art of healing, he might make a good assistant in the herbarium, and would be glad to learn more. It would be something in common, a way in through the sealed door of his silence.

Brother Fidelis fetched and carried, fed, washed, shaved his patient, tended to all his bodily needs, apparently in perfect content so to serve day and night, if Humilis had not ordered him away sometimes into the open air, or to rest in his own cell, or to attend the offices of the church on behalf of both of them; as within two days of slow recovery Humilis increasingly did order, and was obeyed. The broken wound was healing, its lips no longer wet and limp. but drawing together gradually under the plasters of freshly-bruised leaves. Fidelis witnessed the slow improvement, and was glad and grateful, and assisted without revulsion as the dressings were changed. This maimed body was no secret from him.

A favoured family servant? A natural son, as Edmund had hazarded? Or simply a devout young brother of the Order who had fallen under the spell of a charm and nobility all the more irresistible because it was dying? Cadfael could not choose but speculate. The young can be wildly generous, giving away their years and their youth for love, without thought of any gain.

'You wonder about him,' said Humilis from his pillow, when Cadfael was changing his dressing in the early morning, and Fidelis had been sent down with the brothers to Prime.

'Yes,' said Cadfael honestly.

'But you don't ask. Neither have I asked anything. My future,' said Humilis reflectively, 'I left in Palestine. What remained of me I gave to God, and I trust the offering was not all worthless. My novitiate, clipped though it was because of my state, was barely ending when he entered Hyde. I have had good cause to thank God for him.'

'No easy matter,' said Cadfael, musing, 'for a dumb man to vouch for himself and make known his vocation. Had he some elder to speak for him?'

'He had written his plea, how his father was old, and would be glad to see his sons settled, and while his elder brother had the lands, he, the younger, wished to choose the cloister. He brought an endowment with him, but it was his fine hand and his scholarship chiefly commended him. I know no more of him,' said Humilis, 'except what I have learned from him in silence, and that is enough, To me he has been all the sons I shall never father.'

'I have wondered,' said Cadfael, drawing the clean linen carefully over the newly-knit wound, 'about his dumbness. Is it possible that it stems only from some malformation in the tongue? For plainly he is not deaf, to blot out speech from his knowledge. He hears keenly. I have usually found the two go together, but not in him. He learns by ear, and is quick to learn. He was taught, as you say, a fine hand. If I had him with me always among the herbs I could teach him all the years have taught me.'

'I ask no questions of him, he asks none of me,' said Humilis. 'God knows I ought to send him away from me, to a better service than nursing and comforting my too early corruption. He's young, he should be in the sun. But I am too craven to do it. If he goes, I will not hold him, but I have not the courage to dismiss him. And while he stays, I never cease to thank God for him.'

August pursued its unshadowed course, without a cloud, and the harvest filled the barns. Brother Rhun missed his new companion from the gardens and the garth, where the roses burst open daily in the noon and faded by night from the heat. The grapes trained along the north wall of the enclosed garden swelled and changed colour. And far south, in ravaged Winchester, the queen's army closed round the sometime besiegers, severed the roads by which supplies might come in, and began to starve the town. But news from the south was sparse, and travellers few, and here the unbiddable fruit was ripening early.

Of all the cheerful workers in that harvest, Rhun was the blithest. Less than three months ago he had been lame and in pain, now he went in joyous vigour, and could not have enough of his own happy body, or put it to sufficient labours to testify to his gratitude. He had no learning as yet, to admit him to the work of copying or study or colouring of manuscripts, he had a pleasant voice but little musical training; the tasks that fell to him were the unskilled and strenuous, and he delighted in them. There was no one who could fail to reflect the same delight in watching him stretch and lift and stride, dig and hew and carry, he who had lately dragged his own light weight along with crippled effort and constant pain. His elders beheld his beauty and vigour with fond admiration, and gave thanks to the saint who had healed him.

Beauty is a perilous gift, but Rhun had never given a thought to his own face, and would have been astonished to be told that he possessed so rare an endowment. Youth is no less vulnerable, by the very quality it has of making the heart ache that beholds and has lost it.

Brother Urien had lost more than his youth, and had not lost his youth long enough to have grown resigned to its passing. He was thirty-seven years old, and had come into the cloister barely a year past, after a ruinous marriage that had left him contorted in mind and spirit. The woman had wrung and left him, and he was not a mild man, but of strong and passionate appetites and imperious will. Desperation had driven him into the cloister, and there he found no remedy. Deprivation and rage bite just as deeply within as without.

They were working side by side over the first summer apples, at the end of August, up in the dimness of the loft over the barn, laying out the fruit in wooden trays to keep as long as it would. The hot weather had brought on the ripening by at least ten days. The light in there was faintly golden, and heady with motes of dust, they moved as through a shimmering mist. Rhun's flaxen head, as yet unshorn, might have been a fair girl's, the curve of his cheek as he stooped over the shelves was suave as a rose-leaf, and the curling lashes that shadowed his eyes were long and lustrous. Brother Urien watched him sidewise, and his heart turned in him, shrunken and wrung with pain.

Rhun had been thinking of Fidelis, how he would have enjoyed the expedition to the Gaye, and he noticed nothing amiss when his neighbour's hand brushed his as they laid out the apples, or their shoulders touched briefly by chance. But it was not by chance when the outstretched hand, instead of brushing and removing, slid long fingers over his hand and held it, stroking from fingertips to wrist, and there lingering in a palpable caress.

By all the symbols of his innocence he should not have understood, not yet, not until much more had passed. But he did understand. His very candour and purity made him wise. He did not snatch his hand away, but withdrew it very gently and kindly, and turned his fair head to look Urien full in the face with wide, wide-set eyes of the clearest blue-grey, with such comprehension and pity that the wound burned unbearably deep, corrosive with rage and shame. Urien took his hand away and turned aside from him.

Revulsion and shock might have left a morsel of hope that one emotion could yet, with care, be changed gradually into another, since at least he would have known he had made a sharp impression. But this open-eyed understanding and pity repelled him beyond hope. How dared a green, simple virgin, who had never become aware of his body but through his lameness and physical pain, recognise the fire when it scorched him, and respond only with compassion? No fear, no blame, and no uncertainty. Nor would he complain to confessor or superior. Brother Urien went away with grief and desire burning in his bowels, and the remembered face of the woman clear and cruel before his mind's eyes. Prayer was no cure for the memory of her.

Rhun brought away from that encounter, only a moment long and accomplished in silence, his first awareness of the tyranny of the body. Troubles from which he was secure could torture another man. His heart ached a little for Brother Urien, he would mention him in his prayers at Vespers. And so he did, and as Urien beheld still his lost wife's hostile visage, so did Rhun continue to see the dark, tense, handsome face that had winced away from his gaze with burning brow and hooded eyes, bitterly shamed where he, Rhun, had felt no blame, and no bitterness. This was indeed a dark and secret matter.

He said no word to anyone about what had happened. What had happened? Nothing! But he looked at his fellow men with changed eyes, by one dimension enlarged to take in their distresses and open his own being to their needs.

This happened to Rhun two days before he was finally acknowledged as firm in his vocation, and received the tonsure, to become the novice, Brother Rhun.

'So our little saint has made good his resolve,' said Hugh, encountering Cadfael as he came from the ceremony. 'And his cure shows no faltering! I tell you honestly, I go in awe of him. Do you think Winifred had an eye to his comeliness, when she chose to take him for her own? Welshwomen don't baulk their fancy when they see a beautiful youth.'

'You are an unregenerate heathen,' said Cadfael comfortably, 'but the lady should be used to you by now. Never think you'll shock her, there's nothing she has not seen in her time. And had I been in her reliquary I would have drawn that child to me, just as she did. She knew worth when she saw it. Why, he has almost sweetened even Brother Jerome!'

'That will never last!' said Hugh, and laughed. 'He's kept his own name – the boy?'

'It never entered his mind to change it.'

'They do not all so,' said Hugh, growing serious. 'This pair that came from Hyde – Humilis and Fidelis. They made large claims, did they not? Brother Humble we know by his former name, and he needs no other. What do we know of Brother Faithful? And I wonder which name came first?'

'The boy is a younger son,' said Cadfael. 'His elder has the lands, this one chose the cowl. With his burden, who could blame him? Humilis says his own novitiate was not yet completed when the young one came, and they drew together and became fast friends. They may well have been admitted together, and the names . . . Who knows which of them chose first?'

They had halted before the gatehouse to look back at the church. Rhun and Fidelis had come forth together, two notably comely creatures with matched steps, not touching, but close and content. Rhun was talking with animation. Fidelis bore the traces of much watching and anxiety, but shone with a responsive glow. Rhun's new tonsure was bared to the sun, the fair hair round it roused like an aureole.

'He frequents them,' said Cadfael, watching. 'No marvel, he reaches out to every soul who has lost a piece of his being, such as a voice.' He said nothing of what the elder of that pair had lost. 'He talks for both. A pity he has small learning yet. There's neither of those two can read to Humilis, the one for want of a voice, the other for want of letters. But he studies, and he'll learn. Brother Paul thinks well of him.'

The two young men had vanished at the archway of the day stairs, plainly bound for the dortoir cell where Brother Humilis was still confined to his bed. Who would not be heartened by the vision of Brother Rhun just radiant from his admission to his heart's desire? And it was fitting, that reticent kinship between two barren bodies, the one virgin unawakened, the other hollowed out and despoiled in its prime. Two whose seed was not of this world.

It was that same afternoon that a young man in a soldier's serviceable riding gear, with rolled cloak at his saddle-bow, came in towards the town by the main London road to Saint Giles, and there asked directions to the abbey of Saint Peter and Saint Paul. He went bare-headed in the sun, and in his shirt-sleeves, with breast bared, and face and breast and naked forearms were brown as from a hotter sun even than here, where the summer did but paint a further copper shade on a hide already gilded. A neatly-made young man, on a good horse, with an easy seat in the saddle and a light hand on the rein, and a bush of wiry dark hair above a bold, blunt-featured face.

Brother Oswin directed him, and with pricking curiosity watched him ride on, wondering for whom he would enquire there. Evidently a fighting man, but from which army, and from whose household troops, to be heading for Shrewsbury abbey so particularly? He had not asked for town or sheriff. His business was not concerned with the warfare in the south. Oswin went back to his work with mild regret at knowing no more, but dutifully.

The rider, assured that he was near his goal, eased to a walk along the Foregate, looking with interest at all he saw, the blanched grass of the horse-fair ground, still thirsty for rain, the leisurely traffic of porter and cart and pony in the street, the gossiping neighbours out at their gates in the sun, the high, long wall of the abbey enclave on his left hand, and the lofty roof and tower of the church looming over it. Now he knew that he was arriving. He rounded the west end of the church, with its great door ajar outside the enclosure for parish use, and turned in under the arch of the gatehouse.

The porter came amiably to greet him and ask his business. Brother Cadfael and Hugh Beringar, still at their leisurely leave-taking close by, turned to examine the newcomer, noted his business-like and well-used harness and leathern coat slung behind, and the sword he wore, and had him accurately docketed in a moment. Hugh stiffened, attentive, for a man in soldier's gear heading in from the south might well have news.

Moreover, one who came alone and at ease here through these shires loyal to King Stephen was likely to be of the same complexion. Hugh went forward to join the colloquy, eyeing the horseman up and down with restrained approval of his appearance.

'You're not, by chance, seeking me, friend? Hugh Beringar, at your service.'

'This is the lord sheriff,' said Brother Porter by way of introduction; and to Hugh: 'The traveller is asking for Brother Humilis – though by his former name.'

'I was some years in the service of Godfrid Marescot,' said the horseman, and slid his reins loose and lighted down to stand beside them. He was taller than Hugh by half a head, and strongly made, and his brown countenance was open and cheerful, lit by strikingly blue eyes. 'I've been hunting for him among the brothers dispersed in Winchester after Hyde burned to the ground. They told me he'd chosen to come here. I have some business in the north of the shire, and need his approval for what I intend. To tell the truth,' he said with a wry smile, 'I had clean forgotten the name he took when he entered Hyde. To me he's still my lord Godfrid.'

'So he must be to many,' said Hugh, 'who knew him aforetime. Yes, he's here. Are you from Winchester now?'

'From Andover. Where we've burned the town,' said the young man bluntly, and studied Hugh as attentively as he himself was being studied. It was plain they were of the same party.

'You're with the queen's army?'

'I am. Under FitzRobert.'

'Then you'll have cut the roads to the north. I hold this shire for King Stephen, as you must know. I would not keep you from your lord, but will you ride with me into Shrewsbury and sup at my house before you move on? I'll wait your convenience. You can give me what I'm hungry for, news of what goes forward there in the south. May I know your name? I've given you mine.'

'My name is Nicholas Harnage. And very heartily I'll tell you all I know, my lord, when I've done my errand here. How is it with Godfrid?' he asked earnestly, and looked from Hugh to Cadfael, who stood by watching, listening, and until now silent.

'Not in the best of health,' said Cadfael, 'but neither was he, I suppose, when you last parted from him. He has broken an old wound, but that came, I think, after his long ride here. It is mending well now, in a day or two he'll be up and back to the duties he's chosen. He is well loved, and well tended by a young brother who came here with him from Hyde, and had been his attendant there. If you'll wait but a moment I'll tell Father Prior that Brother Humilis has a visitor, and bring you to him.'

That errand he did very briskly, to leave the pair of them together for a few minutes. Hugh needed tidings, all the firsthand knowledge he could get from that distant and confused battlefield, where two factions of his enemies, by their mutual clawings, had now drawn in the whole formidable array of his friends upon one side. A shifty side at best, seeing the bishop had changed his allegiance now for the third time. But at least it held the empress's forces in a steel girdle now in the city of Winchester, and was tightening the girdle to starve them out. Cadfael's warrior blood, long since abjured, had a way of coming to the boil when he heard steel in the offing. His chief uneasiness was that he could not be truly penitent about it. His king was not of this world, but in this world he could not help having a preference.

Prior Robert was taking his afternoon rest, which was known to others as his hour of study and prayer. A good time, since he was not disposed to rouse himself and come out to view the visitor, or exert himself to be ceremoniously hospitable. Cadfael got what he had counted on, a gracious permission to conduct the guest to Brother Humilis in his cell, and attend him to provide whatever assistance he might require. In addition, of course, to Father Prior's greetings and blessing, sent from his daily retreat into meditation.

They had had time to grow familiar and animated while he had been absent, he saw it in their faces, and the easy turn of both heads, hearing his returning step. They would ride together into the town already more than comrades in arms, potential friends.

'Come with me,' said Cadfael, 'and I'll bring you to Brother Humilis.'

On the day stairs the young, earnest voice at his shoulder said quietly: 'Brother, you have been doctoring my lord since this fit came on. So the lord sheriff told me. He says you have great skills in herbs and medicine and healing.'

'The lord sheriff,' said Cadfael, 'is my good friend for some years, and thinks better of me than I deserve. But, yes, I do tend your lord, and thus far we two do well together. You need not fear he is not valued truly, we do know his worth. See him, and judge for yourself. For you must know what he suffered in the east. You were with him there?'

'Yes. I'm from his own lands, I sailed when he sent for a fresh force, and shipped some elders and wounded for home. And I came back with him, when he knew his usefulness there was ended.'

'Here,' said Cadfael, with his foot on the top stair, 'his usefulness is far from ended. There are young men here who live the brighter by his light – under the light by which we all live, that's understood. You may find two of them with him now. If one of them lingers, let him, he has the right. That's his companion from Hyde.'

They emerged into the corridor that ran the whole length of the dortoir, between the partitioned cells, and stood at the opening of the dim, narrow space allotted to Humilis.

'Go in,' said Cadfael. 'You do not need a herald to be welcome.'

FOUR

In the cell the little lamp for reading was not lighted, since one of the young attendants could not read, and the other could not speak, while the incumbent himself still lay propped up with pillows in his cot, too weak to nurse a heavy book. But if Rhun could not read well, he could learn by heart, and recite what he had learned with feeling and warmth, and he was in the middle of a prayer of Saint Augustine which Brother Paul had taught him, when he felt suddenly that he had an audience larger than he had bargained for, and faltered and fell silent, turning towards the open end of the cell.

Nicholas Harnage stood hesitant within the doorway, until his eyes grew accustomed to the dim light. Brother Humilis had opened his eyes in wonder when Rhun faltered. He beheld the best-loved and most trusted of his former squires standing almost timorously at the foot of his bed.

'Nicholas?' he ventured, doubtful and wondering, heaving himself up to stare more intently.

Brother Fidelis stooped at once to prop and raise him, and brace the pillows at his back, and then as silently withdrew into the dark corner of the cell, to leave the field to the visitor.

'Nicholas! It *is* you!'

The young man went forward and fell on his knee to clasp and kiss the thin hand stretched out to him.

'Nicholas, what are you doing here? You're welcome as the morning, but I never looked to see you in this place. It was kind indeed to seek me out in such a distant refuge. Come, sit by me here. Let me see you close!'

Rhun had slipped away silently. From the doorway he made a small reverence before he vanished. Fidelis took a step to follow him, but Humilis laid a hand on his arm to detain him.

45

'No, stay! Don't leave us! Nicholas, to this young brother I owe more than I can ever repay. He serves me as truly in this field as you did in arms.'

'All who have been your men, like me, will be grateful to him,' said Nicholas fervently, looking up into a face shadowed by the cowl, and as featureless as voiceless in this half-darkness. If he wondered at getting no answer, but only an inclination of the head by way of acknowledgement, he shrugged it off without another thought, for it was of no importance that he should reach a closer acquaintance with one he might never see again. He drew the stool close to the bedside, and sat studying the emaciated face of his lord with deep concern.

'They tell me you are mending well. But I see you leaner and more fallen than when I left you, that time in Hyde, and went to do your errand. I had a long search in Winchester to find your prior, and enquire of him where you were gone. Need you have chosen to ride so far? The bishop would have taken you into the Old Minster, and been glad of you.'

'I doubt if I should have been so glad of the bishop,' said Brother Humilis with a wry little smile. 'No, I had my reasons for coming so far north. This shire and this town I knew as a child. A few years only, but they are the years a man remembers later in life. Never trouble for me, Nick, I'm very well here, as well as any other place, and better than most. Let us speak rather of you. How have you fared in your new service, and what has brought you here to my bedside?'

'I've thrived, having your commendation. William of Ypres has mentioned me to the queen, and would have taken me among his officers, but I'd rather stay with FitzRobert's English than go to the Flemings. I have a command. It was you who taught me all I know,' he said, at once glowing and sad, 'you and the mussulmen of Mosul.'

'It was not the Atabeg Zenghi,' said Brother Humilis, smiling, 'whose affairs sent you here so far to seek me out. Leave him to the King of Jerusalem, whose noble and perilous business he is. What of Winchester, since I fled from it?'

'The queen's armies have encircled it. Few men get out, and no food gets in. The empress's men are shut tight in their castle, and their stores must be running very low. We came north to straddle the road by Andover. As yet nothing moves, therefore I got leave to ride north on my own business. But they must attempt to break out soon, or starve where they are.'

'They'll try to reopen one of the roads and bring in supplies, before they abandon Winchester altogether,' said Humilis, frowning thoughtfully over the possibilities. 'If and when they do break, they'll break for Oxford first. Well, if this stalemate has sent you here to me, one good thing has come out of it. And what is this business that brought you to Shrewsbury?'

'My lord,' began Nicholas, leaning forward very earnestly, 'you remember how you sent me here to the manor of Lai, three years ago, to take the word to Humphrey Cruce and his daughter that you could not keep your compact to marry her? – that you were entering the cloister at Hyde Mead?'

'It is not a thing to forget,' agreed Humilis drily.

'My lord, neither can I forget the girl! You never saw her but as a child five years old, before you went to the Crusade. But I saw her a grown lady, nearly nineteen. I did your message to her father and to her, and came away glad to have it delivered and done. But now I cannot get her out of my mind. Such grace she had, and bore the severance with such dignity and courtesy. My lord, if she is still not wed or betrothed, I want to speak for her myself. But I could not go without first asking your blessing and consent.'

'Son,' said Humilis, glowing with astonished pleasure, 'there's nothing could delight me more than to see her happy with you, since I had to fail her. The girl is free to marry whom she will, and I could wish her no better man than you. And if you succeed I shall be relieved of all my guilt towards her, for I shall know she has made a better bargain than ever I should have been to her. Only consider, boy, we who enter the cloister abjure all possessions, how then can we dare lay claim to rights of possession in another creature of God? Go, and may you get her, and my blessing on you both. But come back and tell me how you fare.'

'My lord, with all my heart! How can I fail, if you send me to her?'

He stooped to kiss the hand that held him warmly, and rose blithely from the stool to take his leave. The silent figure in the shadows returned to his consciousness belatedly; it was as if he had been alone with his lord all this time, yet here stood the mute witness. Nicholas turned to him with impulsive warmth.

'Brother, I do thank you for your care of my lord. For this time, farewell. I shall surely see you again on my return.'

It was disconcerting to receive by way of reply only silence, and the courteous inclination of the cowled head.

'Brother Fidelis,' said Humilis gently, 'is dumb. Only his life and works speak for him. But I dare swear his goodwill goes with you on this quest, like mine.'

There was silence in the cell when the last crisp, light echo had died away on the day stairs. Brother Humilis lay still, thinking, it seemed, tranquil and contented thoughts, for he was smiling.

'There are parts of myself I have never given to you,' he said at last, 'things that happened before ever I knew you. There is nothing of myself I would not wish to share with you. Poor girl! What had she to hope for from me, so much her elder, even before I was broken? And I never saw her but once, a little lass with brown hair and a solemn round face. I never felt the want of a wife or children until I was thirty years old, having an elder brother to carry on my father's line after the old man died. I took the Cross, and was fitting out a company to go with me to the east, free as air, when my brother also died, and I was left to balance my vow to God and my duty to my house. I owed it to God to do as I had sworn, and go for ten years to the Holy Land, but also I owed it to my house to marry and breed sons. So I looked for a sturdy, suitable little girl who could well wait all those years for me, and still have all her child-bearing time in its fullness when I returned. Barely six years old she was – Julian Cruce, from a family with manors in the north of this shire, and in Stafford, too.'

He stirred and sighed for the follies of men, and the presumptuous solemnity of the arrangements they made for lives they would never live. The presence beside him drew near, put back the cowl, and sat down on the stool Nicholas had vacated. They looked each other in the eyes gravely and without words, longer than most men can look each other in the eyes and not turn aside.

'God knew better, my son!' said Humilis. 'His plans for me

were not as mine. I am what I am now. She is what she is. Julian Cruce . . . . I am glad she should escape me and go to a better man. I pray she has not yet given herself to any, for this Nicholas of mine would make her a fitting match, one that would set my soul at rest. Only to her do I feel myself a debtor, and forsworn.'

Brother Fidelis shook his head at him, reproachfully smiling, and leaned and laid a finger for an instant over the mouth that spoke heresy.

Cadfael had left Hugh waiting at the gatehouse, and was crossing the court to return to his duties in the herb-garden, when Nicholas Harnage emerged from the arch of the stairway, and recognising him, hailed him loudly and ran to pluck him urgently by the sleeve.

'Brother, a word!'

Cadfael halted and turned to face him. 'How do you find him? The long ride put him to too great a strain, and he did not seek help until his wound was broken and festering, but that's over now. All's clean, wholesome and healing. You need not fear we shall let him founder like that a second time.'

'I believe it, Brother,' said the young man earnestly. 'But I see him now for the first time after three years, and much fallen even from the man he was after he got his injuries. I knew they were grave, the doctors had him in care between life and death a long time, but when he came back to us at least he looked like the man we knew and followed. He made his plans then to come home, I know, but he had served already more years than he had promised, it was time to attend to his lands and his life here at home. I made that voyage with him, he bore it well. Now he has lost flesh, and there's a languor about him when he moves a hand. Tell me the truth of it, how bad is it with him?'

'Where did he ever get such crippling wounds?' asked Cadfael, considering scrupulously how much he could tell, and guessing at how much this boy already knew, or at least hazarded.

'In that last battle with Zenghi and the men of Mosul. He had Syrian doctors after the battle.'

That might very well be why he survived so terrible a

maiming, thought Cadfael, who had learned much of his own craft from both Saracen and Syrian physicians. Aloud he asked cautiously: 'You have not seen his wounds? You don't know their whole import?'

Surprisingly, the seasoned crusader was struck silent for a moment, and a slow wave of blood crept up under his golden tan, but he did not lower his eyes, very wide and direct eyes of a profound blue. 'I never saw his body, no more than when I helped him into his harness. But I could not choose but understand what I can't claim I know. It could not be otherwise, or he would never have abandoned the girl he was betrothed to. Why should he do so? A man of his word! He had nothing left to give her but a position and a parcel of dower lands. He chose rather to give her her freedom, and the residue of himself to God.'

'There was a girl?' said Cadfael.

'There *is* a girl. And I am on my way to her now,' said Nicholas, as defiantly as if his right had been challenged. 'I carried the word to her and her father that he was gone into the monastery at Hyde Mead. Now I am going to Lai to ask for her hand myself, and he has given me his consent and blessing. She was a small child when she was affianced to him, she has never seen him since. There is no reason she should not listen to my suit, and none that her kin should reject me.'

'None in the world!' agreed Cadfael heartily. 'Had I a daughter in such case, I would be glad to see the squire follow in his lord's steps. And if you must report to her of his well-being, you may say with truth that he is doing what he wishes, and enjoys content of mind. And for his body, it is cared for as well as may be. We shall not let him want for anything that can give him aid or comfort.'

'But that does not answer what I need to know,' insisted the young man. 'I have promised to come back and tell him how I've fared. Three or four days, no longer, perhaps not so long. But shall I still find him then?'

'Son,' said Cadfael patiently, 'which of us can answer that for himself or any other man? You want truth, and you deserve it. Yes, Brother Humilis is dying. He got his death-wound long ago in that last battle. Whatever has been done for him, whatever can be done, is staving off an ending. But death is not

50

in such a hurry with him as you fear, and he is in no fear of it. You go and find your girl, and bring him back good news, and he'll be here to be glad of it.'

'And so he will,' said Cadfael to Edmund, as they took the air in the garden together before Compline that evening, 'if that young fellow is brisk about his courting, and I fancy he's the kind to go straight for what he wants. But how much longer we can hold our ground with Humilis I dare not guess. This fashion of collapse we can prevent, but the old harm will devour him in the end. As he knows better than any.'

'I marvel how he lived at all,' agreed Edmund, 'let alone bore the journey home, and has survived three years or more since.'

They were private together down by the banks of the Meole Brook, or they could not have discussed the matter at all. No doubt by this hour Nicholas Harnage was well on his way to the north-east of the county, if he had not already arrived at his destination. Good weather for riding, he would be in shelter at Lai before dark. And a very well-set-up young fellow like Harnage, in a thriving way in arms by his own efforts, was not an offer to be sneezed at. He had the blessing of his lord, and needed nothing more but the girl's liking, her family's approval, and the sanction of the church.

'I have heard it argued,' said Brother Edmund, 'that when an affianced man enters a monastic order, the betrothed lady is not necessarily free of the compact. But it seems a selfish and greedy thing to try to have both worlds, choose the life you want, but prevent the lady from doing likewise. But I think the question seldom arises but where the man cannot bear to loose his hold of what once he called his, and himself fights to keep her in chains. And here that is not so, Brother Humilis is glad there should be so happy a solution. Though of course she may be married already.'

'The manor of Lai,' mused Cadfael. 'What do you know of it, Edmund? What family would that be?'

'Cruce had it. Humphrey Cruce, if I remember rightly, he might well be the girl's father. They hold several manors up there, Ightfield, and Harpecote – and Prees, from the Bishop of Chester. Some lands in Staffordshire, too. They made Lai the head of their honour.'

'That's where he's bound. Now if he comes back in triumph,' said Cadfael contentedly, 'he'll have done a good day's work for Humilis. He's already given him a great heave upward by showing his honest brown face, but if he settles the girl's future for her he may have added a year or more to his lord's life, at the same time.'

They went to Compline at the first sound of the bell. The visitor had indeed given Humilis a heft forward towards health, it seemed, for here he came, habited and erect on Fidelis's arm, having asked no permission of his doctors, bent on observing the night office with the rest. But I'll hound him back as soon as the observance is over, thought Cadfael, concerned for his dressing. Let him brandish his banner this once, it speaks well for his spirit, even if his flesh is drawn with effort. And who am I to say what a brother, my equal, may or may not do for his own salvation?

The evenings were already beginning to draw in, the height of the summer was over while its heat continued as if it would never break. In the dimness of the choir what light remained was coloured like irises, and faintly fragrant with the warm, heady scents of harvest and fruit. In his stall the tall, handsome, emaciated man who was old in his middle forties stood proudly, Fidelis on his left hand, and next to Fidelis, Rhun. Their youth and beauty seemed to gather to itself what light there was, so that they shone with a native radiance of their own, like lighted candles.

Across the choir from them Brother Urien stood, kneeled, genuflected and sang, with the full, assured voice of maturity, and never took his eyes from those two young, shining heads, the flaxen and the brown. Day by day those two drew steadily together, the mute one and the eloquent one, matched unfairly, unjustly, to his absolute exclusion, the one as desirable and as inviolable as the other, while his need burned in his bowels day and night, and prayer could not cool it, nor music lull it to sleep, but it ate him from within like the gnawing of wolves.

They had both begun – dreadful sign! – to look to him like the woman. When he gazed at either of these two, the boy's lineaments would dissolve and change subtly, and there would be her face, not recognising, not despising, simply staring through him to behold someone else. His heart ached beyond bearing, while he sang mellifluously in the Compline psalm.

In the twilight of the softer, more open country in the north-east of the shire, where day lingered longer than among the folded hills of the western border, Nicholas Harnage rode between flat, rich fields, unwontedly dried by the heat, into the wattled enclosure of the manor of Lai. Wrapped round on all sides by the enlarged fields of the plain, sparsely tree'd to make way for wide cultivation, the house rose long and low, a stone-built hall and chambers over a broad undercroft, with stables and barns about the interior of the fence. Fat country, good for grain and for roots, with ample grazing for any amount of cattle. The byres were vocal as Nicholas entered at the gate, the mild, contented lowing of well-fed beasts, milked and drowsy.

A groom heard the entering hooves and came forth from the stables, bared to the waist in the warm night. Seeing one young horseman alone, he was quite easy. They had had comparative peace here while Winchester burned and bled.

'Seeking whom, young sir?'

'Seeking the master, your lord, Humphrey Cruce,' said Nicholas, reining in peacably and shaking the reins free. 'If he still keeps house here?'

'Why, the lord Humphrey's dead, sir, three years ago. His son Reginald is lord here now. Would your errand do as well to him?'

'If he'll admit me, yes, surely to him, then,' said Nicholas, and dismounted. 'Let him know, I was here some three years ago, to speak for Godfrid Marescot. It was his father I saw then, but the son will know of it.'

'Come within,' said the groom placidly, accepting the credentials without question. 'I'll have your beast seen to.'

In the smoky, wood-scented hall they were at meat, or still sitting at ease after the meal was done, but they had heard his step on the stone stairs that led to the open hall door, and Reginald Cruce rose, alert and curious, as the visitor entered. A big, black-haired man of austere features and imperious manner, but well-disposed, it seemed, towards chance

53

travellers. His lady sat aloof and quiet, a pale-haired woman in green, with a boy of about fifteen at her side, and a younger boy and girl about nine or ten, who by their likeness might well be twins. Evidently Reginald Cruce had secured his succession with a well-filled quiver, for by the lady's swelling waist when she rose to muster the hospitality of the house, there was another sibling on the way.

Nicholas made his reverence and offered his name, a little confounded at finding Julian Cruce's brother a man surely turned forty, with a wife and growing children, where he had assumed a young fellow in his twenties, perhaps newly-married since inheriting. But he recalled that Humphrey Cruce had been an old man to have a daughter still so young. Two marriages, surely, the first blessed with an heir, the second undertaken late, when Reginald was a grown man, ready for marriage himself, or even married already to his pale, prolific wife.

'Ah, that!' said Reginald of his guest's former errand to this same house. 'I remember it, though I was not here then. My wife brought me a manor in Staffordshire, we were living there. But I know how it fell out, of course. A strange business altogether. But it happens! Men change their minds. And you were the messenger? Well, but leave it now and take some refreshment. Come to table! There'll be time to talk of all such business afterwards.'

He sat down and kept his visitor company while a servant brought meat and ale, and the lady, having made her grave good night, drove her younger children away to their beds, and the heir sat solemn and silent studying his elders. At last, in the deepening evening, the two men were left alone to their talk.

'So you are the squire who brought that word from Marescot. You'll have noticed there's a generation, as near as need be, between my sister and me – seventeen years. My mother died when I was nine years old, and it was another eight before my father married again. An old man's folly, she brought him nothing, and died when the girl was born, so he had little joy of her.'

At least, thought Nicholas, studying his host dispassionately, there was no second son, to threaten a division of the lands.

That would be a source of satisfaction to this man, he was authentically of his class and kind, and land was his lifeblood.

'He may well have had great joy of his daughter, however,' he said firmly, 'for she is a very gracious and beautiful girl, as I well recall.'

'You'll be better informed of that than I,' said Reginald drily, 'if you saw her only three years ago. It must be eighteen or more since I set eyes on her. She was a stumbling infant then, two years old, or three, it might be. I married about that time, and settled on the lands Cecilia brought me. We exchanged couriers now and then, but I never came back here until my father was on his death-bed, and they sent for me to come to him.'

'I didn't know of his death when I set out to come here on this errand of my own,' said Nicholas. 'I heard it only from your groom at the gate. But I may speak as freely with you as I should have done with him. I was so much taken with your sister's grace and dignity that I've thought of her ever since, and I've spoken with my lord Godfrid, and have his full consent to what I'm asking. As for myself,' he thrust on, leaning eagerly across the board, 'I am heir to two good manors from my father, and shall have some lands also after my mother, I stand well in the queen's armies and my lord will speak for me, that I'm in earnest in this matter, and will provide for Julian as truly as any man could, if you will . . .'

His host was gazing, astonished, smiling at his fervour, and had raised a warning hand to still the flood.

'Did you come all this way to ask me to give you my sister?'

'I did! Is that so strange? I admired her, and I'm come to speak for her. And she might have worse offers,' he added, flushing and stiffening at such a reception.

'I don't doubt it, but, man, man, you should have put in a word to give her due warning then. You come three years too late!'

'Too late?' Nicholas sat back and drew in his hands slowly, stricken. 'Then she's already married?'

'You might call it so!' Reginald hoisted wide shoulders in a helpless gesture. 'But not to any man. And you might have sped well enough if you'd made more haste, for all I know. No, this is quite a different story. There was some discussion, even, about whether she was still bound like a wife to Marescot – a great foolery, but the churchmen have to assert their authority, and my father's chaplain was prim as a virgin – though I suspect, for all that, in private he was none! – and clutched at every point of canon law that gave him power, and he took the extreme line, and would have it she was legally a wife, while the parish priest argued the opposing way, and my father, being a sensible man, took his side and insisted she was free. All this I learned by stages since. I never took part or put my head into the hornets' nest.'

Nicholas was frowning into his cupped hands, feeling the cold heaviness of disappointment drag his heart down. But still this was not a complete answer. He looked up ruefully. 'So how did this end? Why is she not here to use her freedom, if she has not yet given herself to a husband?'

'Ah, but she has! She took her own way. She said that if she was free, then she would make her own choice. And she chose to do as Marescot had done, and took a husband not of this world. She has taken the veil as a Benedictine nun.'

'And they let her?' demanded Nicholas, wrung between rage and pain. 'Then, when she was moved by this broken match, they let her go so easily, throw away her youth so unwisely?'

'They let her, yes. How do I know whether she was wise or no? If it was what she wished, why should she not have it? Since she went I've never had word from her, never has she complained or asked for anything. She must be happy in her choice. You must look elsewhere for a wife, my friend!'

Nicholas sat silent for a time, swallowing a bitterness that burned in his belly like fire. Then he asked, with careful quietness: 'How was it? When did she leave her home? How attended?'

'Very soon after your visit, I judge. It might be a month while they fought out the issue, and she said never a word. But all was done properly. Our father gave her an escort of three men-at-arms and a huntsman who had always been a favourite and made a pet of her, and a good dowry in money, and also some ornaments for her convent, silver candlesticks and a crucifix and such. He was sad to see her go, I know by what he said later, but she wanted it so, and her wants were his commands always.' A very slight chill in his brisk, decisive

56

voice spoke of an old jealousy. The child of Humphrey's age had plainly usurped his whole heart, even though his son would inherit all when that heart no longer beat. 'He lived barely a month longer,' said Reginald. 'Only long enough to see the return of her escort, and know she was safely delivered where she wished to be. He was old and feeble, we knew it. But he should not have dwindled so soon.'

'He might well miss her,' said Nicholas, very low and hesitantly, 'about the place. She had a brightness . . . And you did not send for her, when her father died?'

'To what end? What could she do for him, or he for her? No, we let her be. If she was happy there, why trouble her?'

Nicholas gripped his hands together under the board, and wrung them hard, and asked his last question: 'Where was it she chose to go?' His own voice sounded to him hollow and distant.

'She's in the Benedictine abbey of Wherwell, close by Andover.'

So that was the end of it! All this time she had been within hail of him, the house of her refuge encircled now by armies and factions and contention. If only he had spoken out what he felt in his heart at the first sight of her, even hampered as he had been by the knowledge of the blow he was about to deal her, and gagged by that knowledge when for once he might have been eloquent. She might have listened, and at least delayed, even if she could feel nothing for him then. She might have thought again, and waited, and even remembered him. Now it was far too late, she was a bride for the second time, and even more indissolubly.

This time there was no question of argument. The betrothal vows made by or for a small girl might justifiably be dissolved, but the vocational vows of a grown woman, taken in the full knowledge of their meaning, and of her own choice, never could be undone. He had lost her.

Nicholas lay all night in the small guest-chamber prepared for him, fretting at the knot and knowing he could not untie it. He slept shallowly and uneasily, and in the morning he took his leave, and set out on the road back to Shrewsbury.

FIVE

It so happened that Brother Cadfael was private with Humilis in his cell in the dortoir when Nicholas again rode in at the gatehouse and asked leave to visit his former lord, as he had promised. Humilis had risen with the rest that morning, attended Prime and Mass, and scrupulously performed all the duties of the horarium, though he was not yet allowed to exert himself by any form of labour. Fidelis attended him everywhere, ready to support his steps if need arose, or fetch him whatever he might want, and had spent the afternoon completing, under his elder's approving eye, the initial letter which had been smeared and blotted by his fall. And there they had left the boy to finish the careful elaboration in gold, while they repaired to the dortoir, physician and patient together.

'Well closed,' said Cadfael, content with his work, 'and firming up nicely, clean as ever. You scarcely need the bandages, but as well keep them a day or two yet, to guard against rubbing while the new skin is still frail.'

They were grown quite easy together, these two, and if both of them realised that the mere healing of a broken and festered wound was no sufficient cure for what ailed Humilis, they were both courteously silent on the subject, and took their moderate pleasure in what good they had achieved.

They heard the footsteps on the stone treads of the day stairs, and knew them for booted feet, not sandalled. But there was no spring in the steps now, and no hasty eagerness, and it was a glum young man who appeared, shadowy, in the doorway of the cell. Nor had he been in any hurry on the way back from Lai, since he had nothing but disappointment to report. But he had promised, and he was here.

'Nick!' Humilis greeted him with evident pleasure and affection. 'You're soon back! Welcome as the day, but I had thought . . . ' There he stopped, even in the dim interior light aware that the brightness was gone from the young man's face. 'So long a visage? I see it did not go as you would have wished.'

'No, my lord.' Nicholas came in slowly, and bent his knee to both his elders. 'I have not sped.'

'I am sorry for it, but no man can always succeed. You know Brother Cadfael? I owe the best of care to him.'

'We spoke together the last time,' said Nicholas, and found a half-hearted smile by way of acknowledgement. 'I count myself also in his debt.'

'Spoke of me, no doubt,' said Humilis, smiling and sighing. 'You trouble too much for me, I am well content here. I have found my way. Now sit down a while, and tell us what went wrong for you.'

Nicholas plumped himself down on the stool beside the bed on which Humilis was sitting, and said what he had to say in commendably few words: 'I hesitated three years too long. Barely a month after you took the cowl at Hyde, Julian Cruce took the veil at Wherwell.'

'Did she so!' said Humilis on a long breath, and sat silent to take in all that this news could mean. 'Now I wonder . . . No, why should she do such a thing unless it was truly her wish? It cannot have been because of me! No, she knew nothing of me, she had only once seen me, and must have forgotten me before my back was turned. She may even have been glad . . . It may be this is what she always wished, if she could have her way . . . .' He thought for a moment, frowning, perhaps trying to recall what that little girl looked like. 'You told me, Nick, that I do remember, how she took my message. She was not distressed, but altogether calm and courteous, and gave me her grace and pardon freely. You said so!'

'Truth, my lord,' said Nicholas earnestly, 'though she cannot have been glad.'

'Ah, but she may – she may very well have been glad. No blame to her! Willing though she may have been to accept the match made for her, yet it would have tied her to a man more than twenty years her elder, and a stranger. Why should she not be glad, when I offered her her liberty – no, urged it upon her? Surely she must have made of it the use she preferred, perhaps had longed for.'

'She was not forced,' Nicholas admitted, with somewhat reluctant certainty. 'Her brother says it was the girl's own choice, indeed her father was against it, and only gave in because she would have it so.'

'That's well,' agreed Humilis with a relieved sigh. 'Then we can but hope that she may be happy in her choice.'

'But so great a waste!' blurted Nicholas, grieving. 'If you had seen her, my lord, as I did! To shear such hair as she had, and hide such a form under the black habit! They should never have let her go, not so soon. How if she has regretted it long since?'

Humilis smiled, but very gently, eyeing the downcast face and hooded eyes. 'As you described her to me, so gracious and sensible, of such measured and considered speech, I don't think she will have acted without due thought. No, surely she has done what is right for her. But I'm sorry for your loss, Nick. You must bear it as gallantly as she did – if ever I was any loss!'

The Vesper bell had begun to chime. Humilis rose to go down to the church, and Nicholas rose with him, taking the summons as his dismissal.

'It's late to set out now,' suggested Cadfael, emerging from the silence and withdrawal he had observed while these two talked together. 'And it seems there's no great haste, that you need leave tonight. A bed in the guest-hall, and you could set off fresh in the morning, with the whole day before you. And spend an hour or two more with Brother Humilis this evening, while you have the chance.'

To which sensible notion they both said yes, and Nicholas recovered a little of his spirits, if nothing could restore the ardour with which he had ridden north from Winchester.

What did somewhat surprise Brother Cadfael was the considerate way in which Fidelis, confronted yet again with this visitant from the time before he had known Humilis and established his own intimacy with him, withdrew himself from sight as he was withdrawn from the possibility of conversation, and left them to their shared memories of travel, Crusade and battle, things so far removed from his own experience. An affection which could so self-effacingly make room for a rival and prior affection was generous indeed.

There was a merchant of Shrewsbury who dealt in fleeces all up and down the borders, both from Wales and from such fat sheep-country as the Cotswolds, and had done an interesting side-trade in information, for Hugh's benefit, in these contrary times. His active usefulness was naturally confined to this period of high summer when the wool clip was up for sale, and many dealers had restricted their movements in these dangerous times, but he was a determined man, intrepid enough to venture well south down the border, towards territory held by the empress. His suppliers had sold to him for some years, and had sufficient confidence in him to hold their clip until he made contact. He had good trading relations as far afield as Bruges in Flanders, and was not at all averse to a large risk when calculating on a still larger profit. Moreover, he took his own risks, rather than delegating these unchancy journeys to his underlings. Possibly he even relished the challenge, for he was a stubborn and stalwart man.

Now, in early September, he was on his way home with his purchases, a train of three wagons following from Buckingham, which was as near as he could reasonably go to Oxford. For Oxford had become as alert and nervous as a town itself under siege, every day expecting that the empress must be forced by starvation to retreat from Winchester. The merchant had left his men secure on a road relatively peaceful, to bring up his wagons at leisure, and himself rode ahead at good speed with his news to report to Hugh Beringar in Shrewsbury, even before he went home to his wife and family.

'My lord, things move at last. I had it from a man who saw the end of it, and made good haste away to a safer place. You know how they were walled up there in their castles in Winchester, the bishop and the empress, with the queen's armies closing all round the city and sealing off the roads. No supplies have gone in through that girdle for four weeks now, and they say there's starvation in the town, though I doubt if either empress or bishop is going short.' He was a man who spoke his mind, and no great respecter of high personages. 'A very different tale for the poor townsfolk! But it's biting even the garrison within there at the royal castle, for the queen has been supplying Wolvesey while she starves out the opposing side. Well, they came to the point where they must try to win a way through.'

'I've been expecting it,' said Hugh, intent. 'What did they hit on? They could only hope to move north or west, the queen holds all the south-east.'

'They sent out a force, three or four hundred as I heard it, northwards, to seize on the town of Wherwell, and try to secure a base there to open the Andover road. Whether they were seen on the move, or whether some townsman betrayed them — for they're not loved in Winchester — however it was, William of Ypres and the queen's men closed in on them when they'd barely reached the edge of the town, and cut them to pieces. A great killing! The fellow who told me fled when the houses started to burn, but he saw the remnant of the empress's men put up a desperate fight of it and reach the great nunnery there. And they never scrupled to use it, either, he says. They swarmed into the church itself and turned it into a fortress, although the poor sisters had shut themselves in there for safety. The Flemings threw in firebrands after them. A hellish business it must have been. He could hear from far off as he ran, he said, the women screaming, the flames crackling and the din of fighting within there, until those who remained were forced to come out and surrender, half-scorched as they were. Not a man can have escaped either death or capture.'

'And the women?' demanded Hugh aghast. 'Do you tell me the abbey of Wherwell is burned down, like the convent in the city, like Hyde Mead after it?'

'My man never dallied to see how much was left,' said the messenger drily. 'But certainly the church burned down to the ground, with both men and women in it — the sisters cannot all have come out alive. And as for those who did, God alone knows where they will have found refuge now. Safe places are hard to find in those parts. And for the empress's garrison, I'd say there's no hope for them now but to muster every man they have, and try to burst out by force of numbers through the ring, and run for it. And a poor chance for them, even so.'

A poor chance indeed, after this last loss of three or four hundred fighting men, probably hand-picked for the exploit, which must have been a desperate gamble from the first. The year only at early September, and the fortunes of war had changed and changed again, from the disastrous battle of Lincoln which had made the king prisoner and brought the empress within grasp of the crown itself, to this stranglehold drawn round the same proud lady now. Now only give us the empress herself prisoner, thought Hugh, and we shall have stalemate, recover each our sovereign, and begin this whole struggle all over again, for what sense there is in it! And at the cost of the brothers of Hyde Mead and the nuns of Wherwell. Among many others even more defenceless, like the poor of Winchester.

The name of Wherwell, as yet, meant no more to him than any other convent unlucky enough to fall into the field of battle.

'A good year for me, all the same,' said the wool-merchant, rising to make his way home to his own waiting board and bed. 'The clip measures up well, it was worth the journey.'

Hugh took the latest news down to the abbey next morning, immediately after Prime, for whatever of import came to his ears was at once conveyed to Abbot Radulfus, a service the abbot appreciated and reciprocated. The clerical and secular authorities worked well together in Shropshire, and moreover, in this case a Benedictine house had been desecrated and destroyed, and those of the Rule stood together, and helped one another where they could. Even in more peaceful times, nunneries were apt to have much narrower lands and more restricted resources than the houses of the monks, and often had to depend upon brotherly alms, even under good, shrewd government. Now here was total devastation. Bishops and abbots would be called upon to give aid.

He had come from his colloquy with Radulfus in the abbot's parlour with half an hour still before High Mass and, choosing to stay for the celebration since he was here, he did what he habitually did with time to spare within the precinct of the abbey and went looking for Brother Cadfael in his workshop in the herb-garden.

Cadfael had been up since long before Prime, inspected such wines and distillations as he had working, and done a little watering while the soil was in shade and cooled from the night. At this time of year, with the harvest in, there was little work to be done among the herbs, and he had no need as yet to ask for an assistant in place of Brother Oswin.

When Hugh came to look for Cadfael he found him sitting at ease on the bench under the north wall, which at this time of day was pleasantly warm without being too hot, contemplating between admiration and regret the roses that bloomed with such extravagant splendour and wilted so soon. Hugh sat down beside him, rightly interpreting placid silence as welcome.

'Aline says it's high time you came to see how your godson has grown.'

'I know well enough how much he will have grown,' said Giles Beringar's godfather, between complacency and awe of his formidable responsibility. 'Not two years old until Christmas, and too heavy already for an old man.'

Hugh made a derisive noise. When Cadfael claimed to be an old man he must either be up to something, or inclined to be idle, and giving fair warning.

'Every time he sees me he climbs me like a tree,' said Cadfael dreamily. 'You he daren't treat so, you are but a sapling. Give him fifteen more years, and he'll make two of you.'

'So he will,' agreed the fond father, and stretched his lithe, light body pleasurably in the strengthening sun. 'A long lad from birth – do you remember? That was a Christmas indeed, what with my son – and yours . . . I wonder where Olivier is now? Do you know?'

'How should I know? With d'Angers in Gloucester, I hope. She can't have drawn them all into Winchester with her, she must leave force enough in the west to hold her on to her base there. Why, what made you think of him just now?'

'It did enter my head that he might have been among the empress's chosen at Wherwell.' He had recoiled into grim recollection, and did not at first notice how Cadfael stiffened and turned to stare. 'I pray you're right, and he's well out of it.'

'At Wherwell? Why, what of Wherwell?'

64

'I forgot,' said Hugh, startled, 'you don't yet know the latest news, for I've only just brought it within here, and I got it only last night. Did I not say they'd have to try to break out – the empress's men? They have tried it, Cadfael, disastrously for them. They sent a picked force to try to seize Wherwell, no doubt hoping to straddle the road and the river there, and open a way to bring in supplies. William of Ypres cut them to pieces outside the town, and the remnant fled into the nunnery and shut themselves into the church. The place burned down over them . . . God forgive them for ever violating it, but they were Maud's men who first did it, not ours. The nuns, God help them, had taken refuge there when the fight began . . . .'

Cadfael sat frozen even in the sunlight. 'Do you tell me Wherwell has gone the way of Hyde?'

'Burned to the ground. The church at least. As for the rest . . . But in so hot and dry a season . . . .'

Cadfael, who had gripped him hard and suddenly by the arm, as abruptly loosed him, leaped from the bench, and began to run, veritably to run, as he had not done since hurtling to get out of range from the rogue castle on Titterstone Clee, two years earlier. He had still a very respectable turn of speed when roused, but his gait was wonderful, legless under the habit, like a black ball rolling, with a slight oscillation from side to side, a seaman's walk become a headlong run. And Hugh, who loved him, and rose to pursue him with a very sharp sense of the urgency behind this flight, nevertheless could not help laughing as he ran. Viewed from behind, a Benedictine in a hurry, and a Benedictine of more than sixty years and built like a barrel, at that, may be formidably impressive to one who knows him, but must be comic.

Cadfael's purposeful flight checked in relief as he emerged into the great court; for they were there still, in no haste with their farewells, though the horse stood by with a groom at his bridle, and Brother Fidelis tightening the straps that held Nicholas Harnage's bundle and rolled cloak behind the saddle. They knew nothing yet of any need for haste. There was a whole sunlit day before the rider.

Fidelis wore the cowl always outdoors, as though to cover a personal shyness that stemmed, surely, from his mute tongue.

65

He who could not open his mind to others shrank from claiming any privileged advance from them. Only Humilis had some manner of silent and eloquent speech with him that needed no voice. Having secured the saddle-roll the young man stepped back modestly to a little distance, and waited.

Cadfael arrived more circumspectly than he had set out from the garden. Hugh had not followed him so closely, but halted in shadow by the wall of the guest-hall.

'There's news,' said Cadfael bluntly. 'You should hear it before you leave us. The empress has made an attack on the town of Wherwell, a disastrous attack. Her force is wiped out by the queen's army. But in the fighting the abbey of Wherwell was fired, the church burned to the ground. I know no more detail, but so much is certain. The sheriff here got the word last night.'

'By a reliable man,' said Hugh, drawing close. 'It's certain.'

Nicholas stood staring, eyes and mouth wide, his golden sunburn dulling to an earthen grey as the blood drained from beneath it. He got out in a creaking whisper: 'Wherwell? They've dared . . . ?'

'No daring,' said Hugh ruefully, 'but plain terror. They were men penned in, the raiding party, they sought any place of hiding they could find, surely, and slammed to the door. But the end was the same, whoever tossed in the firebrands. The abbey's laid waste. Sorry I am to say it.'

'And the women . . . ? Oh, God . . . Julian's there . . . Is there any word of the women?'

'They'd taken to the church for sanctuary,' said Hugh. In such civil warfare there were no sanctuaries, not even for women and children. 'The remnant of the raiders surrendered – most may have come out alive. All, I doubt.'

Nicholas turned blindly to grope for his bridle, plucking his sleeve out of the quivering hand Humilis had laid on his arm. 'Let me away! I must go . . . I must go there and find her.' He swung back to catch again briefly at the older man's hand and wring it hard. 'I *will* find her! If she lives I'll find her, and see her safe.' He found his stirrup and heaved himself into the saddle.

'If God's with you, send me word,' said Humilis. 'Let me know that she lives and is safe.'

'I will, my lord, surely I will.'

'Don't trouble her, don't speak to her of me. No questions! All I need, all you must ask, is to know that God has preserved her, and that she has the life she wanted. There'll be a place elsewhere for her, with other sisters. If only she still lives!'

Nicholas nodded mutely, shook himself out of his daze with a great heave, wheeled his horse, and was gone, out through the gatehouse without another word or a look behind. They were left gazing after him, as the light dust of his passing shimmered and settled under the arch of the gate, where the cobbles ended, and the beaten earth of the Foregate began.

All that day Humilis seemed to Cadfael to press his own powers to the limit, as though the stress that drove Nicholas headlong south took its toll here in enforced stillness and inaction, where the heart would rather have been riding with the boy, at whatever cost. And all that day Fidelis, turning his back even on Rhun, shadowed Humilis with a special and grievous solicitude, tenderness and anxiety, as though he had just realised that death stood no great distance away, and advanced one gentle step with every hour that passed.

Humilis went to his bed immediately after Compline, and Cadfael, looking in on him ten minutes later, found him already asleep, and left him undisturbed accordingly. It was not a festering wound and a maimed body that troubled Humilis now, but an obscure feeling of guilt towards the girl who might, had he married her, have been safe in some manor far remote from Winchester and Wherwell and the clash of arms, instead of driven by fire and slaughter even out of her chosen cloister. Sleep could do more for his grieving mind than the changing of a dressing could do now for his body. Sleeping, he had the hieratic calm of a figure already carved on a tomb. He was at peace. Cadfael went quietly away and left him, as Fidelis must have left him, to rest the better alone.

In the sweet-scented twilight Cadfael went to pay his usual nightly visit to his workshop, to make sure all was well there, and stir a brew he had standing to cool overnight. Sometimes, when the nights were so fresh after the heat of the day, the skies so full of stars and so infinitely lofty, and every flower and leaf suddenly so imbued with its own lambent colour and light

67

in despite of the light's departure, he felt it to be a great waste of the gifts of God to be going to bed and shutting his eyes to them. There had been illicit nights of venturing abroad in the past – he trusted for good enough reasons, but did not probe too deeply. Hugh had had his part in them, too. Ah, well!

Making his way back with some reluctance, he went in by the church to the night stairs. All the shapes within the vast stone ship showed dimly by the small altar lamps. Cadfael never passed through without stepping for a moment into the choir, to cast a glance and a thought towards Saint Winifred's altar, in affectionate remembrance of their first encounter, and gratitude for her forbearance. He did so now, and checked abruptly before venturing nearer. For there was one of the brothers kneeling at the foot of the altar, and the tiny red glow of the lamp showed him the uplifted face, fast-closed eyes and prayerfully folded hands of Fidelis. Showed him no less clearly, as he drew softly nearer, the tears glittering on the young man's cheeks. A perfectly still face, but for the mute lips moving soundlessly on his prayers, and the tears welling slowly from beneath his closed eyelids and spilling on to his breast. The shocks of the day might well send him here, now his charge was sleeping, to put up fervent prayers for a better ending to the story. But why should his face seem rather that of a penitent than an innocent appellant? And a penitent unsure of absolution!

Cadfael slipped away very quietly to the night stairs and left the boy the entire sheltering space of the church for his inexplicable pain.

The other figure, motionless in the darkest corner of the choir, did not stir until Cadfael had departed, and even then waited long moments before stealing forward by inches, with held breath, over the chilly paving.

A naked foot touched the hem of Fidelis's habit, and as hastily and delicately drew back again from the contact. A hand was outstretched to hover over the oblivious head, longing to touch and yet not daring until the continued silence and stillness gave it courage. Tensed fingers sank into the curling russet that ringed the tonsure, the light touch set the hand quivering, like the pricking of imminent lightning in the air before a storm. If Fidelis also sensed it, he gave no sign. Even when the fingers stirred lovingly in his hair, and stroked down into the nape of his neck within the cowl he did not move, but rather froze where he knelt, and held his breath.

'Fidelis,' whispered a hushed and aching voice close at his shoulder. 'Brother, never grieve alone! Turn to me . . . I could comfort you, for everything, everything . . . whatever your need . . . .'

The stroking palm circled his neck, but before it reached his cheek Fidelis had started to his feet in one smooth movement, resolute and unalarmed, and swung out of reach. Without haste, or perhaps unwilling to show his face, even by this dim light, until he had mastered it, he turned to look upon the intruder into his solitude, for whispers have no identity, and he had never before taken any particular notice of Brother Urien. He did so now, with wide and wary grey eyes. A dark, passionate, handsome man, one who should never have shut himself in within these walls, one who burned, and might burn others before ever he grew cool at last. He stared back at Fidelis, and his face was wrung and his outstretched hand quaked, yearning towards Fidelis's sleeve, which was withdrawn from him austerely before he could grasp it.

'I've watched you,' breathed the husky, whispering voice, 'I know every motion and grace. Waste, waste of youth, waste of beauty . . . Don't go! No one sees us now . . . .'

Fidelis turned his back steadily, and walked out from the choir towards the night stairs. Silent on the tiled floor, Urien's naked feet followed him, the tormented whisper followed him.

'Why turn your back on loving kindness? You will not always do so. Think of me! I will wait . . . .'

Fidelis began to climb the stairs. The pursuer halted at the foot, too sick with anguish to go where other men might still be wakeful. 'Unkind, unkind . . .' wailed the faintest thread of a voice, receding, and then, with barely audible but extreme bitterness: 'If not here, in another place . . . If not now, at another time!'

SIX

Nicholas commandeered a change of horses twice on the way south, leaving those he had ridden hard to await the early return he foresaw, with the news he had promised to carry faithfully, whether good or bad. The stench of burning, old and acrid now, met him on the wind some miles from Wherwell, and when he entered what was left of the small town it was to find an almost de-peopled desolation. The few whose houses had survived unlooted and almost undamaged were sorting through their premises and salvaging their goods, but those who had lost their dwellings in the fire held off cautiously as yet from coming back to rebuild. For though the raiding party from Winchester had been either wiped out or made prisoner, and William of Ypres had withdrawn the queen's Flemings to their old positions ringing the city and the region, this place was still within the circle, and might yet be subjected to more violence.

Nicholas made his way with a cramped and anxious heart to the enclave of the nunnery, one of the three greatest in the shire, until this disaster fell upon its buildings and laid the half of them flat and the rest uninhabitable. The shell of the church stood up gaunt and blackened against the cloudless sky, the walls jagged and discoloured like decayed teeth. There were new graves in the nuns' cemetery. As for the survivors, they were gone, there was no home for them here. He looked at the newly-turned earth with a sick heart, and wondered whose daughters lay beneath. There had not yet been time to do more for them than bury them, they were nameless.

He would not let himself even consider that she might be there. He looked for the parish church and sought out the priest, who had gathered two homeless families beneath his roof and in his barn. A careworn, tired man, growing old, in a shabby gown that needed mending.

'The nuns?' he said, stepping out from his low, dark doorway. 'They're scattered, poor souls, we hardly know where. Three of them died in the fire. Three that we know of, but there may well be more, lying under the rubble there still. There was fighting all about the court and the Flemings were dragging their prisoners out of the church, but neither side cared for the women. Some are fled into Winchester, they say, though there's little safety to be found there, but the lord bishop must try to do something for them, their house was allied to the Old Minster. Others . . . I don't know! I hear the abbess is fled to a manor near Reading, where she has kin, and some she may have taken with her. But all's confusion – who can tell?'

'Where is this manor?' demanded Nicholas feverishly, and was met by a weary shake of the head.

'It was only a thing I heard – no one said where. It may not even be true.'

'And you do not know, Father, the names of those sisters who died?' He trembled as he asked it.

'Son,' said the priest with infinite resignation, 'what we found could not have a name. And we have yet to seek there for others, when we have found enough food to keep those alive who still live. The empress's men looted our houses first, and after them the Flemings. Those who have, here, must share with those who have nothing. And which of us has very much? God knows not I!'

Nor had he, in material things, only in tired but obstinate compassion. Nicholas had bread and meat in his saddle-bag, brought for provision on the road from his last halt to change horses. He hunted it out and put it into the old man's hands, a meagre drop in a hungry ocean, but the money in his purse could buy nothing here where there was nothing to buy. They would have to milk the countryside to feed their people. He left them to their stubborn labours, and rode slowly through the rubble of Wherwell, asking here and there if anyone had more precise information to impart. Everyone knew the sisters had dispersed, no one could say where. As for one woman's name, it meant nothing, it might not even be the name by which she

71

had entered on her vows. Nevertheless, he continued to utter it wherever he enquired, doggedly proclaiming the irreplaceable uniqueness of Julian Cruce, separate from all other women.

From Wherwell he rode on into Winchester. A soldier of the queen could pass through the iron ring without difficulty, and in the city it was plain that the empress's faction were hard-pressed, and dared not venture far from their tight fortress in the castle. But the nuns of Winchester, themselves earlier endangered and now breathing more easily, could tell him nothing of Julian Cruce. Some sisters from Wherwell they had taken in and cherished, but she was not among them. Nicholas had speech with one of their elder members, who was kind and solicitous, but could not help him.

'Sir, it is a name I do not know. But consider, there is no reason I should know it, for surely this lady may have taken a very different name when she took her vows, and we do not ask our sisters where they came from, nor who they once were, unless they choose to tell us freely. And I had no office that should bring me knowledge of these things. Our abbess would certainly be able to answer you, but we do not know where she is now. Our prioress, also. We are as lost as you. But God will find us, and bring us together again. As he will find for you the one you seek.'

She was a shrewd, agile, withered woman, thin as a gnat but indestructible as scutch grass. She eyed him with mildly amused sympathy, and asked blandly: 'She is kin to you, this Julian?'

'No,' said Nicholas shortly, 'but I would have had her kin, and very close kin, too.'

'And now?'

'I want to know her safe, living, content. There is no more in it. If she is so, God keep her so, and I am satisfied.'

'If I were you,' said the lady, after viewing him closely for some moments in silence, 'I should go on to Romsey. It is far enough removed to be a safer place than here, and it is the greatest of our Bendictine houses in these parts. God knows which of our sisters you may find there, but surely some, and it may be, the highest.'

He was young enough and innocent enough still, for all his travels, to be strongly moved by any evidence of trust and kindness, and he caught and kissed her hand in taking leave, as though she had been his hostess somewhere in hall. She, for her part, was too old and experienced to blush or bridle, but when he was gone she sat smiling a long, quiet while, before she rejoined her sisters. He was a very personable young man.

Nicholas rode the twelve miles or so to Romsey in sobering solemnity, aware he might be drawing near to an answer possibly not to his liking. Once clear of Winchester and on his way further south-west, he was delivered from any threat, for he went through country where the queen's writ ran without challenge. Pleasant, rolling country, well tree'd even before he reached the fringes of the great forest. He came to the abbey gatehouse, in the heart of the small town, in the late evening, and rang the bell at the gate. The portress peered at him through the grille, and asked his business. He stooped entreatingly to the grid, and gazed into a pair of bright, elderly eyes in beds of wrinkles.

'Sister, have you given refuge here to some of the nuns of Wherwell? I am seeking for news of one of them, and could get no answers there.'

The portress eyed him narrowly, and saw a young face soiled and drawn with travel, a young man alone, and in dead earnest, no threat. Even here in Romsey they had learned to be cautious about opening their gates, but the road beyond him was empty and still, and the twilight folded down on the little town peacefully enough.

'The prioress and three sisters reached here,' she said, 'but I doubt if any of them can tell you much of the rest, not yet. But come within, and I'll ask if she will speak with you.'

The wicket clanked open, lock and chain, and he stepped through into the court. 'Who knows?' said the portress kindly, fastening the door again after him. 'One of our three may be the one you're seeking. At least you may try.'

She led him along dim corridors to a small, panelled parlour, lit by a tiny lamp, and there left him. The evening meal would be long over, even Compline past, it was almost time for sleeping. They would want him satisfied, if satisfaction was possible, and out of their precinct before the night.

He could not rest or sit, but was prowling the room like a

caged bear when a further door opened, and the prioress of Wherwell came quietly in. A short, round, rosy woman, but with a formidably strong face and exceedingly direct brown eyes, that studied her visitor from head to foot in one piercing glance as he made his reverence to her.

'You asked for me, I am told. I am here. How can I help you?'

'Madam,' said Nicholas, trembling for awe of what might come, 'I was well north, in Shropshire, when I heard of the sack of Wherwell. There was a sister there of whose vocation I had only just learned, and now all I want is to know that she lives and is safe after that outrage. Perhaps to speak with her, and see for myself that she is well, if that can be permitted. I did ask in Wherwell itself, but could get no word of her – I know only the name she had in the world.'

The prioress waved him to a seat, and herself sat down apart, where she could watch his face. 'May I know your own name, sir?'

'My name is Nicholas Harnage. I was squire to Godfrid Marescot until he took the cowl in Hyde Mead. He was formerly betrothed to this lady, and he is anxious now to know that she is safe and well.'

She nodded at that very natural desire, but nevertheless her brows had drawn together in a thoughtful and somewhat puzzled frown. 'That name I know, Hyde was proud of having gained him. But I never recall hearing . . . What is the name of this sister you seek?'

'In the world she was Julian Cruce, of a Shropshire family. The sister I spoke with in Wherwell had never heard the name, but it may well be that she chose a very different name when she took the veil. But you will know of her both before and after.'

'Julian Cruce?' she repeated, erect and intent now, her sharp eyes narrowing. 'Young sir, are you not in some mistake? You are sure it was Wherwell she entered? Not some other house?'

'No, certainly, madam, Wherwell,' he said earnestly. 'I had it from her brother himself, he could not be mistaken.'

There was a moment of taut silence, while she considered and shook her head over him, frowning. 'When was it that she entered the Order? It cannot be long ago.'

'Three years, madam. The date I cannot tell, but it was about a month after my lord took the cowl, and that was in the middle of July.' He was frightened now by the strangeness of her reception. She was shaking her head dubiously, and regarding him with mingled sympathy and bewilderment. 'It may be that this was before you held office . . . . '

'Son,' she said ruefully, 'I have been prioress for more than seven years now, there is not a name among our sisters that I don't know, whether the world's name or the cloistered, not an entry I have not witnessed. And sorry as I am to say it, and little as I myself understand it, I cannot choose but tell you, past any doubt, that no Julian Cruce ever asked for, or received the veil at Wherwell. It is a name I never heard, and belongs to a woman of whom I know nothing.'

He could not believe it. He sat staring and passing a dazed hand once and again over his forehead. 'But . . . this is impossible! She set out from home with an escort, and a dowry intended for her convent. She declared her intent to come to Wherwell, all her household knew it, her father knew it and sanctioned it. About this, I swear to you, madam, there is no possible mistake. She set out to ride to Wherwell.'

'Then,' said the prioress gravely, 'I fear you have questions to ask elsewhere, and very serious questions. For believe me, if you are certain she set out to come to us, I am no less certain that she never reached us.'

'But what could prevent?' he asked urgently, wrenching at impossibilities. 'Between her home and Wherwell . . . '

'Between her home and Wherwell were many miles,' said the prioress. 'And many things can prevent the fulfilment of the plans of men and women in this world. The disorders of war, the accidents of travel, the malice of other men.'

'But she had an escort to bring her to her journey's end!'

'Then it's of them you should be making enquiries,' she said gently, 'for they signally failed to do so.'

No point whatever in pressing her further. He sat stunned into silence, utterly lost. She knew what she was saying, and at least she had pointed him towards the only lead that remained to him. What was the use of hunting any further in these parts, until he had caught at the clue she offered him, and begun to trace that ride of Julian's from Lai, where it had begun. Three men-at-arms, Reginald had said, went with her, under a huntsman who had an affection for her from her childhood. They must still be there in Reginald's service, there to be questioned, there to be made to account for the mission that had never been completed.

The prioress had yet one more point to make, even as she rose to indicate that the interview was over, and the late visitor dismissed.

'She was carrying, you say, the dowry she intended to bring to Wherwell? I know nothing of its value, of course, but . . . The roads are not entirely free of evil customs . . . .'

'She had four men to guard her,' cried Nicholas, one last flare in desperation.

'And they knew what she carried? God knows,' said the prioress, 'I should be loth to cast suspicion on any upright man, but we live in a world, alas, where of any four men, one at least may be corruptible.'

He went away into the town still dazed, unable to think or reason, unable to grasp and understand what with all his heavy heart he believed. It was growing dark, and he was too weary to continue now without sleep, besides the care he must have for his horse. He found an alehouse that could provide him a rough bed, and stabling and fodder for his beast, and lay wakeful a long time before his own exhaustion of body and mind overcame him.

He had an answer, but what to make of it he did not know. Certain it was that she had never passed through the gates of Wherwell, and therefore had not died there in the fire. But – three years, and never a word or a sign! Her brother had not troubled himself with a half-sister he scarcely knew, believing her to be settled in life according to her own choice. And never a word had come from her. Who was there to wonder or question? Cloistered women are secure in their own community, have all their sisterhood about them, what need have they of the world, and what should the world expect from them? Three years of silence from those vowed to the cultivation of silence is natural enough; but three years without a word now became an abyss, into which Julian Cruce had fallen as into the ocean, and sunk without trace.

Now there was nothing to be done but hasten back to Shrewsbury, confess his shattering failure in his mission, and go on to Lai to tell the same dismal story to Reginald Cruce. Only there could he again hope to find a thread to follow. He set off early in the morning to ride back into Winchester.

It was mid-morning when he drew near to the city. He had left it, prudently, not by the direct way through the west gate, since the royal castle with its hostile and by this time surely desperate garrison lay so close and had complete command of the gate. But some time before he reached the spot where he should, in the name of caution, turn eastward from the Romsey road and circle round the south of the city to a safer approach, he began to be aware of a constant chaotic murmur of sound ahead, that grew from a murmur to a throbbing clamour, to a steely din of clashing and screaming that could mean nothing but battle, and a close and tangled and desperate battle at that. It seemed to centre to his left front, at some distance from the town, and the air in that direction hung hazy with the glittering dust of struggle and flight.

Nicholas abandoned all thought of turning aside towards the bishop's hospital of Saint Cross or the east gate, and rode on full tilt towards the west gate. And there before him he saw the townsfolk of Winchester boiling out into the open sunlight with shouting and excitement, and the streets within full of people, loud, exultant and fearless, all clamouring for news or imparting news at the tops of their voices, throwing off all the creeping caution that had fettered them for so long.

Nicholas caught at a tall fellow's shoulder and bellowed his own question: 'What is it? What's happened?'

'They're gone! Marched out at dawn, that woman and her royal uncle of Scotland and all her lords! Little they cared about the likes of us starving, but when the wolf bit them it was another story. Out they went, the lot of them – in good order, *then*! Now hark to them! The Flemings at least let them get clear of the town before they struck, and let us alone. There'll be pickings, over there!'

They were only waiting, these vengeful tradesmen and craftsmen of Winchester, hovering here until the din of battle moved away into the distance. There would be gleanings

77

before the night. No man can ride his fastest loaded down with casque and coat of mail. Even their swords they might discard to lighten the weight their horses had to bear. And if they had retained enough optimism to believe they could convey their valuables away with them, there would be rich pickings indeed before the day was out.

So it had come, the expected attempt to break out of the iron circle of the queen's army, and it had come too late to have any hope of success. After the holocaust of Wherwell even the empress must have known she could hold out here no longer.

North-west along the Stockbridge road and wavering over the rising downs, the glittering halo of dust rolled and danced, spreading wider as it receded. Nicholas set off to follow it, as the boldest of the townsmen, or the greediest, or the most vindictive, were also doing afoot. He had far outridden them, and was alone in the undulating uplands, when he saw the first traces of the assault which had broken the empress's army. A single fallen body, a lamed horse straying, a heavy shield hurled aside, the first of many. A mile further on and the ground was littered with arms, pieces of armour torn off and flung aside in flight, helmets, coats of mail, saddle-bags, spilling garments and coins and ornaments of silver, fine gowns, pieces of plate from noble tables, all expendable where mere life was the one thing to be valued. Not all had preserved it, even at this cost. There were bodies, tossed and trampled among the grasses, frightened horses running in circles, some ridden almost to death and gasping on the ground. Not a battle, but a rout, a headlong flight in contagious terror.

He had halted, staring in sick wonder at such a spectacle, while the flight and pursuit span forward into the distance under its shining cloud, towards the Test at Stockbridge. He did not follow it further, but turned and rode back towards the city, wanting no part in that day's work. On his way he met the first of the gleaners, hungry and eager, gathering the spoils of victory.

It was three days later, in the early afternoon, when he rode again into the great court at Shrewsbury abbey, to fulfil the promise he had made. Brother Humilis was in the herb-garden with Cadfael, sitting in the shade while Fidelis chose from among the array of plants a few sprigs and tendrils he wanted for an illuminated border, bryony and centaury and bugloss, and the coiled threads of vetches, infinitely adaptable for framing initial letters. The young man had grown interested in the herbs and their uses, and sometimes helped to make the remedies Cadfael used in the treatment of Humilis, tending them with passionate, still devotion, as though his love could add the final ingredient that would make them sovereign.

The porter, knowing Nicholas well by this time, told him without question where he would find his lord. His horse he left tethered at the gatehouse, intending to ride on at once to Lai, and came striding round the clipped bulk of the tall hedge and along the gravel path to where Humilis was sitting on the stone bench against the south wall. So intent was Nicholas upon Humilis that he brushed past Fidelis with barely a glance, and the young brother, startled by his sudden and silent arrival, turned on him for once a head uncovered and a face open to the sun, but as quickly drew aside in his customary reticent manner, and held aloof from their meeting, deferring to a prior loyalty. He even drew the cowl over his head, and sank silently into its shadow.

'My lord,' said Nicholas, bending his knee to Humilis and clasping the two hands that reached to embrace him, 'your sorry servant!'

'No, never that!' said Humilis warmly, and freed his hands to draw the boy up beside him and peer searchingly into his face. 'Well,' he said with a sigh and a small, rueful smile, 'I see you have not the marks of success on you. No fault of yours, I dare swear, and no man can command success. You would not be back so soon if you had found out nothing, but I see it cannot be what you hoped for. You did not find Julian. At least,' he said, peering a little closer, and in a voice careful and low, 'not living . . . .'

'Neither living nor dead,' said Nicholas quickly, warding off the worst assumption. 'No, it's not what you think – it's not what any of us could have dreamed.' Now that it came to the telling, he could only blurt out the whole of it as baldly and honestly as possible, and be done. 'I searched in Wherwell, and in Winchester, until I found the prioress of Wherwell in refuge in Romsey abbey. She has held the office seven years, she knows every sister who has entered there in that time, and none of them is Julian Cruce. Whatever has become of Julian, she never reached Wherwell, never took vows there, never lived there – and cannot have died there. A blind ending!'

'She never came there?' Humilis echoed in an astonished whisper, staring with locked brows across the sunny garden.

'She never did! Always,' said Nicholas bitterly, 'I come three years too late. Three years! And where can she have been all that time, with never a word of her here, where she left home and family, nor there, where she should have come to rest? What can have happened to her, between here and Wherwell? That region was not in turmoil then, the roads should have been safe enough. And there were four men with her, well provided.'

'And they came home,' said Humilis keenly. 'Surely they came home, or Cruce would have been wondering and asking long ago. In God's name, what can they have reported when they returned? No evil! None from other men, or there would have been an instant hue and cry, none of their own, or they would not have returned at all. This grows deeper and deeper.'

'I am going on to Lai,' said Nicholas, rising, 'to let Cruce know, and have him hunt out and question those who rode with her. His father's men will be his men now, whether at Lai or on some other of his manors. They can tell us, at least, where they parted from her, if she foolishly dismissed them and rode the last miles alone. I'll not rest until I find her. If she lives, I *will* find her!'

Humilis held him by the sleeve, doubtfully frowning. 'But your command . . . You cannot leave your duties for so long, surely?'

'My command,' said Nicholas, 'can do very well without me now for a while. I've left them snug enough, encamped near Andover, living off the land, and my sergeants in charge, old soldiers well able to fill my place, the way things are now. For I have not told you the half. I'm so full of my own affairs, I have no time for kings. Did we not say, last time, that the empress must try to break out from Winchester soon, or starve where she was? She has so tried. After the disaster at Wherwell they must have known they could not hold out longer. Three days ago they marched out westward, towards Stockbridge, and

William de Warenne and the Flemings fell on them and broke them to pieces. It was no retreat, it was headlong flight. Everything weighty about them they threw away. If ever they do come safe back to Gloucester it will be half naked. I'll make a stay in the town and let Hugh Beringar know.'

Brother Cadfael, who had gone on with a little desultory weeding between his herb-beds, at a little distance, nevertheless heard all this with stretched ears and kindling blood, and straightened his back now to stare.

'And she – the empress? They have not taken her?' An empress for a king would be fair exchange, and almost inevitable, even if it meant not an ending, but stalemate, and a new beginning over the same exhausted and exhausting ground. Had Stephen been the one to capture the implacable lady, with his mad, endearing chivalry he would probably have given her a fresh horse and an escort, and sent her safely to Gloucester, to her own stronghold, but the queen was no such magnanimous idiot, and would make better use of a captive enemy.

'No, not Maud, she's safely away. Her brother sped her off ahead with Brian FitzCount to watch over her, and stayed to rally the rearguard and hold off the pursuit. No, it's better than Maud! He could have gone on fighting without her, but she'll be hard put to it without him. The Flemings caught them at Stockbridge, trying to ford the river, and rounded up all those who survived. It's the king's match we've taken, the man himself, Robert of Gloucester!'

81

SEVEN

Reginald Cruce, whether he had, or indeed could well be expected to have any deep affection for a half-sister so many years distant from him and so seldom seen, was not the man to be tolerant of any affront or injury towards any of his house. Whatever touched a Cruce reflected upon him, and roused his hackles like those of a pointing hound. He heard the story out in stoic silence but ever-growing resentment and rage, the more formidable for being under steely control.

'And all this is certain?' he said at length. 'Yes, the woman would know her business, surely. The girl never came there. I was not in this matter at all, I was not here and did not witness either the going or the return, but now we will see! At least I know the names of those who rode with her, for my father spoke of the journey on his death-bed. He sent his closest, men he trusted – who would not, with his daughter? And he doted on her. Wait!'

He bellowed from the hall door for his steward, and in from the fading daylight, cooling now towards dusk, came a grey elder dried and tanned like old leather, but very agile and sinewy. He might have been older than the lord he had lost, and was in no awe of either father or son here, but plainly master of his own duties, and aware of his worth. He spoke as an equal, and easy in the relationship.

'Arnulf, you'll remember,' said Reginald, waving him to a seat at the table with them, as free in acknowledgement of the association as his man, 'when my sister went off to her convent, the lads my father sent off with her – the Saxon brothers, Wulfric and Renfred, and John Bonde, and the other, who was he? He went off with the draft, I know, soon after I came here . . . . '

82

'Adam Heriet,' said the steward readily, and drew across the board the horn his lord filled for him. 'Yes, what of them?'

'I want them, Arnulf, all of them – here.'

'Now, my lord?' If he was surprised, he took surprises in his stride.

'Now, or as soon as may be. But first, all these were of my father's close household, you knew them better than ever I did. Would you count them trustworthy?'

'Out of question,' said the steward without hesitation, in a voice as dry and tough as his hide. 'Bonde is a simpleton, or little better, but a hard worker and open as the day. The Saxon pair are clever and subtle, but clever enough to know when they have a good lord, and loyal enough to be grateful for him. Why?'

'And the other, Heriet? Him I hardly knew. That was when Earl Waleran demanded my service of men in arms, and I sent him whatever offered, and this Heriet put himself forward. They told me he was restless because my sister was gone from the manor. He was a favourite of hers, so I heard, and fretted for her.'

'That could be true,' said Arnulf the steward. 'Certainly he was never the same after he came back from that journey. Such girl children can worm their way into a man and get at his heart. So she may have done with him. If you've known them from the cradle, they work deep into your marrow.'

Reginald nodded dourly. 'Well, he went. Twenty men my overlord asked of me, and twenty men he got. It was about the time he had that contention of his against the bishops, and needed reinforcements. Well, wherever he may be now, Heriet is out of our reach. But the rest are all here?'

'The Saxon pair in the stable loft this minute. Bonde should be coming in about this time from the fields.'

'Bring them,' said Reginald. And to Nicholas he said, when the steward had drained his horn and departed down the stone stair into the court as nimbly and rapidly as a youth of twenty: 'Wherever I look among these four, I can see no treachery. Why should they return, if they had somehow betrayed her? And why should they do so, any man of them? Arnulf says right, they knew they had the softest of beds here, my father was of the old, paternal, household kind, easier far than I, and

I am not hated.' He was well aware, to judge by the sharp smile and curl of the lip, yellow-outlined in the low lamplight, of all the tensions that still bound and burned between Saxon and Norman, and was too intelligent to strain them too far. In the countryside memories were very long, and loyalties with them, hard to displace, slow to replace.

'Your steward is Saxon,' said Nicholas drily.

'So he is! And content! Or if not content,' said Reginald, at once dour and bright in the intimate light, 'at least aware of worse, worse by far. I have benefited by my father's example, I know when to bend. But where my sister is concerned, I tell you, I feel my spine stiffen.'

So did Nicholas, as stiff as if the marrow there had petrified into stone. And he viewed the three hinds, when they came marshalled sleepily up the steps into the hall, with the same blank, opaque eyes as did their master. Two long, fair fellows surely no more than thirty years old, with all the lean grace of their northern kin and eyes that caught the light in flashes of pale, blinding blue, and a softer, squat, round-faced man perhaps a little older, bearded and brown.

It might be true enough, thought Nicholas, watching them, that they had no hate for their lord, but rather reckoned themselves lucky by comparison with many of their kind, now for the third generation subject to Norman masters. But for all that, they went in awe of Reginald, and any such summons as this, outside the common order of their labouring day, brought them to questioning alert and wary, their faces closed, like a lid shut down over a box of thoughts that might not all be acceptable to authority. But it was different when they understood the subject of their lord's enquiry. The shut faces opened and eased. It was clear to Nicholas that none of these three felt he had any reason for uneasiness concerning that journey, rather they recalled it with pleasure, as well they might, the one carefree pilgrimage, the one holiday of their lives, when they rode instead of going afoot, and went well-provided and in the pride of arms.

Yes, of course they remembered it. No, they had had no trouble by the way. A lady accompanied by two good bowmen and two swordsmen had had nothing to fear. The taller of the

Saxon pair, it seemed, used the new long-bow, drawn to the shoulder, while John Bonde carried the short Welsh bow, drawn to the breast, of less range and penetration than the long-bow, but wonderfully fast and agile in use at shorter range. The other brother was a swordsman, and so had the fourth member been, the missing Adam Heriet. A good enough company to travel briskly and safely, at whatever speed the lady could maintain without fatigue.

'Three days on the way, my lord,' said the Saxon bowman, spokesman for all three, and encouraged with vehement nods, 'and then we came into Andover, and because it was already evening, we lay there overnight, meaning to finish the journey the next morning. Adam found a lodging for the lady with a merchant's household there, and we lay in the stables. It was but three or four miles more to go, so they told us.'

'And my sister was then in health and spirits? Nothing had gone amiss?'

'No, my lord, we had a good journey. She was glad then to be so close to what she wished. She said so, and thanked us.'

'And in the morning? You brought her on those few miles?'

'Not we, my lord, for she chose to go the rest of the way with only Adam Heriet, and we were to wait in Andover for his return, and so we did as we were ordered. And when he came, then we set out for home.'

To this the other two nodded firm assent, satisfied that their errand had been completed in obedience to the lady's wishes. So it was only one, only her servant and familiar, according to repute, who had gone the rest of the way with Julian Cruce.

'You saw them ride for Wherwell?' demanded Reginald, frowning heavily at every complexity that arose to baulk him. 'She went with him freely, content?'

'Yes, my lord, fresh and early in the morning they went. A fine morning, too. She said farewell to us, and we watched them out of sight.'

No need to doubt it. Only four miles from her goal, and yet she had never reached it. And only one man could know what had become of her in that short distance.

Reginald waved them away irritably. What more could they tell him? To the best of their knowledge she had gone where she had meant to go, and all was well with her. But as the three made for the hall door, glad to be off to their beds, Nicholas said suddenly: 'Wait!' And to his host: 'Two more questions, if I may ask them?'

'Do so, freely.'

'Was it the lady herself who told you it was her wish to go on with only Heriet, and ordered you to remain in Andover and wait for him?'

'No,' said the spokesman, after a moment's thought, 'it was Adam told us.'

'And they set out in the early morning, you said. At what hour did Heriet return?'

'Not until twilight, sir. It was getting dark when he came. Because of that we stayed the night over, to make an early start for home next day.'

'There was another question I might have added,' said Nicholas, when he was alone with his host, and the hall door stood open on the deepening dusk and quiet of the yard, 'but I doubt he would have seen to his own horse, and after a night's rest there'd be no way of judging how far it had been ridden. But see how the time testifies – three or four miles to Wherwell, and he would have had no call to linger, once he had brought her there. Yet he was the whole day away, twelve hours or more. What was he about all that time? Yet he's said to have been her devoted slave from infancy.'

'It got him credit with my father, who also doted,' said Reginald sourly. 'I knew little of him. But there he is at the heart of this, and who else is there? He alone rode with her that last day. And came back here with his fellows, letting it be seen all had gone well, and the matter was finished. But between Andover and Wherwell my sister vanishes. And a month or so later, when our overlord, Earl Waleran, from whom we hold three manors, sends asking for men, who should be first to offer himself but this same man? Why so ready to seize on a way of leaving here? For fear questions should yet be asked, some day? Something untoward come to light, and start the hunt?'

'Would he have come back at all,' wondered Nicholas, 'if he had done her harm or any way betrayed her?'

'If he had wit enough, yes, and wit enough he surely had, for see how he has succeeded! If he had failed to return with the others, there would have been a hue and cry at once. They would have started it before ever they left Andover. As it is, three years are gone without a word or a shadow of doubt, and where is Heriet now?'

He had fastened on the notion now, tearing it with his teeth, savouring the inner rage he felt at any such thing being dared against his house. It was for that he would want revenge, if ever it came to the proof, not for Julian's own injuries. And yet Nicholas could not but tread the same way with him. Who else was there, to have wiped out the very image and memory of that girl committed to his care? Two had ridden from Andover, one had returned. The other was gone from the face of the earth, vanished into air. It was hard to go on believing that she would ever be seen again.

A servant brought in a lamp, and refilled the pitcher of ale on the table. The lady kept her chamber with her children, and left the men to confer without interruption. The night came down almost suddenly, in the brief customary breeze that came with this hour.

'She is dead!' said Reginald abruptly, and spread a large hand flat on the table.

'No, that's not certain. And *why* should he do such a thing? He lost his security here, for he dared not stay, once the chance of leaving offered. What was there to gain that would outweigh that? Is a man-at-arms in Waleran of Meulan's service better off than your trusted people here? I think not!'

'Service for half a year? If he stayed longer it was from choice, half a year was all that was demanded. And as for what he had to gain – and by God, he was the only one of the four who could have known the worth of it – my sister had three hundred silver marks in her saddle-bags, besides a list of valuables meant for her convent. I cannot recite you the whole tally offhand, but they're listed somewhere in the manor books, the clerk can lay hands on the record. I know there was a pair of silver candle-holders. And such jewels as she had from her mother she also took in gift, having no further use for them herself in this world. Enough to tempt a man – even if he had to buy in a confederate to put a better face on the deed.'

And it could be so! A woman carrying her dowry with her,

87

with a father and household satisfied of her well-being at home, and no one to wonder at her silence . . . But no, that could not be right, Nicholas caught himself up hopefully, not if she had already sent word of her coming ahead to Wherwell. Surely a girl intending to take the veil must advance her plea and be sure of acceptance before venturing on the journey south. But if she had done so, then there would have been wonder at her failure to arrive, and rapid enquiry, and the prioress, had there ever been letters or a courier from Julian Cruce, would have known and remembered the name. No, she could not have bargained beforehand. She had taken her dowry and simply gone to knock on the door and ask admittance. He had not the experience in such matters to know if that was very unusual, nor the cynicism to reflect that it would hardly be refused if the portion brought was large enough.

'This man Heriet will have to be found,' said Nicholas, making up his mind. 'If he's still serving with Waleran of Meulan, then I may be able to find him. Waleran is the king's man. If not, he'll be far to seek, but what other choice have we? He's native in this shire, is he? If he has kin, they'll be here?'

'He's second son to a free tenant at Harpecote. Why, what are you thinking?'

'That you'd best have your clerk make two copies of the list of what your sister took with her when she left. The money can't be traced and known, but it may be the valuables can. Have him describe them fully if he can. Plate meant for church use may turn up on sale or be noted somewhere, so may gems. I'll have the list circulated round Winchester – if the bishop's well rid of his empress he may know now where his interest lies! – and try to find Adam Heriet among Meulan's companies, or get word when and how he left them. You do as much here, where if he has kin he may some day visit. Can you think of anything better? Or anything more we can undertake?'

Reginald heaved himself up from the table, making the flame of the lamp gutter. A big, black-avised, affronted man, with a face grimly set. 'That's well reasoned, and we'll do it. Tomorrow I'll have him copy the items – he's a finicky little fellow who has everything at his finger-ends – and I'll ride with you to Shrewsbury and see Hugh Beringar, and have this matter in train before the day's out. If this or any villain has done murder and robbery against my house, I want justice and I want restitution.'

Nicholas rose with his host, and went to the bed prepared for him so weary that he could not fail to sleep. So did he want justice. But what was justice in this matter? He planned and thought as one following a trail, he must pursue it with all his powers, having nothing else left to attempt, but he could not and would not believe in it. What he wanted above everything else in the world was a breath of some fresh breeze, blowing from another quarter, suggesting that she was not dead, that all this coil of suspicion and cupidity and treachery was false, a mere appearance, to be blown away when the morning came. But the morning came, and nothing was new, and nothing changed.

Thus two who had only one quest in common, and nothing besides to make them allies, rode together back into Shrewsbury, armed with two well-scripted copies of the valuables and money Julian Cruce had carried with her as her dowry on entering the cloister.

Hugh had come down from the town to dine with Abbot Radulfus, and acquaint him with the latest developments in the political tangle that was England. The flight of the empress back into her western stronghold, the scattering of a great part of her forces, and the capture of Earl Robert of Gloucester, without whom she was impotent, must transform the whole pattern of events, though its first effect was to freeze them from any action at all. The abbot might not have any interest in factional strife, but he was entitled to the mitre and a place in the great council of the country, and the welfare of people and church was very much his business. They had conferred a long time over the abbot's well-furnished table, and it was mid-afternoon when Hugh came looking for Cadfael in the herb-garden.

'You'll have heard? The word that Nicholas Harnage brought me yesterday? He said he had come here first, to his lord. Robert of Gloucester is penned up in Rochester a prisoner, and everything has halted while both sides think on what comes next – we, how best to make use of him, they, how to survive without him.' Hugh sat down on the stone bench in the shade, and spread his booted feet comfortably. 'Now comes the argument. And she had better order the king loosed from his chains, or Robert may find himself tethered, too.'

'I doubt if she'll see it so,' said Cadfael, pausing to lean on his hoe and pluck out a wisp of weed from between his neat, aromatic beds. 'More than ever, Stephen is her only weapon now. She'll try to exact the highest possible price for him, her brother will scarcely be enough to satisfy her.'

Hugh laughed. 'Robert himself takes the same line, by young Harnage's account. He refuses to consider an exchange for the king, says he's no fair match for a monarch, and to balance it fitly we must turn loose all the rearguard that were taken with him, to make up Stephen's weight in the scale. But wait a while! If the empress argues in the same way now, within a month wiser men will have shown her she can do nothing, nothing at all, without Robert. London will never let her enter again, much less get within reach of the crown, and for all she has Stephen in a dungeon, he is still king.'

'It's Robert they'll have trouble persuading,' Cadfael reasoned.

'Even he will have to see the truth in the end. If she is to continue her fight, it can only be with Robert beside her. They'll convince him. Reluctant as they all may be to loose their hold on him, we shall have Stephen back before the year's end.'

They were still there together in the garden when Nicholas and Reginald Cruce, having enquired in vain for Hugh at the castle, as they entered the town, and again at Hugh's house by Saint Mary's church, as they passed through, followed the directions given by his porter, and came purposefully hunting for him at the abbey. At the sound of their boots on the gravel, and the sight of them rounding the box hedge, Hugh rose alertly to meet them.

'You're back in good time. What news?' And to the second man he said, eyeing him with interest: 'I have not enjoyed your acquaintance until now, sir, but you are surely the lord of Lai. Nicholas here has told me how things stood at Wherwell. You're welcome to whatever service I can offer. And what now?'

'My lord sheriff,' said Cruce loudly and firmly, as one accustomed to setting the pace for others to follow, 'in the matter of my sister there's ground for suspicion of robbery and murder, and I want justice.'

'So do all decent men, and so do I. Sit down here, and let me hear what grounds you have for such suspicions, and where the finger points. I grant you the matter looks ugly enough. Let me know what you've found at home to add to it.'

It was over-hot in the afternoon sun, and even in shirt-sleeves Cruce was sweating freely. They moved back into the shade, and there sat down together, and Cadfael, hospitable in his own domain, and by no means inclined to be ousted from it in the middle of his work, went instead to bring a pitcher of wine from his workshop, and beakers for their use. He served them and went aside, but not so far that he did not hear what passed. All that had gone before he already knew, and on certain points his curiosity was already pricked into wakefulness, and foresaw circumstances in which he might yet be needed. His patient fretted over the girl, and could not afford further fraying away of what little flesh he had. Cadfael clove to his fellow-crusader in a solidarity of shared experience and mutual respect. One of those few, like Guimar de Massard, who came clean and chivalrous out of a very deformed and marred holy war. And however gradually, dying of it. Whatever concerned his welfare, body or soul, Cadfael wanted to know.

'My lord,' said Nicholas earnestly, 'you'll remember all I told you of the men of my lord Cruce's household who escorted his sister to Wherwell. Three of the four we have questioned at Lai, and I am sure they have told us truth. But the fourth . . . and he the only one who accompanied her on the last day of her journey, the last few miles – he is no longer there, and him we must find.'

They told the whole story between them, at times in chorus, very vehemently.

'He left with her from Andover early in the morning, and the other three, who had orders to remain there, watched them away.'

'And he did not return until late evening, too late to set out for home that night. Yet Wherwell is but three or four miles from Andover.'

'And he, alone of those four,' said Cruce fiercely, 'was so deep in her confidence from old familiarity that he may well have known, must have known, the dowry she carried with her.'

'And that was?' demanded Hugh sharply. His memory was excellent. There was nothing he needed to be told twice.

'Three hundred marks in coin, and certain valuables for church use. My lord, we have had my clerk, who keeps good accounts, write a list of what she took, and here we have two copies. The one we hold you should circulate in these parts, where the man is native, and so was my sister, and the other Harnage here will carry to make known round Winchester, Wherwell and Andover, where she vanished.'

'Good!' said Hugh heartily. 'The coins can never be certainly traced, but the pieces of church ornaments may.' He took the scroll Nicholas held out to him, and read with lowered and frowning brows: 'Item, a pair of candlesticks of silver, made in the form of tall sconces entwined with the vine, with snuffers attached by silver chains, also ornamented with grape leaves. Item, a standing cross a man's hand-length in height, on a silver pedestal of three steps, and studded with semi-precious stones of yellow pebble, amethyst and agate, together with a similar cross of the same metal and stones, a little finger's length, on a thin silver neck-chain for a priest's wear. Item, a silver pyx, small, engraved with ferns. Also certain pieces of jewellery to her belonging, as, a necklet of polished stones from the hills above Pontesbury, a bracelet of silver engraved with tendrils of vetch, and a curious ring of silver set with enamels all round, in the form of yellow and blue flowers.' He looked up. 'Surely identifiable if they can be found, almost any of these. Your clerk did well. Yes, I'll have this made known to all officers and tenants of mine here in the shire, but it seems to me that in the south they're more likely to be traced. As for the man, if he's native here he has kin, and may well keep in touch with them. You say he went to do fighting service?'

'Only a matter of weeks after he returned to my father's household, yes. My father was newly dead, and the Earl of Worcester, my overlord, demanded a draft of men, and this

Adam Heriet offered himself.'

'How old?' asked Hugh.

'A year or so past fifty. A strong man with sword or bow. He had been forester and huntsman to my father, Waleran would think himself lucky to get him. The rest were younger, but raw.'

'And where did this Heriet hail from? Your father's man must belong to one of your own manors.'

'Born at Harpecote, a younger son of a free man who farmed a yardland there. His elder brother farmed it after him. A nephew has it now. They were not on good terms, or so my father said. But for all that there may be some trace of him to be picked up there.'

'Had they any other kin? And the fellow never took a wife?'

'No, he never did. I know of no others of his family, but there well may be some around Harpecote.'

'Let them be,' said Hugh decidedly. 'It had best be left to me to probe there. Though I doubt if a man with no ties here will have come back to the shire, once having taken to the fighting life. More likely to be found where you're bound for, Nicholas. Do your best!'

'I mean to,' said Nicholas grimly, and rose to be off about the work without delay. The scroll of Julian's possessions he rolled and thrust into the breast of his coat. 'I must say a word first to my lord Godfrid, and let him know I'll not abandon this hunt while there's a grain of hope left. Then I'm on the road!' And he was away at a fast stride that became a light, long-paced run before he was out of sight. Cruce rose in his turn, eyeing Hugh somewhat grudgingly, as if he doubted to find in him a sufficient force of vengeful fury for the undertaking.

'Then I may leave this with you, my lord? And you will pursue it vigorously?'

'I will,' said Hugh drily. 'And you will be at Lai? That I may know where to find you, at need?'

Cruce went away silenced, for the time being, but none too content, and looked back from the turn of the hedge dubiously, as if he felt that the lord sheriff should already have been on horseback, or at least shaping for it, in the cause of Cruce vengeance. Hugh stared him out coolly, and watched him

93

round the thick screen of box and disappear.

'Though I had best move speedily,' he said then, wryly smiling, 'for if that one found the fellow first I would not give much for his chances of escaping a few broken bones, if not a stretched neck. And even if it may come to that in the end, it shall not be at Reginald Cruce's hands, nor without a fair trial.' He clapped Cadfael heartily on the back, and turned to go. 'Well, if it's close season for kings and empresses, at least it gives us time to hunt the smaller creatures.'

Cadfael went to Vespers with an unquiet mind, troubled by imaginings of a girl on horseback, with silver and rough gems and coin in her saddle-bags, parting from her last known companions only a few miles from her goal, and then vanishing like morning mist in the summer sun, as if she had never been. A wisp of vapour over the meadow, and then gone. If those who agonised after her, the old and the young, had known her dead and with God, they, too, could have been at peace. Now there was no peace for any man drawn into this elaborate web of uncertainty.

Among the novices and schoolboys and the child oblates, last of their kind, for Abbot Radulfus would accept no more infants into a cloistered life decreed for them by others, Rhun stood rapt and radiant, smiling as he sang. A virgin by nature and aptitude, as well as by years, untroubled by the bodily agonies that tore most men, but miraculously aware of them and tender towards them, as few are to pains that leave their own flesh unwrung.

Vespers at this time of year shone with with filtered summer light, that showed Rhun's flaxen beauty in crystalline pallor, and flashed across into the ranks of the brothers to burn in the sullen, smouldering darkness of Brother Urien, and the dilated brilliance of his black eyes, and cool into discreet shade where Brother Fidelis stood withdrawn into the shadows of the wall, alert at his lord's elbow, with no eyes and no thought for what went on around him, as he had no voice to join in the chant. His shadowed eyes looked nowhere but at Humilis, his slight body stood braced to receive and support at any moment the even frailer form that stood lance-straight beside him.

Well, worship has its own priorities, and a duty once

assumed is a duty to the end. God and Saint Benedict would understand and respect that.

Cadfael, whose mind should also have been on higher things, found himself thinking: he dwindles before our eyes. It will be even sooner than I had thought. There is nothing that can prevent, or even greatly delay it now.

EIGHT

If Robert of Gloucester had not been trapped and captured in the waters of the river Test, and the Empress Maud in headlong flight with the remnant of her army into Gloucester, by way of Ludgershall and Devizes, the hunt for Adam Heriet might have gone on for a much longer time. But the freezing chill of stalemate between the two armies, each with a king in check, had loosed many a serving man, bored with inaction and glad of a change, to stretch his legs and take his leisure elsewhere, while the lull lasted and the politicians argued and bargained. And among them an ageing, experienced practitioner of sword and bow, among the Earl of Worcester's forces.

Hugh was a man of the northern part of the shire himself, but from the Welsh border; and the manors to the north-east, dwindling into the plain of Cheshire, were less familiar to him and less congenial. Over in the tamer country of the hundred of Hodnet the soil was fat and well-farmed, and the gleaned grain-fields full of plump, contented cattle at graze, at once making good use of what aftermath there was in a dry season, and leaving their droppings to feed the following year's tilth. There were abbey tenants here and there in these parts, and abbey stock turned into the fields now the crop was reaped. Their treading and manuring of the ground was almost as valuable as their fleeces.

The manor of Harpecote lay in open plain, with a small coppiced woodland on the windward side, and a low ridge of common land to the south. The house was small and of timber, but the fields were extensive, and the barns and byres that clung within the boundary fence were well-kept, and probably well-filled. Cruce's steward came out into the yard to greet the sheriff and his two sergeants, and direct them to the homestead of Edric Heriet.

It was one of the more substantial cottages of the hamlet, with a kitchen-garden before it and a small orchard behind, where a tousled girl with kilted skirts was hanging out washing on the hedge. Hens ran in the orchard grass, and a she-goat was tethered to graze there. A free man, this Edric was said to be, farming a yardland as a rent-paying tenant of his lord, a dwindling phenomenon in a country where a tiller of the soil was increasingly tied to it by customary services. These Heriets must be good husbandmen and hard workers to continue to hold their land and make it provide them a living. Such families could make good use of younger sons, needing all the hands they could muster. Adam was clearly the self-willed stray who had gone to serve for pay, and cultivated the skills of arms and forestry and hunting instead of the land.

A big, tow-headed, shaggy fellow in a frayed leather coat came ducking out of the low byre as Hugh and his officers halted at the gate. He stared, stiffening, and stood fronting them with a wary face, recognising authority though he did not know the man who wore it.

'You're wanting something here, masters?' Civil but not servile, he eyed them narrowly, and straddled his own gateway like a man on guard.

Hugh gave him good-day with the special amiability he used towards uneasy poor men bitterly aware of their disadvantages. 'You'll be Edric Heriet, I'm told. We're looking for word of where to find one Adam of that name, who should be your uncle. And you're all his kin that we know of, and may be able to tell us where to seek him. And that's the whole of it, friend.'

The big young man, surely no more than thirty years old, and most likely husband to the dishevelled but comely girl in the orchard, and father to the baby that was howling somewhere within the croft, shifted uncertainly from foot to foot, made up his mind, and stood squarely, his face inclined to clear.

'I'm Edric Heriet. What is it you want with uncle of mine? What has he done?'

Hugh was not displeased with that. There might be small warmth of kinship between them, but this one was not going to open his mouth until he knew what was in the wind. Blood thickened at the hint of offence and danger.

'To the best of my knowledge, nothing amiss. But we need to have out of him as witness what he knows about a matter he had a hand in some years ago, sent by his lord on an errand from Lai. I know he is – or was – in the service of the Earl of Worcester since then, which is why he may be hard to find, the times being what they are. If you've had word from him, or can tell us where to look for him, we'll be thankful to you.'

He was curious now, though still uncertain. 'I have but one uncle, and Adam he's called. Yes, he was huntsman at Lai, and I did hear from my father that he went into arms for his lord's overlord, though I never knew who that might be. But as long as I recall, he never came near us here. I never remember him but from when I was a child shooing the birds off the ploughland. They never got on well, those brothers. Sorry I am, my lord,' he said, and though it was doubtful if he felt much sorrow, it was plain he spoke truth as to his ignorance. 'I have no notion where he may be now, nor where he's been these several years.'

Hugh accepted that, perforce, and considered a moment. 'Two brothers, were they? And no more? Never a sister between them? No tie to fetch him back into the shire?'

'There's an aunt I have, sir, only the one. It was a thin family, ours, my father was hard put to it to work the land after his brother left, until I grew up, and two younger brothers after me. We do well enough now between us. Aunt Elfrid was the youngest of the three, she married a cooper, bastard Norman he was, a little dark fellow from Brigge, called Walter.' He looked up, unaware of indiscretion, at the little dark Norman lord on the tall, raw-boned dapple-grey horse, and wondered at Hugh's blazing smile. 'They're settled in Brigge, I think she has childer. She might know. They were nearer.'

'And no other beside?'

'No, my lord, that was all of them. I think,' he said, hesitant but softening, 'he was godfather to her first. He might take that to heart.'

'So he might,' said Hugh mildly, thinking of his own masterful heir, to whom Cadfael stood godfather, 'so he very well might. I'm obliged to you, friend. At least we'll ask there.'

He wheeled his horse, without haste, to the homeward way. 'A good harvest to you!' he said over his shoulder, smiling, and chirruped to the grey and was off, with his sergeants at his heels.

Walter the cooper had a shop in the hilltop town of Brigge, in a narrow alley no great way from the shadow of the castle walls. His booth was a narrow-fronted cave that drove deep within, and backed on an open, well-lit yard smelling of cut timber, and stacked with his finished and half-finished barrels, butts and pails, and the tools and materials of his craft. Over the low wall the ground fell away by steep, grassy terraces to where the Severn coiled, almost as it coiled at Shrewsbury, close about the foot of the town, broad and placid now at low summer water, with sandy shoals breaking its surface, but ready to wake and rage if sudden rains should come.

Hugh left his sergeants in the alley, and himself dismounted and went in through the dark booth to the yard beyond. A freckled boy of about seventeen was stooped over his jointer, busy bevelling a barrel-stave, and another a year or two younger was carefully paring long bands of willow for binding the staves together when the barrel was set up in its truss hoop. Yet a third boy, perhaps ten years old, was energetically sweeping up shavings and cramming them into bags for firing. It seemed that Walter had a full quiver of helpers in his business, for they were all alike, and all plainly sons of one father, and he the small, spry, dark man who straightened up from his shaving-horse, knife in hand.

'Serve you, sir?'

'Master cooper,' said Hugh, 'I'm looking for one Adam Heriet, who I'm told is brother to your wife. They know nothing of his whereabouts at his nephew's croft at Harpecote, but thought you might be in closer touch with him. If you can tell me where he's to be found, I shall be grateful.'

There was a silence, sudden and profound. Walter stood gravely staring, and the hand that held the draw-knife with its curved blade sank quite slowly to hang at his side while he thought. Manual dexterity was natural to him, but thought came with deliberation, and slowly. All three boys stood equally mute and stared as their father stared. The eldest,

Hugh supposed, must be Adam's godson, if Edric had the matter aright.

'Sir,' said Walter at length, 'I don't know you. What's your will with my wife's kin?'

'You shall know me, Walter,' said Hugh easily. 'My name is Hugh Beringar, I am sheriff of this shire, and my business with Adam Heriet is to ask him some questions concerning a matter three years old now, in which I trust he'll be able to help us do right. If you can bring me to have speech with him, you may be helping him no less than me.'

Even a law-abiding man, in the circumstances, might have his doubts of that, but a law-abiding man with a decent business and a wife and family to look after would also take a careful look all round the matter before denying the sheriff a fair answer. Walter was no fool. He shuffled his feet thoughtfully in the sawdust and the small shavings his youngest son had missed in his sweeping, and said with every appearance of candour and goodwill: 'Why, my lord, Adam's been away soldiering some years, but now it seems there's almost quiet down in the southern parts, and he's free to take his pleasure for a few days. You come very apt to your time, sir, as it chances, for he's here within the house this minute.'

The eldest boy had made to start forward softly towards the house door by this, but his father plucked him unobtrusively back by the sleeve, and gave him a swift glance that froze him where he stood. 'This lad here is Adam's godson and namesake,' said Walter guilelessly, putting him forward by the hand which had restrained him. 'You show the lord sheriff into the room, boy, and I'll put on my coat and follow.'

It was not what the younger Adam had intended, but he obeyed, whether in awe of his father or trusting him to know best. But his freckled face was glum as he led the way through the door into the large single room that served as hall and sleeping-quarters for his elders. An uncovered window, open over the descent to the river, let in ample light on the centre of the room, but the corners receded into a wood-scented darkness. At a big trestle table sat a solid, brown-bearded, balding man with his elbows spread comfortably on the board, and a beaker of ale before him. He had the weathered look of a man who lives out of doors in all but the bleakest seasons, and

100

an air of untroubled strength about his easy stillness. The woman who had just come in from her cupboard of a kitchen, ladle in hand, was built on the same generous fashion, and had the same rich brown colouring. It was from their father that the boys got their wiry build and dark hair, and the fair skins that dappled in the sun.

'Mother,' said the youth, 'here's the lord sheriff asking after Uncle Adam.'

His voice was flat and loud, and he halted a moment, blocking the doorway, before he moved within and let Hugh pass by him. It was the best he could do. The unshuttered window was large enough for an active man, if he had anything on his conscience, to vault through it and make off down the slope to a river he could wade now without wetting his knees. Hugh warmed to the loyal godson, and refrained from letting him see even the trace of a smile. A dreaming soul, evidently, who saw no use in a sheriff but to bring trouble to lesser men. But Adam the elder sat attentive and interested a reasonable moment before he got to his feet and gave amiable greeting.

'My lord, you have your asking. That name and title belongs to me.'

One of Hugh's sergeants would be circling the slope below the window by now, while the other stayed with the horses. But neither the man nor the boy could have known that. Evidently Adam had seen action enough not to be easily startled or affrighted, and here had no reason he could see, so far, to be either.

'Be easy,' he said. 'If it's a matter of some of King Stephen's men quitting their service, no need to look here. I have leave to visit my sister. You may have a few strays running loose, for all I know, but I'm none.'

The woman came to his side slowly and wonderingly, bewildered but not alarmed. She had a round, wholesome, rosy face, and honest eyes.

'My lord, here's my good brother come so far to see me. Surely there's no wrong in that?'

'None in the world,' said Hugh, and went on without preamble, and in the same mild manner: 'I'm seeking news of a lady who vanished three years since. What do you know of

Julian Cruce?'

That was sheer blank bewilderment to mother and son, and to Walter, who had just come into the room at Hugh's back, but it was plain enough vernacular to Adam Heriet. He froze where he stood, half-risen from the bench, leaning on the trestle table, and hung there staring into Hugh's face, his own countenance wary and still. He knew the name, it had flung him back through the years, every detail of that journey he was recalling now, threading them frantically through his mind like the beads of a rosary in the hands of a terrified man. But he was not terrified, only alerted to danger, to the pains of memory, to the necessity to think fast, and perhaps select between truth, partial truth and lying. Behind that firm, impenetrable face he might have been thinking anything.

'My lord,' said Adam, stirring slowly out of his stillness, 'yes, of her certainly I know. I rode with her, I and three others from her father's household, when she went to take the veil at Wherwell. And I do know, seeing I serve in those parts, I do know how the nunnery there was burned out. But vanished three years since? How is that possible, seeing it was well known to her kin where she was living? Vanished now – yes, all too certainly, for I've been asking in vain since the fire. If you know more of my lady Julian since then than I, I beg you tell me. I could get no word whether she's living or dead.'

It had all the ring of truth, if he had not so strongly contained himself in those few moments of silence. It might be more than half truth, even so. If he was honest, he would have looked for her there, after the holocaust. If dishonest – well, he knew and could use the recent circumstances.

'You went with her to Wherwell,' said Hugh, answering nothing and volunteering nothing. 'Did you then see her safe within the convent gates there?'

This silence was brief indeed, but pregnant. If he said yes, boldly, he lied. If not, at least he might be telling truth.

'No, my lord, I did not,' said Adam heavily. 'I wish I had, but she would not have it so. We lay the last night at Andover, and then went on with her the last few miles. When we came within a mile – but it was not within sight yet, and there were small woodlands between – she sent me back, and said she would go the end of the way alone. I did what she wished. I had done what she wished since I carried her in my arms, barely a year old,' he said, with the first flash of fire out of his dark composure, like brief lightning out of banked clouds.

'And the other three?' asked Hugh mildly.

'We left them in Andover. When I returned we set out for home all together.'

Hugh said nothing yet about the discrepancy in time. That might well be held in reserve, to be sprung on him when he was away from this family solidarity, and less sure of himself.

'And you know nothing of Julian Cruce since that day?'

'No, my lord, nothing. And if you do, for God's sake let me know of it, worst or best!'

'You were devoted to this lady?'

'I would have died for her. I would die for her now.'

Well, so you may yet, thought Hugh, if you turn out to be the best player of a part that ever put on a false face. He was in two minds about this man, whose brief flashes of passion had all the force of truth, and yet who picked his way among words with a rare subtlety.

Why, if he had nothing to hide?

'You have a horse here, Adam?'

The man lifted upon him a long, calculating stare, from eyes deep-set beneath bushy brows. 'I have, my lord.'

'Then I must ask you to saddle and ride with me.'

It was an asking that could not be refused, and Adam Heriet was well aware of it, but at least it was put in a fashion which enabled him to rise and go with composed dignity. He pushed back the bench and stood clear.

'Ride where, my lord?' And to the freckled boy, watching dubiously from the shadows, he said: 'Go and saddle for me, lad, make yourself useful.'

Adam the younger went, though not willingly, and with a long backward glance over his shoulder, and in a moment or two hooves thudded on the hard-beaten earth of the yard.

'You must know,' said Hugh, 'all the circumstances of the lady's decision to enter a convent. You know she was betrothed as a child to Godfrid Marescot, and that he broke off the match to become a monk at Hyde Mead.'

'Yes, I do know.'

'After the burning of Hyde, Godfrid Marescot came to

103

Shrewsbury in the dispersal that followed. Since the sack of Wherwell, he frets for news of the girl, and whether you can bring him any or no, Adam, I would have you come with me and visit him.' Not a word yet of the small matter of her non-arrival at the refuge she had chosen. Nor was there any way of knowing from this experienced and well-regulated face whether Adam knew of it or no. 'If you cannot shed light,' said Hugh amiably, 'at least you can speak to him of her, share a remembrance heavy enough, as things are now, to carry alone.'

Adam drew a long, slow, cautious breath. 'I will well, my lord. He was a fine man, so everyone reports of him. Old for her, but a fine man. It was great pity. She used to prattle about him, proud as if he was making a queen of her. Pity such a lass should ever take to the cloister. She would have been his fair match. I knew her. I'll ride with you in goodwill.' And to the husband and wife who stood close together, wondering and distrustful, he said calmly: 'Shrewsbury is not far. You'll see me back again before you know it.'

It was a strange and yet an everyday ride back to Shrewsbury. All the way this hardened and resilient man-at-arms conducted himself as though he did not know he was a prisoner, and suspect of something not yet revealed, while very well knowing that two sergeants rode one at either quarter behind him, in case he should make a break for freedom. He rode well, and had a very decent horse beneath him, and must be a man held in good repute and trusted by his commander to be loosed as he pleased, and thus well provided. Concerning his own situation he asked nothing, and betrayed no anxiety; but three times at least before they came in sight of Saint Giles he asked:

'My lord, did you ever hear word of her at all, after the troubles fell on Winchester?'

'Sir, if you have made enquiries round Wherwell, did you come upon any trace? There must have been many nuns scattered there.'

And last, in abrupt pleading: 'My lord, if you do know, is she living or dead?'

To none of which could he get a direct answer, since there was none to give him. Last, as they passed the low hillock of

Saint Giles, with its squat roofs and modest little turret, he said reflectively: 'That must have been a hard journey for a sick and ageing man, all this way from Hyde alone. I marvel how the lord Godfrid bore it.'

'He was not alone,' said Hugh almost absently. 'They were two who came here from Hyde Mead.'

'As well,' said Adam, nodding approval, 'for they said he was a sorely wounded man. He might have foundered on the way, without a helper.' And he drew a slow, cautious breath.

After that he went in silence, perhaps because of the looming shadow of the abbey wall on his left, that cut off the afternoon sun with a sharp black knife-stroke along the dusty road.

They rode in under the arch of the gatehouse to the usual stir of afternoon, following the half-hour or so allowed for the younger brothers to play, and the older ones to sleep after dinner. Now they were rousing and going forth to their various occupations, to their desks in the scriptorium, or their labours in the gardens along the Gaye, or at the mill or the hatcheries of the fishponds. Brother Porter came out from his lodge at sight of Hugh's gangling grey horse, observed the attendant officers, and looked with some natural curiosity at the unknown who rode with them.

'Brother Humilis? No, you won't find him in the scriptorium, nor in the dortoir, either. After Mass this morning he swooned, here crossing the court, and though the fall did him no great harm, the young one catching him in his arms and bringing him down gently, it took some time to bring him round afterwards. They've carried him to the infirmary. Brother Cadfael is there with him now.'

'I'm sorry to hear it,' said Hugh, checking in dismayed concern. 'Then I can hardly trouble him now . . . ' And yet, if this was one more step towards the end which Cadfael said was inevitable and daily drawing nearer, Hugh could not afford to delay any enquiry which might shed light on the fate of Julian Cruce. Humilis himself most urgently desired knowledge.

'Oh, he's come to himself now,' said the porter, 'and as much his own master – under God, the master of us all! – as ever he was. He wants to come back to his own cell in the dortoir, and says he can still fulfil all his duties a while longer here, but they'll keep him where he is. He's in his full wits, and has all his will. If you have word for him of any import, I would at least go and see if they'll let you in to him.'

'They', when it came to authority in the infirmary, meant Brother Edmund and Brother Cadfael, and their judgement would be decisive.

'Wait here!' said Hugh, making up his mind, and swung down from the saddle to stride across the court to its north-western corner, where the infirmary stood withdrawn into the angle of the precinct wall. The two sergeants also dismounted, and stood in close and watchful attendance on their charge, though it seemed that Adam was quite prepared to brazen out whatever there was to be answered, for he sat his horse stolidly for a few moments, and then lit down and freely surrendered his bridle to the groom who had come to see to Hugh's mount. They waited in silence, while Adam looked about the clustered buildings round the court with wary interest.

Hugh encountered Brother Edmund just emerging from the doorway of the infirmary, and put his question to him briskly. 'I hear you have Brother Humilis within. Is he fit to have visitors? I have the one missing man here under guard, with luck we may start something out of him between us, before he has too much time to think out his cover and make it impregnable.'

Edmund blinked at him for a moment, hard put to it to leave his own preoccupations for another man's. Then he said, after some hesitation: 'He grows daily feebler, but he's resting well now, and he has been fretting over this matter of the girl, feeling his own acts brought her to this. His mind is strong and determined. I think he would certainly wish to see you. Cadfael is there with him – his wound broke again when he fell, where it was newly healed, but it's clean. Yes, go in to him.' His face said, though his lips did not utter it: 'Who knows how long his time may be? An easy mind could lengthen it.'

Hugh went back to his men. 'Come, we may go in.' And to the two sergeants he said: 'Wait outside the door.'

He heard the familiar tones of Cadfael's voice as soon as he entered the infirmary with Adam docile at his heels. They had not taken Brother Humilis into the open ward, but into one of the small, quiet cells apart, and the door stood open between. A cot, a stool and a small desk to support book or candle were all the furnishings, and wide-open door and small, unshuttered window let in light and air. Brother Fidelis was on his knees by the bed, supporting the sick man in his arm while Cadfael completed the bandaging of hip and groin where the frail new scar tissue had split slightly when Humilis fell. They had stripped him naked, and the cover was drawn back, but Cadfael's solid body blocked the view of the bed from the doorway, and at the sound of feet entering Fidelis quickly drew up the sheet to the patient's waist. So emaciated was the long body that the young man could lift it briefly on one arm, but the gaunt face showed clear and firm as ever, and the hollow eyes were bright. He submitted to being handled with a wry and patient smile, as to a salutary discipline. It was the boy who so jealously reached to conceal the ruined body from uninitiated eyes. Having drawn up the sheet, he turned to take up and shake out the clean linen shirt that lay ready, lifted it over Humilis's head, and very adroitly helped his thin arms into the sleeves, and lifted him to smooth the folds comfortably under him. Only then did he turn and look towards the doorway.

Hugh was known and accepted, even welcomed. Humilis and Fidelis as one looked beyond him to see who followed.

From behind Hugh's shoulder the taller stranger looked quickly from face to face, the mere flicker of a sharp glance that touched and took flight, a lightning assessment by way of taking stock of what he might have to deal with. Brother Cadfael, clearly, belonged here and was no threat, the sick man in the bed was known by repute, but the third brother, who stood close by the cot utterly still, wide eyes gleaming within the shadow of the cowl, was perhaps not so easily placed. Adam Heriet looked last and longest at Fidelis, before he lowered his eyes and composed his face into a closed book.

'Brother Edmund said we might come in,' said Hugh, 'but if we tire you, turn us out. I am sorry to hear you are not so well.'

'It will be the best of medicines,' said Humilis, 'if you have any better news for me. Brother Cadfael will not grudge another doctor having a say. I am not so sick, it was only a faintness – the heat gets ever more oppressive.' His voice was a little less steady than usual, and slower in utterance, but he breathed evenly, and his eyes were clear and calm. 'Who is this you have brought with you?'

'Nicholas will have told you, before he left,' said Hugh, 'that we have already questioned three of the four who rode as escort to the lady Julian when she left for Wherwell. This is the fourth – Adam Heriet, who went the last part of the way with her, leaving his fellows in Andover to wait for his return.'

Brother Humilis stiffened his frail body and sat upright to gaze, and Brother Fidelis kneeled and braced an arm about him, behind the supporting pillow, stooping his head into shadow behind his lord's lean shoulder.

'Is it so? Then we know all those who guarded her now. So you,' said Humilis, urgently studying the stalwart figure and blunt, brow-bent face that stooped a sunburned forehead to him, like a challenged bull, 'you must be that one they said loved her from a child.'

'So I did,' said Adam Heriet firmly.

'Tell him,' said Hugh, 'how and when you last parted from the lady. Speak up, it is your story.'

Heriet drew breath long and deeply, but without any evidence of fear or stress, and told it again as he had told it to Hugh at Brigge. 'She bade me go and leave her. And so I did. She was my lady, to command me as she chose. What she asked of me, that I did.'

'And returned to Andover?' asked Hugh mildly.

'Yes, my lord.'

'Scarcely in haste,' said Hugh with the same deceptive gentleness. 'From Andover to Wherwell is but a few short miles, and you say you were dismissed a mile short of that. Yet you returned to Andover in the dusk, many hours later. Where were you all that time?'

There was no mistaking the icy shock that went through Adam, stopping his breath for an instant. His carefully hooded eyes rolled wide and flashed one wild glance at Hugh, then were again lowered. It took him a brief and perceptible struggle to master voice and thoughts, but he did it with heroic smoothness, and even the pause seemed too brief for the inspired concoction of lies.

'My lord, I had never been so far south before, and reckoned at that time I never should again. She dismissed me, and the city of Winchester was there close. I had heard tell of it, but never thought to see it. I know I had no right so to borrow time, but I did it. I rode into the town, and there I stayed all that day. It was peace there, then, a man could walk abroad, view the great church, eat at an alehouse, all without fear. And so I did, and went back to Andover only late in the evening. If they have told you so, they tell truth. We never set out for home until next morning.'

It was Humilis, who knew the city of Winchester like his own palm, who took up the interrogation there, drily and calmly, eyes and voice again alert and vigorous. 'Who could blame you for taking a few hours to yourself, with your errand done? And what did you see and do in Winchester?'

Adam's wary breathing eased again readily. This was no problem for him. He launched into a very full and detailed account of Bishop Henry's city, from the north gate, where he had entered, to the meadows of St Cross, and from the cathedral and the castle of Wolvesey to the north-western fields of Hyde Mead. He could describe in detail the frontages of the steep High Street, the golden shrine of Saint Swithun, and the magnificent cross presented by Bishop Henry to his predecessor Bishop Walkelin's cathedral. No doubt but he had seen all he claimed to have seen. Humilis exchanged glances with Hugh and assured him of that. Neither Hugh nor Cadfael, who stood a little apart, taking note of all, had ever been in Winchester.

'So that is all you know of Julian Cruce's fate,' said Hugh at length.

'Never word of her, my lord, since we parted that day,' said Adam, with every appearance of truth. 'Unless there is something you can tell me now, as you know I have asked and asked.' But he was asking no longer, even this repetition had lost all its former urgency.

'Something I can and will tell you,' said Hugh abruptly and harshly. 'Julian Cruce never entered Wherwell. The prioress of Wherwell never heard of her. From that day she has vanished, and you were the last ever to see her. What's your answer to that?'

Adam stood mute, staring, a long minute. 'Do you tell me this is true?' he said slowly.

'I do tell you so, though I think there never was any need to tell you, for you knew it, none better. As you are now left, the only one who may, who must, know where she did go, since she never reached Wherwell. Where she went and what befell her, and whether she is now on this earth or under it.'

'I swear to God,' said Adam slowly, 'that when I parted from my lady at her wish, I left her whole and well, and I pray she is now, wherever she may be.'

'You knew, did you not, what valuables she carried with her? Was that enough to tempt you? Did you, I ask you now in due form, did you rob your mistress and do her violence when she was left alone with you, and no witness by?'

Fidelis laid Humilis gently back against his pillows, and stood up tall and straight beside him. The movement drew Adam's gaze, and for a moment held it. He said loudly and clearly: 'So far from that, I would have died for her then, and so I would, gladly, now, rather than she should suffer even one moment's grief.'

'Very well!' said Hugh shortly. 'That's your plea. But I must and will keep you in hold until I know more. For I will know more, Adam, before I let go of this knot.' He went to the door, where his sergeants waited for their orders, and called them in. 'Take this man and lodge him in the castle. Securely!'

Adam went out between them without a word of surprise or protest. He had looked for nothing else, events had hedged him in too closely not to lock the door on him now. It seemed that he was not greatly discomforted or alarmed, either, though he was a stout, practised man who would not betray his thoughts. He did cast one look back from the doorway, a look that embraced them all, but said nothing and conveyed nothing to Hugh, and little enough to Cadfael. A mere spark, too small as yet to cast any light.

NINE

Brother Humilis watched the departure of prisoner and guards with a long, unwavering stare, and when they had vanished he sank back on his bed with a deep sigh, and lay gazing up into the low stone vault over him.

'We've tired you out,' said Hugh. 'We'll leave you now to rest.'

'No, wait!' There was a fine dew of sweat breaking on his high forehead. Fidelis leaned and wiped it away, and a preoccupied smile flashed up at him for a moment, and lingered to darken into a frown.

'Son, go out from here, take the sun and the air, you spend too much time caring for me, and you see I am in need of nothing now. It is not right that you should make me your only work here. In a little while I shall sleep.' It was not clear, from the serenity of his voice, weak though it was, whether he spoke of a mere restful slumber on a hot afternoon, or the last sleep of the body at the awakening of the soul. He laid his hand for a moment on the young man's hand, in the most delicate touch possible, austerely short of a caress. 'Yes, go, I wish it. Finish my work for me, your touch is steadier than mine, and the detail – too fine for me now.'

Fidelis looked down at him with a composed face, looked up briefly at the two who watched, and again lowered submissively those clear grey eyes that rang so striking a contrast with the curling bronze ring of his tonsure. He went as he was bidden, perhaps gladly, certainly with a free and rapid step.

'Nicholas never stopped to tell me,' said Humilis, when silence had closed over the last light footstep, 'what these valuables were, that my affianced wife took with her. Were they so distinctive as to be recognisable, should they ever be traced?'

'I doubt if there were any two such,' said Hugh. 'Gold and silversmiths generally make to their own designs, even when they aim at pairs I wonder if they ever match exactly. These were singular enough. Once known, known for all time.'

'May I know what they were? She had coined money, I understand – that is at the service of whoever takes it. But the rest?'

Hugh, whose memory for words was exact as a mirror, willingly described them: 'A pair of candlesticks of silver, made in the form of tall sconces entwined with the vine, with snuffers attached by silver chains, also ornamented with grapeleaves. A standing cross a man's hand-length in height, on a silver pedestal of three steps, and studded with semi-precious stones of yellow pebble, amethyst and agate, together with a similar cross of the same metal and stones, a little finger's length, on a thin silver neck-chain for a priest's wear. Also some pieces of jewellery, a necklet of polished stones from the hills above Pontesbury, a bracelet of silver engraved with tendrils of vetch, and a curious ring of silver set with enamels all round, in the form of yellow and blue flowers. That's the tally. They must surely all have left this shire. They'll be found, if ever found at all, somewhere in the south, where they and she vanished.'

Humilis lay quiet, his eyelids closed, his lips moving soundlessly on the details of these chattels. 'A very small fortune,' he said in a whisper. 'But not small to some poor wretched souls. Do you truly believe she may have died for these few things?'

'Men, and women too,' said Hugh starkly, 'have died for very much less.'

'Yes, true! A small cross,' said Humilis, lips moving again upon the recollected phrases, 'the length of a little finger, set with yellow stones, and green agate and amethyst . . . Fellow to an altar cross of the same, but made for wearing. Yes, a man would know that again.'

The faint dew of weakness was budding again on his forehead, a great drop ran down into the folds of a closed eyelid. Cadfael wiped the corroding drops away, and frowned Hugh before him out at the door.

'I shall sleep . . . ' said Humilis, and faintly and fleetingly smiled.

In the large room across the stone passage, where a dozen beds lay spaced in two rows, either side an open corridor, Brother Edmund and another brother, his back turned and his strong, erect figure unidentifiable from behind, were lifting a cot and the lay brother in it, to move them a short way along the wall, and make room for a new pallet and a new patient. The helper set down his end of the bed as Cadfael and Hugh passed by the open doorway. He straightened and turned, brushing his hands together to rub out the dents left by the weight, and showed them the dark, level brows and burning eyes of Brother Urien. In unaccustomed content with himself and the walls and persons about him, he wore a slight, taut smile that curled his lips but never damped the smouldering of his eyes. He watched them pass as if a shadow had passed, and crossed their tracks as soon as they were by, to stack an armful of washed linen in the press that stood in the passage.

In the infirmary, by custom, all doors stood open, so that a call for help might safely reach attentive ears, and help come hurrying. Voices, the chant of the office, even birdsong, circulated freely. Only in times of storm or heavy rain or winter cold were doors closed and shutters secured, never as now, in the heat of summer.

'The man is lying,' said Hugh, pacing beside Cadfael in the great court, and worrying at the texture of truth and deceit. 'But also half the time he is telling the truth, and which half holds the lies? Tell me that!'

'If I could,' said Cadfael mildly, 'I should be more than mortal.'

'He had her trust, he knew what she was worth, he rode alone with her the last few miles, and no trace of her since,' said Hugh, gnawing the evidence savagely. 'And yet, on the road there, he asked me time and again if I knew whether she lived or was dead, and I would have sworn he was honest in asking. But now see him! Halfway through that business, he stands there unmoved as a rock, and never makes protest against being held, nor shows any further trouble over *her* fate. What's to be made of him?'

'Or of any of this,' agreed Cadfael ruefully. 'I'm of your mind, he is certainly lying. He knows what he has not declared. Yet if he has possessed himself of all she had, what has he done with it? It may not be great riches, but it would be worth more to a man than the low pay and danger and sweat of a simple soldier, yet here is he manifestly a simple soldier still, and nothing more.'

'Soldier he may be,' said Hugh wryly, 'but simple he is not. His twists and turns have me baffled. Winchester he knows well – yes, maybe, but wherever he has served the greater part of these three years, since this winter all forces have closed in on Winchester. How could he not know it? And yet I'd have sworn, at first, that he truly did not know, and longed to know, what had become of the girl. Either that, or he's the cunningest mime that ever twisted his face to deceive.'

'He did not seem to me greatly uneasy,' said Cadfael thoughtfully, 'when you brought him in. Wary, yes, and picking his words with care – and that gives them all the more meaning,' he added, brightening. 'I'll be thinking on that. But fearful or anxious, no, I would not say so.'

They had reached the gatehouse, where the groom waited with Hugh's horse. Hugh gathered the reins and set toe in stirrup, and paused there to look over his shoulder at his friend.

'I tell you what, Cadfael, the only sure way out of this tangle is for that girl to turn up somewhere, alive and well. Then we can all be easy. But there, you've had more than your fair share of miracles already this year, not even you dare ask for more.'

'And yet,' said Cadfael, fretting at the disorderly confusion of shards that would not fit together, 'there's something winks at me in the corner of my mind's eye, and is gone when I look towards it. A mere will-o'-wisp – not even a spark . . . .'

'Let it alone,' said Hugh, wheeling his horse towards the gate. 'Never blow on it for fear it may go out altogether. If you breathe the other way, who knows? It may grow into a candle-flame, and bring the moths in to singe their wings.'

Brother Urien lingered long over stacking the laundered linen in its press in the infirmary. He had let Fidelis pass without a sign, his mind still intent upon the three who were left within the sickroom, and the stone walls brought hollow echoes ringing across the passage, through the open doors. Brother Urien's senses were all honed into acute sensitivity by his inward anguish, to the point where his skin crawled and his short hairs stood on end at the torture of sounds which might seem soft and gentle to another ear.

He moved with precision and obedience to fulfil whatever Edmund required of him: a bed to be moved, without disturbing its occupant, who was half-paralysed and very old, a new cot to be installed ready for another sufferer. He turned to watch the departure of sheriff and herbalist brother without conceal, his mind still revolving words sharply remembered. All those artifacts of precious metal and semi-precious stones, vanished with a vanished woman. An altar cross – no, that was of no importance here. But a cross made to match, on a silver neck-chain . . . Benedictine brothers may not retain the trappings of the person, the fruit of the world, however slight, without special permission, seldom granted. Yet there are brothers who wear chains about the neck – one, at least. He had touched, once, to bitter humiliation, and he knew.

The time, too, spoke aloud, the time and the place. Those who have killed for a desperate venture, for gain, and find themselves hard pressed, may seek refuge wherever it offers. Gains may be hidden until flight is again possible and safe. But why, then, follow that broken crusader here into Shrewsbury? Flight would have been easy after Hyde burned, in that inferno who could count heads?

Yet no one knew better than he how love, or whatever the name for this torment truly is, may be generated, nursed, take tyrannical possession of a man's soul, with far greater fury and intensity here in the cloister than out in the world. If he could be made to suffer it thus, driven blind and mad, why should not another? And how could two such victims not have something to bind them together, if nothing else, their inescapable guilt and pain? And Humilis was a sick man, and could not live long. There would be room for another when he vacated his place, when the void left after him began to ache intolerably. Urien's heart melted in him like wax, thinking on what Fidelis might be enduring in his impenetrable silence.

He finished the work to which he had been called in the infirmary, closed the press, glanced once round the open ward, and went out to the court. He had been a body-servant and groom in the world, and was without craft skills, and barely literate until entering the Order. He lent his sinews and strength where they were needed, indoors or out, to any labour. He did not grudge the effort such labour cost him, nor feel his unskilled aid to be menial, for the fuel that fired him within demanded a means of expending itself without, or there could be no sleep for him in his bed, nor ease when he awoke. But whatever he did he could not rid himself of the too well remembered face of the woman who had spurned and left him in his insatiable hunger and thirst. He had seen again her smooth young face, the image of innocence, and her great, lucid grey eyes in the boy Rhun, until those eyes turned on him full and seared him to the bone by their sweetness and pity. But her rich, burning russet hair, not red but brown in its brightness, he had found only in Brother Fidelis, crowning and corroborating those same wide grey eyes, the pure crystals of memory. The woman's voice had been clear, high and bold. This mirror image was voiceless, and therefore could never be harsh or malicious, never condemn, never scarify. And it was male, blessedly not of the woman's cruel and treacherous clan. Once Fidelis might have recoiled from him, startled and affrighted. But he had said and believed then that it would not always be so.

He had achieved the measured monastic pace, but not the tranquillity of mind that should have gone with it. By lowering his eyes and folding his hands before him in his sheltering sleeves he could go anywhere within these walls, and pass for one among many. He went where he knew Fidelis had been sent, and where he would surely go, valuing the bench where he sat by the true tenant who should have been sitting there, and the vellum leaf on the desk before him, and the little pots of colour deployed there, by the work Humilis had begun, and bade him finish.

At the far end of the scriptorium range in the cloister, under the south wall of the church, Brother Anselm the precentor was trying out a chant on his small hand-organ, a sequence of a half-dozen notes repeated over and over, like an inspired bird-call, sweet and sad. One of the boy pupils was there with him, lifting his childish voice unconcernedly, as gifted children will, wondering why the elders make so much fuss about what comes by nature and costs no pain. Urien knew little of music, but felt it acutely, as he felt everything, like arrows piercing his flesh. The boy rang purer and truer than any instrument, and did not know he could wring the heart. He would rather have been playing with his fellow-pupils, out in the Gaye.

The carrels of the scriptorium were deep, and the stone partitions cut off sound. Fidelis had moved his desk so that he could sit half in shade, while the full sunlight lit his leaf. His left side was turned to the sun, so that his hand cast no shadow as he worked, though the coiled tendril which was his model for the decoration of the capital letter M was wilting in the heat. He worked with a steady hand and a very fine brush, twining the delicate curls of the stem and starring them with pale, bright flowers frail as gossamer. When the singing boy, released from his schooling, passed by at a skipping run, Fidelis never raised his head. When Urien cast a long shadow and did not pass by, the hand that held the brush halted for a moment, then resumed its smooth, long strokes, but still Fidelis did not look up. By which token Brother Urien was aware that he was known. For any other this mute painter would have looked up briefly, for many among the brothers he would have smiled. And without looking, how could he know? By a silence as heavy as his own, or by some quickening that flushed his flesh and caused the hairs of his neck to rise when this one man of all men came near?

Urien stepped within the carrel, and stood close at Fidelis's shoulder, looking down at the intricate M that still lacked its touches of gold. Looking down also, with more intense awareness, at the inch or two of thin silver chain that showed within the dropped folds of collar and cowl, threading the short russet hairs on the bent neck. A cross a little finger long, on a neck-chain, and studded with yellow, green and purple stones . . . He could have inserted a finger under the chain and

117

plucked it forth, but he did not touch. He had learned that a touch is witchcraft, instant separation, putting cold distance between.

'Fidelis,' said the softest of yearning voices at Fidelis's shoulder, 'you keep from me. Why do you so? I can be the truest friend ever you had, if you will let me. What is there I will not do for you? And you have need of a friend. One who will keep secrets and be as silent as you are. Let me in to you, Fidelis . . . .' He did not say 'brother'. 'Brother' is a title beyond desire, an easy title, no shaker of the mind or spirit. 'Let me in, and I can be to you all you need of love and loyalty. To the death!'

Fidelis laid aside his brush very slowly, and set both hands to the edge of the desk as though bracing himself to rise, and all this with rigid body and held breath. Urien pressed on in hushed haste.

'You need not fear me, I mean you only good. Don't stir, don't draw away! I know what you have done, I know what you have to hide . . . No one else will ever hear it from me, if only you'll do your part. Silence deserves a reward . . . love deserves love!'

Fidelis slid along the polished wood of the bench and stood clear, putting the desk between them. His face was pale and fixed, the dilated grey eyes enormous. He shook his head vehemently, and moved round to push past Urien and quit the carrel, but Urien spread his arms and blocked the way.

'Oh, no, not this time! Not now! That's over. I've asked, I've begged, now I give you to know even asking is over.' His tight control had burned into abrupt and savage anger, his eyes flared redly. 'I have ears, I could be your ruin if I were so minded. You had best be kind to me.' His voice was still very low, no one would hear, and no one passed along the cloister flagstones to see and wonder. He moved closer, driving Fidelis deeper into shadow within the carrel. 'What is it you wear round your neck, under your habit, Fidelis? Will you show it to me? Or shall I tell you what it is? And what it means! There are those who would give a good deal to know. To your cost, Fidelis, unless you grow kind to me.'

He had backed his quarry into the deepest corner, and pinned him there with arms outspread, and a palm flattened against the wall on either side, preventing escape. Still the pale, oval face confronted him icily, even scornfully, and the grey eyes had burned into a slow blaze of anger, utterly rejecting him.

Urien struck like a snake, flashing a hand into the bosom of Fidelis's habit, down within the ample folds, to drag out of hiding the length of the silver chain, and the trophy that hung hidden upon it, warmed by the flesh and the heart beneath. Fidelis uttered a strange, breathy sound, and leaned back hard against the wall, and Urien started back from him one unsteady step, himself appalled, and echoed the gasp. For an instant there was a silence so deep that both seemed to drown in it, then Fidelis gathered up the slack of the chain in his hand, and stowed his treasure away again in its hiding place. For that one moment he had closed his eyes, but instantly he opened them again and kept them fixed with a bleak, unbending stare upon his persecutor.

'Now, more than ever,' said Urien in a whisper, 'now you shall lower those proud eyes of yours, and stoop that stiff neck, and come to me pliantly, or go to whatever fate such an offence as yours brings down on the offender. But no need to threaten, if you will but listen to me. I pledge you my help, oh, yes, faithfully, with my whole heart – you have only to let me in to yours. Why not? And what choice have you, now? You need me, Fidelis, as cruelly as I need you. But we two together – and there need be no cruelty, only tenderness, only love . . . .'

Fidelis burned up abruptly like a candle-flame, and with the hand that was not clutching his profaned treasure to his breast he struck Urien in the mouth and silenced him.

For a moment they hung staring, eye to eye, with never a sound or a breath between them. Then Urien said thickly, in a grating whisper that was barely audible: 'Enough! Now you shall come to me! Now you shall be the beggar. Of your own need and your own will you shall come, and beg me for what you now refuse. Or I will tell all that I know, and what I know is enough to damn you. You shall come to me and plead, and follow me like a little dog at my heels, or else I will destroy you, as now you *know* I can. Three days I give you, Fidelis! If you do not seek me out and give yourself to me by Vespers of the third day from now, *Brother*, I will let loose hell to swallow you, and smile to watch you burn!'

He swung on his heel then, and flew out of the carrel. The long black shadow vanished, the afternoon light came in again placidly. Fidelis leaned in the darkness of his corner a long moment with eyes closed and breast heaving in deep, exhausted rise and fall. Then he groped his way heavily back to his bench and sat down, and took up his brush in a hand too unsteady to be able to use it. Holding it gave him a hold on normality, and presented a fitting picture of an illuminator at work, if anyone should come to witness it. Within, there was a numbed desperation past which he could not see any light or any deliverance.

It was Rhun who came to be a witness. He had met Brother Urien in the garth, and seen the set face and smouldering, wounded eyes. He had not seen from which carrel Urien had issued, but here he sensed, smelled, felt in the prickling of his own flesh where Urien in his rank rage and pain had been.

He said no word of it to Fidelis, nor remarked on the pallor of his friend's face or the strange stiffness of his movements as he greeted him. He sat down beside him on the bench, and talked of the simple matters of the day, and the pattern of the capital letter still unfinished, and took up the fine brush for the gilding and laid in carefully the gold edges of two or three leaves, the tip of his tongue arching at the corner of his mouth, like a child at his letters.

When the bell rang for Vespers they went in together, both with calm faces, neither with a quiet heart.

Rhun absented himself from supper, and went instead to the infirmary, and into the small room where Brother Humilis lay sleeping. He sat beside the bed patiently for a long time, but the sick man slept on. And now, in this silence and solitude, Rhun could scan every line of the worn, ageing face, and see how the eyes were sunk deep into the skull, the cheeks fallen into gaunt hollows, and the flesh slack and grey. He was so full of life himself that he recognised with exquisite clarity the approach of another man's death. He abandoned his first purpose. For even if Humilis should awaken, and however ardently he would exert what life was left to him for the sake of Fidelis, Rhun could not now cast any part of this load upon a man already burdened with the spiritual baggage of his own departure. But he sat there still, and waited, and after supper Brother Edmund came to make the rounds of his patients before nightfall.

Rhun approached him in the stone-flagged passage.

'Brother Edmund, I'm anxious about Humilis. I've been sitting with him, and surely he grows weaker before our eyes. I know you keep good care of him always, but I thought – could not a cot be put in with him for Fidelis? It would be much to the comfort of them both. In the dortoir with the rest of us Fidelis will fret, and not sleep. And if Humilis should wake in the night, it would be a grace to see Fidelis close by him, ready to serve as he always is. They went through the fire at Hyde together . . . .' He drew breath, watching Brother Edmund's face. 'They are closer,' he said gravely, 'than ever were father and son.'

Brother Edmund went himself to look at the sleeping man. Breath came shallowly and rapidly. The single light cover lay very flat and lean over the long body.

'It might be well so,' said Edmund. 'There is an empty cot in the anteroom of the chapel, and it would go in here, though the space is a little tight for it. Come and help me to carry it, and then you may tell Brother Fidelis he can come and sleep here this night, if that's his wish.'

'He will be glad,' said Rhun with certainty.

The message was delivered to Fidelis simply as a decision by Brother Edmund, taken for the peace of mind and better care of his patient, which seemed sensible enough. And certainly Fidelis was glad. If he suspected that Rhun had had a hand in procuring the dispensation, that was acknowledged only with a fleeting smile that flashed and faded in his grave face too rapidly to be noticed. He took his breviary and went gratefully across the court, and into the room where Humilis still slept his shallow, old man's sleep, he who was barely forty-seven years old, and had lived at a gallop the foreshortened life that now crept so softly and resignedly towards death. Fidelis kneeled by the bedside to shape the night prayers with his mute lips.

It was the most sultry night of the hot, oppressive summer, a low cloud cover had veiled the stars. Even within stone walls the heat hung too heavy to bear. And here at last there was true privacy, apart from the necessities and duties of brotherhood, not low panelled partitions separating them from their chosen kin, but walls of stone, and the width of the great court, and the suffocating weight of the night. Fidelis stripped off his habit and lay down to sleep in his linen. Between the two narrow cots, on the stand beside the breviary, the little oil lamp burned all night long with a dwindling golden flame.

TEN

In his shallow half-sleep, half-swoon Brother Humilis dreamed that he heard someone weeping, very softly, almost without sound but for the break in the breath, the controlled but extreme weeping of a strong being brought to a desperation from which there was no escape. It so stirred and troubled him that he was lifted gradually out of his dream and into a wakeful reality, but by then there was only silence. He knew that he was not alone in the room, though he had not heard the second cot carried in, nor the coming of the one who was to lie beside him. But even before he turned his head, and saw by the faint glimmer of lamplight the white shape stretched on the pallet, he knew who it was. The presence or absence of this one creature was the pulse of his life now. If Fidelis was by, the beat of his blood was strong and comforting, without him it flagged and weakened.

And therefore it must be Fidelis who had grieved alone in the night, enduring what he could not change, whatever burden of sin or sorrow it was that swelled in him speechless and found no remedy.

Humilis put back the single cover from over him, and sat up, swinging his feet to the stone floor between the two beds. He had no need to stand, only to lift the little lamp carefully and lean towards the sleeper, shielding the light so that it should not fall too sharply upon the young man's face.

Seen thus, aloof and impenetrable, it was a daunting face. Under the ring of curling hair, the colour of ripe chestnuts, the forehead was both lofty and broad, ivory-smooth above level, strong brows darker than the hair. Large, arched eyelids, faintly veined like the petals of a flower, hid the clear grey eyes. An austere face, the jaw sharply outlined and resolute, the

th fastidious, the cheekbones high and proud. If he had
eed shed tears, they were gone. There was only a fine dew
sweat on his upper lip. Humilis sat studying him steadily for
a long time.

The boy had shed his habit in order to sleep in better
comfort. He lay on his side, cheek pressed into the pillow, the
loose linen shirt open at his throat, and the chain that he wore
had slid its links down in a silver coil into the hollow of his
neck, and laid bare to view on the pillow the token that hung
upon it.

Not a cross studded with semi-precious stones, but a ring, a
thin gold finger-ring made in the spiral form of a coiled snake,
with two splinters of red for eyes. An old ring, very old, for the
finer chasing of head and scales was worn smooth with time,
and the coils were wafer-thin.

Humilis sat gazing at this small, significant thing, and could
not turn his eyes away. The lamp shook in his hand, and he
laid it back on its stand in careful haste, for fear he should spill
a drop of hot oil on the naked throat or outflung arm, and
startle Fidelis out of what was at least oblivion, if not genuine
rest. Now he knew everything, the best and the worst, all there
was to know, except how to find a way out of this web. Not for
himself – his own way out opened clear before him, and was no
long journey. But for this sleeper . . . .

Humilis lay back on his bed, trembling with the knowledge
of a great wonder and a great danger, and waited for morning.

Brother Cadfael rose at dawn, long before Prime, and went out
into the garden, but even there there was little air to breathe. A
leaden stillness hung over the world, under a thin ceiling of
cloud, through which the rising sun seemed to burn unimpeded. He went down to the Meole Brook, down the bleached
slopes of the pease-fields, from which the haulms had long
since been sickled and taken in for stable-bedding, leaving the
white stubble to be ploughed into the ground for the next
year's crop. Cadfael shed his sandals and waded into the slack,
shallow water that was left, and found it warm where he had
hoped for a little coolness. This weather, he thought, cannot
continue much longer, it must break. Someone will get the
brunt of the storm, and if it's thunder, as by the smell in the air

124

and the prickling of my skin it surely will be, Shrewsbury wil
get its share. Thunder, like commerce, followed the river
valleys.

Once out of his bed, he had lost the fine art of being idle. He
filled in the time until Prime with some work among the herbs,
and some early watering while the sun was still climbing,
round and dull gold behind its veil of haze. These functions his
hands and eyes could take care of, while his mind was free to
fret and speculate over the complicated fortunes of people for
whom he had formed a strong affection. No question but
Godfrid Marescot – to think of him as an affianced man was to
give him his old name – was busy leaving this world at a
steady, unflinching walk, and every day he quickened his pace
like a man anxious to be gone, and yet every day looked back
over his shoulder in case that lost bride of his might be
following on his heels rather than waiting for him patiently
along the road ahead. And what could any man tell him for his
reassurance? And what could afford any comfort to Nicholas
Harnage, who had been too slow in prizing her fitly and
making his bid for her favour?

A mile from Wherwell, and never seen again. And gone with
her, temptation enough for harm, the valuables and the money
she carried. And one man only as visible and obvious suspect,
Adam Heriet, with everything against him except for Hugh's
scrupulous conviction that he had been in genuine desperation
to get news of her. He had asked and asked, and never desisted
until he reached Shrewsbury. Or had he simply been fishing,
not for news of her so much as for a glimpse, any glimpse, into
Hugh's mind, any unwary word that would tell him how much
the law already knew, and what chance he still had, by silence
or lies or any other means, of brazening his way safely through
his present peril?

Other inconsequent questions jutted from the obscurity like
the untrimmed overgrowths from the hedges of a neglected
maze. Why did the girl choose Wherwell, in the first place?
Certainly she might have preferred it as being far from her
home, no bad principle when beginning a new life. Or because
it was one of the chief houses of Benedictine nuns in all the
south country, with scope for a gifted sister to rise to office and
power. And why did she give orders to three of her escort to

remain in Andover instead of accompanying her all the way? True, the one she retained was her confidant and willing slave from infancy. If that was indeed true of him? It was reputed of him, yes, but truth and reputation sometimes part company. And if true, why did she dismiss even him short of her goal? Perhaps better phrase that more carefully: *Did* she dismiss him short of her goal? Then where did he spend the lost hours before he returned to Andover? Gaping at the wonders of Winchester, as he claimed? Or attending to more sinister business? What became of the treasures she carried? No great fortune, except to a man who lacked any fortune, but to him wealth enough. And always: *What became of her?*

And through the tangle he was beginning to glimpse a possible answer, and that uncertain inkling dismayed and terrified him more than all the rest. For if he was right, there could be no good end to this that he could see, every way he probed thorns closed the path. No way out, without worse ruin. Or a miracle.

He went to Prime at last, prompt to the bell, and prayed earnestly for a beckoning light. The need and the deserving must surely be known elsewhere even better than here, he thought, who am I to presume to fill a place far too big for me?

Brother Fidelis did not attend Prime, his empty place ached like the soreness left after a pulled tooth. Rhun shone beside his friend's vacant stall, and never once glanced at Brother Urien. Such problems must not be allowed to distract his rapt attention from the office and the liturgy. There would be a time later in the day to give some thought to Urien, whose aggression had not been absolved, but only temporarily prevented. Rhun had no fear of shouldering the responsibility for another man's soul, being still half-child, with a child's certainty and clarity. To go to his confessor and tell what he suspected and knew of Urien would be to deprive Urien of the whole value of the sacrament of confession, and to tell tales upon a comrade in travail; the former was arrogant in Rhun's eyes, a kind of spiritual theft, and the latter was despicable, a schoolboy's treachery. Yet something would have to be done, something more than merely removing Fidelis from the sphere of Urien's torment and greed. Meantime, Rhun prayed and sang and worshipped with a whole happy heart, and trusted his saint to give him guidance.

Cadfael made short work of breakfast, asked leave, and went to visit Humilis. Coming armed with clean linen pad and green healing salve, he found his patient propped up in his bed freshly washed and shaven, already fed, if indeed he had managed to swallow anything, his toilet seen to in devoted privacy, and a cup of wine and water ready to his hand. Fidelis sat on a low stool beside the bed, ready to stir at once in answer even to a guessed-at need, in any look or gesture. When Cadfael entered, Humilis smiled, though the smile was pallidly blue of lip and cheek, translucent as ice. It is true, thought Cadfael, receiving that salutation, he is fast bound out of this world. It cannot be many days. The flesh melts from his bones as you watch, into smoke, into air. His spirit outgrows his body, soon it must burst out and become visible, there is no room for it in this fragile parcel of bones.

Fidelis looked up and echoed his master's smile, and leaned to turn back the single light cover from the shrunken shanks, then rose from the stool to give place to Cadfael, and stood ready to offer a deft, assisting hand. Those menial services he offered with so much love must be called on frequently now. It was marvel this body could function of itself at all, but there was a will that would not let it surrender its rights – certainly not to anything less than love.

'Have you slept?' asked Cadfael, smoothing his new dressing into place.

'I have, and well,' said Humilis. 'The better for having Fidelis by me. I have not deserved such privilege, but I am meek enough to entreat for it to be continued. Will you speak with Father Abbot for me?'

'I would, if there was need,' said Cadfael heartily, 'but he already knows and approves.'

'Then if I'm to have my indulgence,' said Humilis, 'speak for me now to this nurse and confessor and tyrant of mine, that he use a little kindness also to himself. At least he should go now to Mass, since I cannot, and take a turn in the garden for a little while, before he shuts himself here again with me.'

Fidelis heard all this smiling, but with a smile of inexpressible sadness. The boy, thought Cadfael, knows all too well the time cannot be long, and numbers every moment, charging it

127

with meaning. Love in ignorance squanders what love, informed, crowds and overfills with tokens of eternity.

'He says rightly,' said Cadfael. 'You go to Mass, and I'll stay here until you come again. No need to hurry, I fancy you'll find Brother Rhun waiting for you.'

Fidelis accepted what he recognised as his purposeful dismissal, and went out silently, leaving them no less silent until his slight shadow had passed from the threshold of the room and out into the open court.

Humilis lay back in his raised pillows, and drew a great breath that should have floated his diminished body into the air, like thistledown.

'Will Rhun truly be looking for him?'

'He surely will,' said Cadfael.

'That's well! Of such a one he has need. An innocent, of such native power! Oh, Cadfael, for the simplicity and the wisdom of the dove! I wish Fidelis were such a one, but he is the other, the complement, the inward one. I had to send him away, I must talk with you. Cadfael, I am troubled in my mind for Fidelis.'

It was not news. Cadfael honestly nodded, and said nothing.

'Cadfael,' said the patient voice, delivered from stress now that they were alone. 'I've grown to know you a little, in this time you have been tending me. You know as well as I that I am dying. Why should I grieve for that? I owe a death that has been all but claimed of me a hundred times already. It is not for myself I'm troubled, it is for Fidelis. I dread leaving him alone here, trapped in this life without me.'

'He will not be alone,' said Cadfael. 'He is a brother of this house. He will have the service and fellowship of all here.' The sharp, wry smile did not surprise him. 'And mine,' he said, 'if that means anything more to you. Rhun's, certainly. You have said yourself that Rhun's loyalty is not to be despised.'

'No, truly. The saints of simplicity are made of his metal. But you are not simple, Brother Cadfael. You are sometimes of frightening subtlety, and that also has its place. Moreover, I believe you understand me. You understand the nature of the need. Will you take care of Fidelis for me, stand his friend, believe in him, be shield and sword to him if need be, after I am gone?'

'To the best of my power,' said Cadfael, 'yes, I will.' He leaned to wipe away a slow trickle of spittle from the corner of a mouth wearied with speaking and slack at the lip, and Humilis sighed, and let him serve, docile under the brief touch. 'You know,' said Cadfael gently, 'what I only guess at. If I have guessed right, there is here a problem beyond my wit or yours to solve. I promise my endeavour. The ending is not mine, it belongs only to God. But what I can do, I will do.'

'I would happily die,' said Humilis, 'if my death can serve and save Fidelis. But what I dread is that my death, which cannot delay long, may only aggravate his trouble and his suffering. Could I take them with me into the judgement, how gladly would I embrace them and go. God forbid he should ever be brought to shame and punishment for what he has done.'

'If God forbids, man cannot touch him,' said Cadfael. 'I see what needs to be done, but how to achieve it, God knows, I cannot see. Well, God's vision is clearer than mine, he may both see a way out of this tangle and open my eyes to it when the time is ripe. There's a path through every forest, and a safe passage somewhere through every marsh, it needs only the finding.'

A faint grey smile passed slowly over the sick man's face, and left him grave again. 'I am the marsh out of which Fidelis must find safe passage. I should have Englished that name of mine, it would have been more fitting, with more than half my blood Saxon – Godfrid of the Marsh for Godfrid de Marisco. My father and my grandfather thought best to turn fully Norman. Now it's all one, we leave here all by the same gate.' He lay still and silent for a while, visibly gathering his thoughts and such strength as he had. 'There is one other longing I have, before I die. I should like to see again the manor of Salton, where I was born. I should like to take Fidelis there, just once to be with him outside the monastery walls, in the place that saw my beginning. I ought to have asked permission earlier, but there is still time. It's only a few miles up-river from us. Will you speak for me to the lord abbot, and ask this one kindness?'

Cadfael eyed him in doubt and consternation. 'You cannot ride, that's certain. Whatever means we might take to get you there, it would be asking too much of such strength as you have left.'

'No effort on my part can now alter by more than hours what is left of my life, but it would be a happiness to exchange some part of my time remaining for a glimpse of the place where I was a child. Ask it for me, Cadfael.'

'There is the river,' said Cadfael dubiously, 'but such twists and turns, it adds double to the journey. And such low water, you'd need a boatman who knows every shoal and current.'

'You must know of such a one. I remember how we used to swim and fish off our own shore. Shrewsbury lads were watermen from birth, I could swim before I could walk. There must be many such adepts along this riverside.'

And so there were, and Cadfael knew the best of them, whose knowledge of the Severn spanned every islet, every bend and shallow, and who at any season could judge accurately where anything cast into the water would again be cast ashore. Madog of the Dead Boat had earned his title through the many sad services he had rendered in his time to distracted families who had lost sons or brothers into the flood after the melting of the Welsh snows far up-river, or too venturesome infants left unguarded for a moment while their mothers spread the washing on the bushes of the shore, or fishermen fathers putting out in their coracles with too much ale already under their belts. He did not resent his title, though his preferred trade was fishing and ferrying. What he did for the dead someone had to do, in grace, and since he could do it better than any other, why should he not take pride in it? Cadfael had known him many years, an elderly Welshman like himself, and had several times had occasion to seek his help, which was never grudged.

'Even in this low water,' said Cadfael thoughtfully, 'Madog could get a coracle up the brook from the river, but a coracle wouldn't carry you and Fidelis besides. But his light skiff draws very little water, I daresay he could bring it into the mill pond, there's still depth enough that far up the brook, with the mill race fed back into it. We could carry you out by the wicket to the mill, and see you bestowed . . . .'

'That far I could walk,' said Humilis resolutely.

'You'd be wise to save your energy for Salton. Who knows?'

marvelled Cadfael, noting the slight flush of blood that warmed the thin grey face at the very prospect of returning to the first remembered home of his childhood – perhaps to end where he began. 'Who knows, it may yet do you a world of good!'

'And you will ask the lord abbot?'

'I will,' said Cadfael. 'When Fidelis returns, I'll go to him.'

'Tell him there may be need for haste,' said Humilis, and smiled.

Abbot Radulfus listened with his usual shrewd gravity, and considered for a while in silence before making any comment. Outside the dim, wood-panelled parlour in his lodging the hot sun climbed, still veiled with a thin haze that turned it copper-colour, and made it seem to burn even more fiercely. The roses budded, flowered and fell all in one day.

'Is he strong enough to bear it?' asked the abbot at length. 'And is it not too great a load to lay upon Brother Fidelis, to bear responsibility for him all that time.'

'It's the passing of his strength that makes him ask so urgently,' said Cadfael. 'If his wish is to be granted at all, it must be now, quickly. And he says rightly, it can make very little difference to the tale of his remaining days, whether they end tomorrow or after another week. But to his peace of mind this visit might make all the difference. As for Brother Fidelis, he has never yet shrunk from any burden laid upon him for love, and will not now. And if Madog takes them, they'll be in the best of hands. No one knows the river as he does. And he is to be trusted utterly.'

'For that I take your word,' said Radulfus equably. 'But it is a desperate enterprise for so frail a man. Granted it is his heart's wish, and he has every right to advance it. But how will you get him to the boat? And at the other end, is he sure of his welcome at Salton? Will there be willing attendants there to care for him?'

'Salton is a part of the honour he has relinquished now to a cousin he hardly knows, Father, but tenant and servants there will remember him. We can make a sling chair for him and carry him down to the mill. The infirmary lies close to the wall there, it's no distance to the mill wicket.'

'Very well,' said the abbot. 'It had better be very soon. If you know where to find this Madog, I give you leave, seek him out today, and if he's willing this journey had better be made tomorrow.'

Cadfael thanked him and departed, well pleased on his own account. He was no longer quite as ready as he would once have been to take leave of absence without asking, unless for a life-or-death reason, but he had no objection to making the very most of official leave when it was given. The prospect of a meal with Hugh and Aline in the town, instead of the hushed austerity of the refectory, and then a leisurely hunt along the waterside for Madog or news of him, and a comradely gossip when he was found, had all the attractions of a feast-day. But he looked in again on Humilis before he left the enclave, and told him how he had fared. Fidelis was again in careful attendance at the bedside, withdrawn and unobtrusive as ever.

'Abbot Radulfus grants your wish,' said Cadfael, 'and gives me leave to go and find Madog for you this very day. If he's agreeable, you can go to Salton tomorrow.'

Hugh's house by Saint Mary's church had an enclosed garden behind it, a small central herber with grassed benches round it, and fruit trees to give shade. There Aline Beringar was sitting on the clipped seat sown with close-growing, fragrant herbs, with her son playing beside her. Not two years old until Christmas, Giles stood tall and sturdy and firm on his feet, made on a bigger scale than either his dark, trim father or his slender, fair mother. He had a rich colouring somewhere between the two, light bronze hair and round brown eyes, and a will of steel inherited, perhaps, from both, but not yet disciplined. He was wearing, in this hot summer, nothing at all, and was brown as a hazel-nut from brow to toes.

He had a pair of cut-out wooden knights, garishly painted and strung by two strings through their middles, their feet weighted with little blobs of lead, their legs and sword-arms jointed so that when the cords were tweaked from both ends they flourished their weapons and danced and slashed at each other in a very bloodthirsty manner. Constance, his willing slave, had forsaken him to go and supervise the preparations for dinner, and he clamoured imperiously for his godfather to supply the vacated place. Cadfael kneeled in the turf, only mildly complaining of the creaks in his joints, and manned the cords doughtily. In these arts he was well practised since the birth of Giles. Moreover, he must be careful not to be seen to give his opponent the better of the exchange by design, or there would be a shriek of knightly outrage. The heir and pride of the Beringars knew when he was being condescended to, and wholeheartedly resented it, convinced he was any man's equal. But he was none too pleased when he was defeated, either. It was necessary to walk a mountebank's tightrope to avoid his displeasure.

'You'll be wanting Hugh,' said Aline serenely through her son's squeals of delight, and drew in her feet to give them full play for their strings. 'He'll be home for dinner in a little while. There's venison – they've started the cull.'

'So have a few other law-abiding citizens of the town, I daresay,' said Cadfael, energetically manipulating the cords to make the twin wooden swords flail like windmills.

'One here and there, what does it matter? Hugh knows how long to turn a blind eye. Good meat, and enough of it – and the king with little use for it, as things are! But it may not be long now,' said Aline, and smiled over her needlework, inclining her pale gold head and fair face above her naked son, sprawled on the grass tugging his strings in two plump brown fists. 'His own friends are beginning to work upon Robert of Gloucester, urging him to agree to the exchange. He knows she can do nothing without him. He must give way.'

Cadfael sat back on his heels, letting the cords fall slack. The two wooden warriors fell flat in one embrace, both slain, and Giles tugged indignantly to bring them to life again, and was left to struggle in vain for a while.

'Aline,' said Cadfael earnestly, looking up into her gentle face, 'if ever I should have need of you suddenly, and come to fetch you, or send you word to come – would you come? Wherever it was? And bring whatever I asked you to bring?'

'Short of the sun or the moon,' said Aline, smiling, 'whatever you asked, I would bring, and wherever you wanted me, I would come. Why? What's in your mind? Is it secret?'

'As yet,' said Cadfael ruefully, 'it is. For I'm almost as blind as I must leave you, girl dear, until I see my way, if ever I do.

But indeed, some day soon I might need you.'

The imp Giles, distracted from his game and losing interest in the inexplicable conversation of his elders, hoisted his fallen knights, and went off hopefully after the floating savour of his dinner.

Hugh came hungry and in haste from the castle, and listened to Cadfael's account of developments at the abbey with meditative interest, over the venison Aline brought to the board.

'I remember it was said when they came here – was it you who told me so? It might well be! – that Marescot was born at Salton, and had a hankering to see it again. A pity he's brought so low. It seems this matter of the girl may not be solved for him this side of death. Why should he not have what can best make his going pleasant and endurable? It can cost him nothing but a few hours or days of surely burdensome living. But I wish we could have done better for him over the girl.'

'We may yet,' said Cadfael, 'if God wills. You've had no further word from Nicholas in Winchester?'

'Nothing as yet. And small wonder, in a town and a countryside torn to pieces by fire and war. Hard to find anything among the ashes.'

'And how is it with your prisoner? He has not conveniently remembered anything more from his journey to Winchester?'

Hugh laughed. 'Heriet has the good sense to know where he's safe, and sits very contentedly in his cell, well fed, well housed and well bedded. Solitude is no hardship to him. Question him, and he says again what he has already said, and never falls foul of a detail, either, no matter how you try to trip him. Not all the king's lawyers would get anything more out of him. Besides, I took care to let him know that Cruce has been here twice, thirsty for his blood. It may be necessary to put a guard on his prison to keep Cruce out, but certainly not to keep Heriet in. He sits quietly and bides his time, sure we must loose him at last for want of proof.'

'Do you believe he ever harmed the girl?' said Cadfael.

'Do you?'

'No. But he is the one man who knows what did happen to

her, and if he but knew it, he would be wise to speak, but to you only. No need for any witness besides. Do you think you could bring him to speak, by giving him to understand it was between you two only?'

'No,' said Hugh simply. 'What cause has he to trust me so far, if he has gone three years without trusting any other, and keeps his mouth shut still, even to his own peril? No, I think I know his mettle. He'll continue secret as the grave.'

And indeed, thought Cadfael, there are secrets which should be buried beyond discovery, things, even people, lost beyond finding, for their own sake, for all our sakes.

He took his leave, and went on through the town, and down to the waterside under the western bridge that led out towards Wales, and there was Madog of the Dead Boat working at his usual small enclosure, weaving the rim of a new coracle with intertwined hazel withies, peeled and soaked in the shallows under the bridge. A squat, square, hairy, bandy-legged Welshman of unknown age, though apparently made to last for ever, since no one could remember a time when he had looked any younger, and the turning of the years did not seem to make him look any older. He squinted up at Cadfael from under thick, jutting eyebrows that had turned grey while his hair was still black, and gave leisurely greeting, his brown hands still plaiting at the wands with practised dexterity.

'Well, old friend, you've become almost a stranger this summer. What's the word with you, to bring you here looking for me – for I take it that was your purpose, this side the town? Sit down and be neighbourly for a while.'

Cadfael sat down beside him in the bleached grass, and measured the diminished level of the Severn with a considering eye.

'You'll be saying I never come near but when I want something of you. But indeed we've had a crowded year, what with one thing and another. How do you find working the water now, in this drought? There must be a deal of tricky shallows upstream, after so long without rain.'

'None that I don't know,' said Madog comfortably. 'True, the fishing's profitless, and I wouldn't say you could get a loaded barge up as far as Pool, but I can get where I want to go. Why? Have you work for me? I could do with a day's pay, easy come by.'

'Easy enough, if you can get yourself and two more up as far as Salton. Lightweights both, for the one's skin and bone, and the other young and slender.'

Madog leaned back from his work, interested, and asked simply: 'When?'

'Tomorrow, if nothing prevents.'

'It would be far shorter to ride,' Madog observed, studying his friend with kindling curiosity.

'Too late for one of these ever to ride again. He's a dying man, and wants to see again the place where he was born.'

'Salton?' Shrewd dark eyes blinked through their thick silver brows. 'That should be a de Marisco. We heard you had the last of them in your house.'

'Marescot, they're calling it now. Of the Marsh, Godfrid says it should better have been, his line being Saxon. Yes, the same. His time is not long. He wants to complete the circle of birth to death before he goes.'

'Tell me,' said Madog simply, and listened with still and serene attention as Cadfael told him the nature of his cargo, and all that was required of him.

'Now,' he said, when all was told, 'I'll tell what I think. This weather will not hold much longer, but for all that, it may still tarry a week or so. If your paladin is as set on his pilgrimage as you say, if he's willing to venture whatever comes, then I'll bring my boat into the mill-pool tomorrow after Prime. I'll have something aboard to shelter him if the rain does come. I keep a waxed sheet to cover goods that will as well cover a knight or a brother of the Benedictines at need.'

'Such a cerecloth,' said Brother Cadfael very soberly, 'may be only too fitting for Brother Humilis. And he will not despise it.'

ELEVEN

In the streets of Winchester the stinking, blackened debris of fire was beginning to give place to the timid sparks of new hope, as those who had fled returned to pick over the remnants of their shops and households, and those who had stayed set to work briskly clearing the wreckage and carting timber to rebuild. The merchant classes of England were a tough and resilient breed, after every reverse they came back with fresh vigour, grimly determined upon restoration and willing to retrench until a profit was again possible. Warehouses were swept clear of what was spoiled, and made ready within to receive new merchandise. Shops collected what was still saleable, cleaned out ravaged rooms and set up temporary stalls. Life resumed, with astonishing speed and energy, its accustomed rhythms, with an additional beat in defiance of misfortune. As often as you fell us, said the tradesmen of the town, we will get up again and take up where we left off, and you will tire of it first.

The armies of the queen, secure in possession here and well to westward, as well as through the south-east, went leisurely about their business, consolidating what they held, and secure in the knowledge that they had only to sit still and wait, and King Stephen must now be restored to them. There must have been a few shrewd captains, both English and Flemish, who saw no great reason to rejoice at the exchange of generals, for however vital Stephen might be as a figurehead to be prized and protected at all costs, and however doughty a fighter, he was no match for his valiant wife as a strategist in war. Still, his release was essential. They sat stolidly on their winnings, and waited for the enemy to surrender him, as sooner or later they must. There was a degree of boredom to be endured, while the negotiators parleyed and wrangled. The end was assured.

Nicholas Harnage, with the list of Julian Cruce's valuables in his pouch, went doggedly about the city of Winchester, enquiring wherever such articles might have surfaced, whether stolen, sold or given in reverence. And he had begun with the highest, the Holy Father's representative in England, the Prince-Bishop of Winchester, Henry of Blois, just shaking together his violated dignity and emerging with formidable resolution into the field of discussion, as if he had never changed and rechanged his coat, nor been shut up fast in his own castle in his own city, in peril of his life. It took a deal of persistence to get admission to his lordship's presence, but Nicholas, in his present cause, had persistence enough to force his way through even these prickly defences.

'Do you trouble me with such trifles?' Bishop Henry had demanded, after perusing, with a blackly frowning countenance, the list Nicholas presented to him. 'I know nothing of any such tawdry trinkets. None of these have I ever seen, none belongs to any house of worship known here to me. What is there here to concern me?'

'My lord, there is a lady's life,' said Nicholas, stung. 'She intended what she never achieved, a life of dedication in the abbey of Wherwell. Before ever reaching there she was lost, and what I intend is to find her, if she lives, and avenge her, if she is dead. And only by these, as you say, tawdry trinkets can I hope to trace her.'

'In that,' said the bishop shortly, 'I cannot help you. I tell you certainly, none of these things ever came into the possession of the Old Minster, nor of any church or convent under my supervision. But you may enquire where you will among other houses in this city, and say that I have sanctioned your search. That is all I can do.'

And with that Nicholas had had to be content, and indeed it did give him a considerable authority, should he be questioned as to what right he had in the matter. However eclipsed for a time, Henry of Blois would rise again like the phoenix, as formidable as ever, and the fire that had all but consumed him could be relied upon to scorch whoever dared his enmity afterwards.

From church to church and priest to priest Nicholas carried his list, and found nothing but shaken heads and helplessly knitted brows everywhere, even where there was manifest goodwill towards him. No house of religion surviving in Winchester knew anything of the twin candlesticks, the stone-studded cross or the silver pyx that had been a part of Julian Cruce's dowry. There was no reason to doubt their word, they had no reason to lie, none even to prevaricate.

There remained the streets, the shops of goldsmiths, silversmiths, even the casual market-traders who would buy and sell whatever came to hand. Nicholas began the systematic examination of them all, and in so rich a city, with so wealthy a clientele of lofty churchmen and rich foundations, they were many.

Thus he came, on the morning of this same day when Brother Humilis entreated passage to the place of his birth, into a small, scarred shop in the High Street, close under the shadow of Saint Maurice's church. The frontage had suffered in the fires, and the silversmith had rigged a shuttered opening like a fairground booth, and drawn his work-bench close to it, to have the full daylight on his work. The raised shutter overhead protected his face from glare, but let in the morning shine to the brooch he was handling, and the fine stones he was setting in it. A man in his prime, probably well-fleshed when times were good, but now somewhat shrunken after the privations of the long siege, for his skin hung on him flaccid and greyish, like a too-large coat on a fasting man. He looked up alertly through a forelock of greying hair, and asked if he could serve the gentleman.

'I begin to think it a thin enough chance,' admitted Nicholas ruefully, 'but at least let's make the assay. I am hunting for word, any word, of certain pieces of church plate and ornaments that went astray in these parts three years ago. Do you handle such things?'

'I handle anything of gold or silver. I have made church plate in my time. But three years is a long while. What is so notable about them? Stolen, you think? I deal in no suspect goods. If there's anything dubious about what's offered, I never touch it.'

'There need not have been anything here to deter you. True

139

enough they might have been stolen, but there need be nothing to tell you so. They belonged to no southern church or convent, they were brought from Shropshire, and most likely made in that region, and to a man like you they'd be recognisable as northern work. The crosses might well be old, and Saxon.'

'And what are these items? Read me your list. My memory is not infallible, but I may recall, even after three years.'

Nicholas went through the list slowly, watching for a gleam of recognition. 'A pair of silver candlesticks with tall sconces entwined with vines, with snuffers attached by silver chains, these also decorated with vine-leaves. Two crosses made to match in silver, the larger a standing cross a man's hand in height, on a three-stepped silver pedestal, the other a small replica on a neck-chain for a priest's wear, both ornamented with semi-precious stones, yellow pebble, agate and amethyst . . . .'

'No,' said the silversmith, shaking his head decidedly, 'those I should not have forgotten. Nor the candlesticks, either.'

'. . . a small silver pyx engraved with ferns . . .'

'No. Sir, I recall none of these. If I had still my books I could look back for you. The clerk who kept them for me was always exact, he could find you every item even after years. But they're gone, every record, in the fire. It was all we could do to rescue the best of my stock, the books are all ash.'

The common fate in Winchester this summer, Nicholas thought resignedly. The most meticulous of book-keepers would abandon his records when his life was at risk, and if he had time to take anything but his life with him, he would certainly snatch up the most precious of his goods, and let the parchments go. It seemed hardly worth listing the small personal things which had belonged to Julian, for they would be less memorable. He was hesitating whether to persist when a narrow door opened and let in light from a yard behind the shop, and a woman came in.

When the outer door was closed behind her she vanished again briefly into the dimness of the interior, but once more emerged into light as she approached her husband's bench and the bright sunlight of the street, and leaned forward to set a beaker of ale ready at the silversmith's right hand. She looked up, as she did so, at Nicholas, with candid and composed interest, a good-looking woman some years younger than her husband. Her face was still shadowed by the awning that protected her husband's eyes, but her hand emerged fully into the sun as she laid the cup down, a pale, shapely hand cut off startlingly at the wrist by the black sleeve.

Nicholas stood staring in fascination at that hand, so fixedly that she remained still in wonder, and did not withdraw it from the light. On the little finger, too small, perhaps, to go over the knuckle of any other, was a ring, wider than was common, its edge showing silver, but its surface so closely patterned with coloured enamels that the metal was hidden. The design was of tiny flowers with four spread petals, the florets alternately yellow and blue, spiked between with small green leaves. Nicholas gazed at it in disbelief, as at a miraculous apparition, but it remained clear and unmistakable. There could not be two such. Its value might not be great, but the workmanship and imagination that had created it set it apart from all others.

'I pray your pardon, madam!' he said, stammering as he drew his wits together. 'But that ring . . . May I know where it came from?'

Both husband and wife were looking at him intently now, surprised but not troubled.

'It was come by honestly,' she said, and smiled in mild amusement at his gravity. 'It was brought in for sale some years back, and since I liked it, my husband gave it to me.'

'When was this? Believe me, I have good reasons for asking.'

'It *was* three years back,' said the silversmith readily. 'In the summer, but the date . . . that I can't be sure of now.'

'But *I* can,' said his wife, and laughed. 'And shame on you for forgetting, for it was my birthday, and that was how I wooed the ring out of you. And my birthday, sir, is the twentieth day of August. Three years I've had this pretty thing. The bailiff's wife wanted my husband to copy it for her once, but I wouldn't have it. This must still be the only one of its kind. Primrose and periwinkle . . . such soft colours!' She turned her hand in the sun to admire the glow of the enamels. 'The other pieces that came with it were sold, long ago. But they were not so fine as this.'

141

'There were other pieces that came with it?' demanded Nicholas.

'A necklace of polished pebbles,' said the smith, 'I remember it now. And a silver bracelet chased with tendrils of pease – or it might have been vetch.'

The ring alone would have been enough; these three together were certainty. The three small items of personal jewellery belonging to Julian Cruce had been brought into this shop for sale on the twentieth of August, three years ago. The first clear echo, and its note was wholly sinister.

'Master silversmith,' said Nicholas, 'I had not completed the tale of all I sought. These three things came south, to my certain knowledge, in the keeping of a lady who was bound for Wherwell, but never reached her destination.'

'Do you tell me so?' The smith had paled, and was gazing warily and doubtfully at his visitor. 'I bought the things honestly, I've done nothing amiss, and know nothing, beyond that some fellow, decent enough to all appearance, brought them in here openly for sale . . . .'

'Oh, no, don't mistake me! I don't doubt your good faith, but see, you are the first I have found that even may help me to discover what is become of the lady. Think back, tell me, who was this man who came? What like was he? What age, what style of man? He was not known to you?'

'Never seen before nor since,' said the silversmith, cautiously relieved, but not sure that telling too much might not somehow implicate him in dangerous business. 'A man much of my years, fifty he might be. Ordinary enough, plain in his dress, I took him for what he claimed, a servant sent on an errand.'

The woman did better. She was much interested by this time, and saw no reason to fear involvement, and some sympathetic cause to help, insofar as she could. She had a sharper eye for a man than had her husband, and was disposed to approve of Nicholas and desire his goodwill.

'A solid, square-made man he was,' she said, 'brown as his leather coat. That was not a hot summer like this, his brown was the everlasting kind that would only yellow a little in winter, the kind that comes with living out of doors year-round – forester or huntsman, perhaps. Brown-bearded, brown-haired but for his crown, he was balding. He had a bold, oaken face on him, and a quick eye. I should never have remembered him so well, but that he was the one who brought my ring. But I tell you what, I fancy he remembered me for a good while. He gave me long enough looks before he left the shop.'

She was used to that, being well aware that she was handsome, and it was one more reason why she had recalled the man so well. Good reason, also, for paying close attention to all she had to say of him.

Nicholas swallowed burning bitterness. It was not the fifty years, nor the beard, nor' the bald crown, nor even the weathered hide that identified the man, for Nicholas had never seen Adam Heriet. It was the whole circumstance, possession of the jewellery, the evidence of the date, the fact that the other three had been left in Andover, and in any case Nicholas had seen them for himself, and none of them resembled this description. The fourth man, the devoted servant, the fifty-year-old huntsman and forester, a stout man of his hands, a man Waleran of Meulan would think himself lucky to get . . . yes, every word Nicholas had heard said of Adam Heriet fitted with what this woman had to say of the man who had sold Julian's jewels.

'I did question possession,' said the silversmith, still uneasy, 'seeing they were clearly a lady's property. I asked how he came by them, and why he was offering them for sale. He said he was simply a servant sent on an errand, his business to do as he was told, and he had too much sense to quibble over it, seeing whoever questioned the orders that man gave might find himself short of his ears, or with a back striped like a tabby cat. I could well believe it, there are many such masters. He was quite easy about it, why should I be less so?'

'Why, indeed!' said Nicholas heavily. 'So you bought, and he departed. Did he argue over the price?'

'No, he said his orders were to sell, he was no valuer and was not expected to be. He took what I gave. It was a fair price.'

With room for a fair profit, no doubt, but why not? Silversmiths were not in the business to dole out charity to chance vendors.

'And was that all? He left you so?'

'He was going, when I did call after him, and asked him

143

what was become of the lady who had worn these things, and had she no further use for them, and he turned back in the doorway and looked at me, and said no, for such she had no further use at all, for that this lady who had owned them was dead.'

The hardness of the answer, its cold force, was there in the silversmith's voice as he repeated it. Remembering had brought it back far more vividly than ever he had dreamed, it shook him as he voiced it. Even more fiercely it stabbed at Nicholas, a knife in the heart, driving the breath out of him. It rang so hideously true, and named Adam Heriet almost beyond doubt. She who had owned them was dead. Ornaments were of no further concern to her.

Out of the chill rage that consumed him he heard the woman, roused now and eager, saying: 'No, but that's not all! For it so chanced I followed the man out when he left, but softly, not to be seen too soon.' Had he given her an appraising look, smiled, flashed an admiring eye, to draw her on a string? No, not if he had anything to hide, no, he would rather have slid away unobtrusively, glad to be rid of his winnings for money. No, she was female, curious, and had time on her hands to spare, she went out to see whatever was to be seen. And what was it she saw? 'He slipped along to the left here,' she said, 'and there was another man, a young fellow, pressed close against the wall there, waiting for him. Whether he gave him the money, all of it or some of it, I could not be sure, but something was handed over. And then the older one looked over his shoulder and saw me, and they slipped away very quickly round the corner into the side street by the market, and that was all I saw of them. And more than I was meant to see,' she reflected, herself surprised now that she came to see more in it than was natural.

'You're sure of that?' asked Nicholas intently. 'There was a second with him, a younger man?' For the three innocents from Lai had been left waiting in Andover. If it had not been true, one or other of them, the simpleton surely, would have given the game away at once.

'I am sure. A young fellow, neat enough but homespun, such as you might see hanging around inns or fairs or markets, the best of them hoping for work, and the worst hoping for a chance to get a hand in some other man's pouch.'

Hoping for work or hoping to thieve! Or both, if the work offered took that shape – yes, even to the point of murder.

'What was he like, this second?'

She furrowed her brow and considered, gnawing a lip. She was in strong earnest, searching her memory, which was proving tenacious and long. 'Tallish but not too tall, much the older one's height when they stood together, but half his bulk. I say young because he was slender and fast when he slipped away, and light on his feet. But I never saw his face, he had the capuchon over his head.'

'I did wonder,' said the silversmith defensively. 'But it was done, I'd paid, and I had the goods. There was no more I could do.'

'No. No, there's no blame. You could not know.' Nicholas looked again at the bright ring on the woman's finger. 'Madam, will you let me buy that ring of you? For double what your husband paid for it? Or if you will not, will you let me borrow it of you for a fee, and my promise to return it when I can? To you,' he said earnestly, 'it is dear as a gift, and prized, but I need it.'

She stared back at him wide-eyed and captivated, clasping and turning the ring on her finger. 'Why do you need it? More than I?'

'I need it to confront that man who brought it here, the man who has procured, I do believe, the death of the lady who wore it before you. Put a price on it, and you shall have it.'

She closed her free hand round it defensively, but she was flushed and bright-eyed with excitement, too. She looked at her husband, who had the merchant's calculating, far-off look in his eyes, and was surely about to fix a price that would pay the repairs of his shop for him. She tugged suddenly at the ring, twisted it briskly over her knuckle, and held it out to Nicholas.

'I lend it to you, for no fee. But bring it back to me yourself, when you have done, and tell me how this matter ends. And should you find you are mistaken, and she is still living, and wants her ring, then give it back to her, and pay me for it whatever you think fair.'

The hand she had extended to him with her bounty he caught and kissed. 'Madam, I will! All you bid me, I will! I pledge you my faith!' He had nothing fit to offer her as a return pledge, she had the better of him at all points. Her husband was looking at her indulgently, as one accustomed to the whims of a very handsome wife, and made no demur, at least until the visitor was gone. 'I serve here under FitzRobert,' said Nicholas. 'Should I fail you, or you ever come to suppose that I have so failed you, complain to him, and he will show you justice. But I will not fail you!'

'Are you so ready to say farewell to my gifts?' asked the silversmith, when Nicholas was out of sight. But he sounded amused rather than offended, and had turned back to his close work on the brooch with unperturbed concentration.

'I have not said farewell to it,' she said serenely. 'I trust my judgement. He will be back, and I shall have my ring again.'

'And how if he finds the lady living, and takes you at your word? What then?'

'Why, then,' said his wife, 'I think I may earn enough out of his gratitude to buy myself all the rings I could want. And I know you have the skill to make me a copy of that one, if I so wish. Trust me, whichever way his luck runs – and I wish him better than he expects! – we shall not be the losers.'

Nicholas rode out of Winchester within the hour, in burning haste, by the north gate towards Hyde, passing close by the blackened ground and broken-toothed walls of the ill-fated abbey from which Humilis and Fidelis had fled to Shrewsbury for refuge. These witnesses to tragedy and loss fell behind him unnoticed now. His sights were set far ahead.

The inertia of despair had lasted no longer than the length of the street, and given place to the most implacable fury of rage and vengefulness. Now he had something as good as certain, a small circlet of witness, evidence of the foulest treachery and ingratitude. There could be no doubt whatever that these modest ornaments were the same that Julian had carried with her, no chance could possibly have thrown together for sale three such others. Two witnesses could tell of the disposal of that ill-gotten plunder, one could describe the seller only too well, with even more certainty once she was brought face to face with him, as, by God, she should be before all was done. Moreover, she had seen him meet with his hired assassin in the street, and pay him for his services. There was no possibility of finding the hireling, nameless and faceless as he was, except through the man who had hired him, and such enquiries as Nicholas had set in motion after Adam Heriet had so far failed to trace his present whereabouts. Only one company of Waleran's men remained near Winchester, and Heriet was not with them. But the search should go on until he was found, and when found, he had more now to explain away than a few stolen hours – possession of the lost girl's goods, the disposal of them for money, the sharing of his gains with some furtive unknown. For whatever conceivable purpose, but to pay him for his part in robbery and murder?

Once the principal villain was found, so would his tool be. And the first thing to do now was inform Hugh Beringar, and accelerate the hunt for Adam Heriet in Shropshire as in the south, until he was run to earth at last, and confronted with the ring.

It was barely past noon when Nicholas rode out of the city. By dusk he was near Oxford, secured a remount, and rode on at a steadier and more sparing pace through the night. A hot, sultry night it was, all the more as he went north into the midlands. The sky was clear of cloud, yet without moon or stars, very black. And all about him, in the mid hours of the night, lightnings flared and instantly died again into blackness, conjuring up, for the twinkling of an eye, trees and roofs and distant hills, only to obliterate them again before the eye could truly perceive them. And all in absolute silence, with nowhere any murmur of thunder to break the leaden hush. Forewarnings of the wrath of God, or of his inscrutable mercies.

TWELVE

The morning came bright, veiled and still, the rising sun a disc of copper, the mill pond flat and dull like a pewter dish. The ripples evoked by Madog's oars did no more than heave sluggishly and settle again with an oily heaviness, as he brought his boat in from the river after Prime.

Brother Edmund had fussed and hesitated over the whole enterprise, unhappy at allowing the risk to his patient, but unable to prevent, since the abbot had given his permission. By way of a compromise with his conscience, he saw to it that every possible provision was made for the comfort of Humilis on the journey, but absented himself from the embarkation to busy himself about his other duties. It was Cadfael and Fidelis who carried Humilis in a simple litter out through the wicket in the enclave wall which led directly to the mill, and down to the waterside. For all his long bones, he weighed hardly as much as a half-grown boy. Madog, shorter by head and shoulders, hoisted him bodily in his arms without noticeable effort, and bade Fidelis first take his place on the thwart, so that the sick man could be settled on brychans against the young man's knees, and propped comfortably with pillows. Thus he might travel with as little fatigue as possible. Fidelis drew the thin shoulders gently back to rest against him, the tonsured head, bared to the morning air, pillowed on his knees. The ring of dark hair still showed vigorous and young where all else was enfeebled, drained and old. Only the eyes had kindled to unusual brightness in the excitement of this venture, the fulfilment of a dear wish. After all the great endeavours, all the crossing and recrossing of oceans and continents, all the battles and victories and strivings, adventure at last was a voyage of a few miles up an English river, to revisit a modest manor in a peaceful English shire.

Happiness, thought Cadfael, watching him, consists in small things, not in great. It is the small things we remember, when time and mortality close in, and by small landmarks we may make our way at last humbly into another world.

He drew Madog aside for a moment before he let them go. The two in the boat were already engrossed, the one in the open day, the sky above him, the green and brightness of the land outside the cloister, the other in his beloved charge. Neither was paying attention to anything else.

'Madog,' said Cadfael earnestly, 'if anything untoward should come to your notice — if there should be anything strange, anything to astonish you ... for God's sake say no word to any other, only bring it to me.'

Madog looked sideways at him, blinking knowingly through the thorn-bushes of his brows, and said: 'And you, I suppose, will be no way astonished! I know you! I can see as far into a dark night as most men. If there's anything to tell, you shall be the first, and from me the only one to hear it.'

He clapped Cadfael weightily on the shoulder, slipped loose the mooring rope he had twined about a stooping willow stump, and set foot with a boy's agility on the side of the boat, at once pushing it off from the shore and sliding down to the thwart in one movement. The dull sheen of the water heaved and sank lethargically between boat and bank. Madog took the oars, and pulled the boat round easily into the outflowing current, lax and sleepy in the heat like a human creature, but still alive and in languid motion.

Cadfael stood to watch them go. The morning light, hazy though it was, shone on the faces of the two travellers as the boat swung round, the young face and the older face, the one hovering, solicitous and grave, the other upturned and pallidly smiling for pleasure in his chosen day. Both great-eyed, intent, perhaps even a little intimidated by the enterprise they had undertaken. Then the boat came round, the oars dipped, and it was on Madog's squat, capable figure the eastern light fell.

There was a ferryman called Charon, Cadfael recalled from his few forays into the writings of antiquity, who had the care of souls bound out of this world. He, too, took pay from his passengers, indeed he refused them if they had not their fare.

But he did not provide rugs and pillows and cerecloth for the souls he ferried across to eternity. Nor had he ever cared to seek and salvage the forlorn bodies of those the river took as its prey. Madog of the Dead Boat was the better man.

There is always a degree of coolness on the water, however sultry the air and sunken the level of the stream. On the still, metallic lustre of the Severn there was at least the illusion of a breeze, and a breath from below that seemed to temper the glow from above, and Humilis could just reach a frail arm over the side and dip his fingers in the familiar waters of the river beside which he had been born. Fidelis nursed him anxiously, his hands braced to steady the pillowed head, so that it lay in a chalice of his cupped palms, quite at rest. Later he might seek to withdraw the touch of his hands, flesh against flesh, for the sake of coolness, but as yet there was no need. He hung above the upturned, dreaming face, delicately shifting his hands as Humilis turned his head from side to side, trying to take in and recall both banks as they slid by. Fidelis felt no cramp, no weariness, almost no grief. He had lived so long with one particular grief that it had settled amicably into his being, a welcome and kindly guest. Here in the boat, thus islanded together, he found also an equally profound and poignant joy.

They had circled the whole of the town in their early passage, for the Severn, upstream from the abbey, made a great moat about the walls, turning the town almost into an island, but for the neck of land covered and protected by the castle. Once under Madog's western bridge, that gave passage to the roads into Wales, the meanderings of the river grew tortuous, and turned first one cheek, then the other, to the climbing, copper sun. Here there was ample water still, though below its common summer level, and the few shoals clung inshore, and Madog was familiar with all of them, and rowed strongly and leisurely, conscious of his mastery.

'All this stretch I remember well,' said Humilis, smiling towards the Frankwell shore, as the great bend north of the town brought them back on their westward course. 'This is pure pleasure to me, friend, but I fear it must be hard labour to you.'

'No,' said Madog, taciturn in English, but able to hold his

own, 'no, this water is my living and my life. I go gladly.'

'Even in wintry weather?'

'In all weathers,' said Madog, and glanced up briefly at the sky, which continued a brazen vault, cloudless but hazy.

Beyond the suburb of Frankwell, outside the town walls and the loop of the river, they were between wide stretches of water-meadows, still moist enough to be greener than the grass on high ground, and a little coolness came up from the reedy shores, as though the earth breathed here, that elsewhere seemed to hold its breath. For a while the banks rose on either side, and old, tall trees overhung the water, casting a leaden shade. Heavy willows leaned from the banks, half their roots exposed by the erosion of the soil. Then the ground levelled and opened out again on their right hand, while on the left the bank rose in low, sandy terraces below and a slope of grass above, leading up to hillocks of woodland.

'It is not far now,' said Humilis, his eyes fixed eagerly ahead. 'I remember well. Nothing here is changed.'

He had gathered a degree of strength from his pleasure in this expedition, and his voice was clear and calm, but there were beads of sweat on his brow and lip. Fidelis wiped them away, and leaned over him to give him shade without touching.

'I am a child given a holiday,' said Humilis, smiling. 'It's fitting that I should spend it where I was a child. Life is a circle, Fidelis. We go outward from our source for half our time, leave behind our kin and our familiar places, value far countries and new-made friends. But then at the furthest point we begin the roundabout return, drawing in again towards the place from which we came. When the circle joins, there is nowhere beyond to go in this world, and it's time to depart. There is nothing sad in that. It's right and good.'

He made to raise himself a little in the boat to look ahead, and Fidelis lifted and supported him under the arms. 'Yonder, behind the screen of trees, there is the manor. We're home!'

The soil was reddish and sandy here, and provided a long, narrow beach, beyond which a slope of grass climbed, and a trodden path went up through the trees. Madog ran his boat into the sand, shipped his oars, and stepped ashore to haul the boat firmly aground and moor it.

'Bide quiet here a while, and I'll go and tell them at the house.'

The tenant of Salton was a man of fifty-five, and had not forgotten the boy, nine years or so his junior, who had been born to his lord in this manor, and lived the first few years of his life there. He came himself in haste down to the river, with a pair of servants and an improvised chair to carry Godfrid up to the house. It was not the paladin of the Kingdom of Jerusalem he came hurrying to welcome, but the boy he had taught to fish and swim, and lifted on to his first pony at three years old. The early companionship had not lasted many years, and perhaps he had not given it a thought now for thirty years or more, being busy marrying and raising a family of his own, but the memories were readily reawakened. And in spite of Madog's dry warning, he checked in sharp and shocked dismay at sight of the frail spectre that awaited him in the boat. He was quick to recover and run to offer hand and knee and service, but Humilis had seen.

'You find me much changed, Aelred,' he said, fetching the name out of the well of his memory by instinct when it was needed. 'We are none of us the boys we once were. I have not worn well, but never let that trouble you. I'm well content. And glad, most glad, to see you here again on this same soil where I left you so long ago, and looking in such good heart.'

'My lord Godfrid, you do me great honour,' said Aelred. 'All here is at your service. My wife and my sons will be proud.'

He lifted his guest bodily out of the boat, startled by the light weight, and set him carefully in the sling chair. As a boy of twelve, long ago, son of his lord's steward, he had more than once carried the little boy in his arms. The elder brother, Marescot's heir, had scorned, at ten, to play nursemaid to a mere baby. Now the same arms carried the last wisp of a life, and found it scarcely heavier than the child.

'I am not come to put you to any trouble,' said Humilis, 'but only to sit here a while with you, and hear your news, and see how your fields prosper and your children grow. That will be great pleasure. And this is my good friend and helper, Brother Fidelis, who takes such good care of me that I lack nothing.'

Up the green slope and through the windbreak of trees they carried their burden, and there in the fields of the demesne, small but **well** husbanded, was the manor-house of Salton in its ring fence lined with byres and barns. A low, modest house, no more than a hall and one small chamber over a stone undercroft, and a separate kitchen in the yard. There was a little orchard outside the fence, and a wooden bench in the cool under the apple-trees. There they installed Humilis, with brychans and pillows to ease his sparsely covered bones, and ran busily back and forth in attendance on him with ale, fruit, new-baked bread, every gift they could offer. The wife came, fluttered and shy, dissembling startled pity as well as she could. Two big sons came, the elder about thirty, the younger surely achieved after one or two infant losses, for he was fifteen years younger. The elder son brought a young wife to make her reverence beside him, a dark, elfin girl, already pregnant.

Under the apple-trees Fidelis sat silent in the grass, leaving the bench for host and guest, while Aelred talked with sudden unwonted eloquence of days long past, and recounted all that had happened to him since those times. A quiet, settled, hard-working life, while crusaders roamed the world and came home childless, unfruitful and maimed. And Humilis listened with a faint, contented smile, his own voice used less and less, for he was tiring, and much of the stimulus of excitement was ebbing away. The sun was in the zenith, still a hazed and angry sun, but in the west swags of cloud were gathering and massing.

'Leave us now a little while,' said Humilis, 'for I tire easily, and I would not wear you out, as well. Perhaps I may sleep. Fidelis will watch by me.'

When they were alone he drew breath deep, and was silent a long time, but certainly not sleeping. He reached a lean hand to pluck Fidelis up by the sleeve, and have him sit beside him, in the place Aelred had vacated. A soft, drowsy lowing came to them from the byres, preoccupied as the humming of bees. The bees had had a hectic summer, frenziedly harvesting the flowers that bloomed so lavishly but died so soon. There were three hives at the end of the orchard. There would be honey in store.

'Fidelis . . . .' The voice that had begun to flag and fail him had recovered clarity and calm, only it sounded at a little distance, as though he had already begun to depart. 'My heart, I brought you here to be with you, you only, you of all the world, here where I began. No one but you should hear what I say now. I know you better than I know my own soul. I value you as I value my own soul and my hope of heaven. I love you above any creature on this earth. Oh, hush . . . still!'

The arm on which his hand lay so gently had jerked and stiffened, the mute throat had uttered some small sound like a sob.

'God forbid I should cause you any manner of pain, even by speaking too freely, but time is short. We both know it. And I have things to say while there's time. Fidelis . . . your sweet companionship has been the blessing, the bliss, the joy and comfort of these last years of mine. There is no way I can recompense you but by loving you as you have loved me. And so I do. There can be nothing beyond that. Remember it, when I am gone, and remember that I go exulting, knowing you now as you know me, and loving as you have loved me.'

Beside him Fidelis sat still and mute as stone, but stones do not weep, and Fidelis was weeping, for when Humilis stooped and kissed his cheek he tasted tears.

That was all that passed. And shortly thereafter Madog stood before them, saying practically that there was a possible storm brewing, and they had better either make up their minds to stay where they were, or else get aboard at once and make their way briskly down with what current there was in this slack water, back to Shrewsbury.

The day belonged to Humilis, and so did the decision, and Humilis looked up at the western sky, darkening into an ominous twilight, looked at his companion, who sat like one straining to prolong a dream, remote and passive, and said, smiling, that they should go.

Aelred's sons carried him down to the shore, Aelred lifted him to his place in the bottom of the boat on his bed of rugs, with Fidelis to prop and cherish him. The east was still sullenly bright, they launched towards the light. Behind them the looming clouds multiplied with black and ominous speed, dangling like overfull udders of venomous milk. Under that darkness, Wales had vanished, distance became a matter of three miles or four. Somewhere there to westward there had already been torrential rain. The first turgid impulse of storm-water, creeping insidiously, began to muddy the Severn under them, and push them purposefully downstream.

They were well down the first reach between the water-meadows when the east suddenly darkened, almost instantly, to reflect back the purple-black frown of the west, and suddenly the light died into dimness, and the rumblings of thunder began, coming from the west at speed, like rolls of drums following them, or peals of deep-mouthed hounds on their trail in a hunt by demi-gods. Madog, untroubled but ready, rested on his oars to unfold the waxed cloth he used for covering goods in passage, and spread it over Humilis and across the body of the boat, making a canopy for his head, which Fidelis held over spread hands to prevent it from impeding the sick man's breathing.

Then the rain began, first great, heavy, single drops striking the stretched cloth loud as stones, then the heavens opened and let fall all the drowning accumulation of water of which the bleached earth was creditor, a downpour that set the Severn seething as if it boiled, and spat abrupt fountains of sand and soil from the banks. Fidelis covered his head, and bent to sustain the cover over Humilis. Madog made out into the centre of the stream, for the lightning, though it followed the course of the river, would strike first and most readily at whatever stood tallest along the banks.

Already soaked, he shook off water merrily as a fish, as much at home in it as beside it. He had been out in storms quite as sudden and drastic as this, and furious though it might be, he was assured it would not last very long.

But somewhere far upstream they had received this baptism several hours ago, for flood water was coming down by this time in a great, foul brown wave, sweeping them before it. Madog ran with it, using his oars only to keep his boat well out in midstream. And steadily and viciously the torrent of rain fell, and the rolls and peals and slashes of thunder hounded them down towards Shrewsbury, and the lightnings, hot on the heels of the thunder, flashed and flamed and criss-crossed their path, the only light in a howling darkness. They could barely see either bank except when the lightning flared and

155

vanished, and the blindness after its passing made the succeeding blaze even more blinding.

Wet and streaming as a seal, Fidelis shook off water on either side, and held the cover over Humilis with braced and aching forearms. His eyes were tight-shut against the deluge of the rain, he opened them only by burdened glimpses, peering through the downpour. He did not know where they were, except by flaming visions that forced light through his very eyelids, and caused him to blink the torment away. Such a flare showed him trees leaning, gaunt and sinister, magnified by the lurid light before they were swallowed in the darkness. So they were already past the open water-meadows, surely by now morasses dimpled and pitted with heavy rain. They were being driven fast between the trees, not far now from possible shelter in Frankwell.

In spite of the covering cloth they were awash. Water swirled in the bottom of the boat, cold and sluggish, a discomfort, but not a danger. They ran with the current, fouled and littered with leaves and the debris of branches, muddied and turgid and curling in perverse eddies. But very soon now they could come ashore in Frankwell and take cover in the nearest dwelling, hardly the worse for all this turmoil and violence.

The thunder gathered and shrieked, one ear-bursting bellow. The lightning struck in time with it, a blinding glare. Fidelis opened his drowned eyes in shock at the blow, in time to see the thickest, oldest, most misshapen willow on the left bank leap, split asunder in flame, wrench out half its roots from the slithering, sodden shore, and burst into a tremendous blossom of fire, hurled into midstream over them, and blazing as it fell.

Madog flung himself forward over Humilis in the shell of the boat. Like a bolt from a mangonel the shattered tree crashed down upon the bow of the skiff, smashed through its sides and split it apart like a cracked egg. Trunk and boat and cargo went down deep together into the murky waters. The fire died in an immense hissing. Everything was dark, everything suddenly cold and in motion and heavier than lead, dragging body and soul down among the weed and debris of storm, turning and turning and drifting fast, drawn irresistibly towards the ease and languor of death.

Fidelis fought and kicked his way upward with bursting heart, against the comforting persuasion of despair, the cramping, crippling weight of his habit, and the swirling and battering of drifting branches and tangling weeds. He came to the surface and drew deep breath, clutching at leaves that slid through his fingers, and fastening greedily on a branch that held fast, and supported him with his head above water. Gasping, he shook off water and opened his eyes upon howling darkness. A cage of shattered branches surrounded and held him. Torn but still tenacious roots anchored the willow, heaving and plunging, against the surging current. A brychan from the boat wound itself about his arm like a snake, and almost tore him from his hold. He dragged himself along the branch, peering and straining after any glimpse of a floating hand, a pale face, phantom-like in all that chaotic gloom.

A fold of black cloth coiled past, driven through the threshing leaves. The end of a sleeve surfaced, a pallid hand trailed by and went under again. Fidelis loosed his hold, and launched himself after it, clear of the tree, diving beneath the trammelling branches. The hem of the habit slid through his fingers, but he got a grip on the billowing folds of the cowl, and struck out towards the Frankwell shore to escape the trailing wreckage of the willow. Clinging desperately, he shifted to a better hold, holding the lax body of Humilis above him. Once they went down together. Then Madog was beside them, hoisting the weight of the unconscious body from arms that could not have sustained it longer.

Fidelis drifted for a moment on the edge of acceptance, in an exhaustion which rendered the idea of death perilously attractive. Better by far to let go, abandon struggle, go wherever the current might take him.

And the current took him and stranded him quite gently in the muddied grass of the shore, and laid him face-down beside the body of Brother Humilis, over which Madog of the Dead Boat was labouring all in vain.

The rain slackened suddenly, briefly, the wind, which had the whistle of anguish on its driving breath, subsided for an instant, and the demons of thunder rolled and rumbled away downstream, leaving a breath of utter silence and almost stillness, between frenzies. And piercing through the lull, a great scream of deprivation and loss and grief shrilled aloft over Severn, startling the hunched and silent birds out of the bushes, and echoing down the flood in a long ululation from bank to bank, crying a bereavement beyond remedy.

THIRTEEN

Nicholas was approaching Shrewsbury when the sky began to darken ominously, and he quickened his pace in the hope of reaching shelter in the town before the storm broke. But the first heavy drops fell as he reached the Foregate, and before his eyes the street was emptied of life, all its inhabitants going to ground within their houses, and closing doors and shutters against the rage to come. By the time he rode past the gatehouse of the abbey, abandoning the thought of waiting out the storm there, since he was now so close, the sky had opened, in a downpour so opaque and blinding that he found himself veering from side to side as he crossed the bridge, unable to steer a straight course. It seemed he was the only man left in a depopulated town in an empty world, for there was not another soul stirring.

Under the arch of the town gate he halted to draw breath and clear his eyes, shaking off the weight of the rain. The whole width of Shrewsbury lay between him and the castle, but Hugh's house by Saint Mary's was no great distance, only up the curve of the Wyle and the level street beyond. Hugh was as likely to be there as at the castle. At least he could call in and ask, on his way through to the High Cross, and the descent to the castle gatehouse. He could hardly get wetter than he already was. He set off up the hill. Saner folk peered out through the chinks in their shuttered windows, and watched him scurrying head-down through the deluge. Overhead the thunder rolled and rattled round a sky dark as midnight, and lightnings flickered, drawing the peals ever closer after them. The horse was unhappy but well-trained, and pressed on obedient but quivering with fear.

The gates of Hugh's courtyard stood open, there was a

159

degree of shelter under the lee of the house, and as soon as hooves were heard on the cobbles the hall door opened, and a groom came haring across from the stables to take the horse to cover. Aline stood peering anxiously out into the murky gloom, and beckoned the traveller in.

'Before you drown, sir,' she said, all concern, as Nicholas plunged into the shelter of the doorway and let fall his streaming cloak, to avoid bringing it within. They stood looking earnestly at each other, for the light was too dim for instant recognition. Then she tilted her head, recaptured a memory, and smiled. 'You are Nicholas Harnage! You came here with Hugh, when first you came to Shrewsbury. I remember now. Forgive such a slow welcome back, but I am not used to midnight in the afternoon. Come within, and let me find you some dry clothes – though I fear Hugh's will be a tight fit for you.'

He was warmed by her candour and kindness, but it could not divert him from the black intensity of his purpose here. He looked beyond her, where Constance hovered, clutching her tyrant Giles firmly by the hand, for fear he should mistake the deluge for a new amusement, and dart out into it.

'The lord sheriff is not here? I must see him as soon as may be. I bring grim news.'

'Hugh is at the castle, but he'll come by evening. Can it not wait? At least until this storm blows by. It cannot last long.'

No, he could not wait. He would go on the rest of the way, fair or foul. He thanked her, almost ungraciously in his preoccupation, swung the wet cloak about him again, took back his horse from the groom, and was off again at a trot towards the High Cross. Aline sighed, shrugged, and went in, closing the door on the chaos without. Grim news! What could that mean? Something to do with King Stephen and Robert of Gloucester? Had the attempts at an exchange foundered? Or was it something to do with that young man's personal quest? Aline knew the bare bones of the story, and felt a mild, rueful interest – a girl set free by her affianced husband, a favoured squire sent to tell her so, and too modest or too sensitive to pursue at once the attraction he felt towards her on his own account. Was the girl alive or dead? Better to know, once for all, than to go on tormented by uncertainty. But surely 'grim

160

news' could only mean the worst.

Nicholas reached the High Cross, spectral through the streaming rain, and turned down the slight slope towards the castle, and the broad ramp to the gatehouse. Water lay ankle-deep in the outer ward, draining off far too slowly to keep pace with the flood. A sergeant leaned out from the guard-room, and called the stranger within.

'The lord sheriff? He's in the hall. If you bear round into the inner ward close to the wall you'll escape the worst. I'll have your horse stabled. Or wait a while here in the dry, if you choose, for this can't last for ever . . . .'

But no, he could not wait. The ring burned in his pouch, and the acid bitterness in his mind. He must get his tale at once to the ears of authority, and his teeth into the throat of Adam Heriet. He dared not stop hating, or the remaining grief became more than he could stand. He bore down on Hugh in the huge dark hall with the briefest of greetings and the most abrupt of challenges, an unkempt apparition, his wet brown hair plastered to forehead and temples, and water streaking his face.

'My lord, I'm back from Winchester, with plain proof Julian is dead and her goods made away with long ago. And we must leave all else and turn every man you have here and I can raise in the south, to hunt down Adam Heriet. It was his doing – Heriet and his hired murderer, some footpad paid for his work with the price of Julian's jewellery. Once we lay hands on him, he won't be able to deny it. I have proof, I have witnesses that he said himself she was dead!'

'Come, now!' said Hugh, his eyes rounding. 'That's a large enough claim. You've been a busy man in the south, I see, but so have we here. Come, sit, and let's have the full story. But first, let's have those wet clothes off you, and find you a man who matches, before you catch your death.' He shouted for the servants, and sent them running for towels and coats and hose.

'No matter for me,' protested Nicholas feverishly, catching at his arm. 'What matters is the proof I have, that fits only one man, to my mind, and he going free, and God knows where . . .'

'Ah, but Nicholas, if it's Adam Heriet you're after, then you need fret no longer. Adam Heriet is safe behind a locked door here in the castle, and has been for a matter of days.'

'You have him? You found Heriet? He's taken?' Nicholas drew deep and vengeful breath, and heaved a great sigh.

'We have him, and he'll keep. He has a sister married to a craftsman in Brigge, and was visiting his kin like any honest man. Now he's the sheriff's guest, and stays so until we have the rights of it, so no more sweat for him.'

'And have you got any part of it out of him? What has he said?'

'Nothing to the purpose. Nothing an honest man might not have said in his place.'

'That shall change,' said Nicholas grimly, and allowed himself to notice his own sodden condition for the first time, and to accept the use of the small chamber provided him, and the clothes put at his disposal. But he was half into his tale before he had dried his face and his tousled hair and shrugged his way into dry garments.

'. . . . never a trace anywhere of the church ornaments, which should be the most notable if ever they were marketed. And I was in two minds whether it was worth enquiring further, when the man's wife came in, and I knew the ring she was wearing for Julian's. No, that's to press it too far, I know – say rather I saw that it fitted only too well the description we had of Julian's. You remember? Enamelled all round with flowers in yellow and blue . . . .'

'I have the whole register by heart,' said Hugh drily.

'Then you'll see why I was so sure. I asked where she got it, and she said it was brought into the shop for sale along with two other pieces of jewellery, by a man about fifty years old. Three years back, on the twentieth day of August, for that was the day of her birth, and she asked the ring as a present, and got it from her husband. And the other two pieces, both sold since, they described to me as a necklace of polished stones and a silver bracelet engraved with sprays of vetch or pease. Three such, and all together! They could only be Julian's.'

Hugh nodded emphatic agreement to that. 'And the man?'

'The description the woman gave me fits what little I have been told of Adam Heriet, for till now I have not seen him. Fifty years old, tanned from living outdoor like forester or huntsman . . . You have seen him, you know more. Brown-

162

bearded, she said, and balding, a face of oak . . . Is that in tune?'

'To the letter and the note.'

'And the ring I have. Here, see! I asked it of the woman for this need, and she trusted me with it, though she valued it and would not sell, and I must give it back – when its work is done! Could this be mistaken?'

'It could not. Cruce and all his household will confirm it, but truth, we hardly need them. Is there more?'

'There is! For the jeweller questioned the ownership, seeing these were all a woman's things, and asked if the lady who owned them had no further use for them. And the man said, as for the lady who had owned them, no, she had no further use for them, seeing she was dead!'

'He said so? Thus baldly?'

'He did. Wait, there's more! The woman was a little curious about him, and followed him out of the shop when he left. And she saw him meet with a young fellow who was lurking by the wall outside, and give something over to him – a part of the money or the whole, or so she thought. And when they were aware of her watching, they slipped away round the corner out of sight, very quickly.'

'All this she will testify to?'

'I am sure she will. And a good witness, careful and clear.'

'So it seems,' said Hugh, and shut his fingers decisively over the ring. 'Nicholas, you must take some food and wine now, while this downpour continues – for why should you drown a second time when we have our quarry already in safe hold? But as soon as it stops, you and I will go and confront Master Heriet with this pretty thing, and see if we cannot prise more out of him this time than a child's tale of gaping at the wonders of Winchester.'

Ever since dinner Brother Cadfael had been dividing his time between the mill and the gatehouse, forewarned of possible trouble by the massing of the clouds long before the rain began. When the storm broke he took refuge in the mill, from which vantage-point he could keep an eye on both the pond and its outlet to the brook, and the road from the town, in case

Madog should have found it advisable to land his charges for shelter in Frankwell, rather than completing the long circuit of the town, in which case he would come afoot to report as much.

The mill's busy season was over, it was quiet and dim within, no sound but the monotonous dull drumming of the rain. It was there that Madog found him, a drowned rat of a Madog, alone. He had come by the path outside the abbey enclave, by which the town customers approached with their grain to be milled, rather than enter at the gatehouse. He loomed shadowy against the open doorway, and stood mute, dangling long, helpless arms. No man's strength could fight off the powers of weather and storm and thunder. Even his long endurance had its limits.

'Well?' said Cadfael, chilled with foreboding.

'Not well, but very ill.' Madog came slowly within, and what light there was showed the dour set of his face. 'Anything to astonish me, you said! I have had my fill of astonishment, and I bring it straight to you, as you wished. God knows,' he said, wringing out beard and hair, and shaking rivulets of rain from his shoulders, 'I'm at a loss to know what to do about it. If you had foreknowledge, you may be able to see a way forward – I'm blind!' He drew deep breath, and told it all in words blunt and brief. 'The rain alone would not have troubled us. The lightning struck a tree, heaved it at us as we passed, and split us asunder. The boat's gone piecemeal down the river, where the shreds will fetch up there's no guessing. And those two brothers of yours . . . .'

'*Drowned?*' said Cadfael in a stunned whisper.

'The older one, Marescot, yes . . . Dead, at any rate. I got him out, the young one helping, though him I had to loose, I could not grapple with both. But I could get no breath back into Marescot. There was barely time for him to drown, the shock more likely stopped his heart, frail as he was – the cold, even the noise of the thunder. However it was, he's dead. There's an end. As for the other – what is there I could tell you of the other, that you do not know?' He was searching Cadfael's face with close and wondering attention. 'No, there's no astonishment in it for you, is there? You knew it all before. Now what do we do?'

Cadfael stirred out of his stillness, gnawed a cautious lip, and stared out into the rain. The worst had passed, the sky was growing lighter. Far along the river valley the diminishing rolls of thunder followed the foul brown flood-water downstream.

'Where have you left them?'

'On the far side of Frankwell, not a mile from the bridge, there's a hut on the bank, the fishermen use it. We fetched up close by, and I got them into cover there. We'll need a litter to bring Marescot home, but what of the other?'

'Nothing of the other! The other's gone, drowned, the Severn has taken him. And no alarm, no litter, not yet. Bear with me, Madog, for this is a desperate business, but if we tread carefully now we may come through it unscathed. Go back to them, and wait for me there. I'm coming with you as far as the town, then you go on to the hut, and I'll come to you there as soon as I can. And never a word of this, never to any, for the sake of us all.'

The rain had stopped by the time Cadfael turned in at the gate of Hugh's house. Every roof glistened, every gutter streamed, as the grey remnants of cloud cleared from a sun now bright and benevolent, all its coppery malignancy gone down-river with the storm.

'Hugh is still at the castle,' said Aline, surprised and pleased as she rose to meet him. 'He has a visitor with him there – Nicholas Harnage is come back, he says with grim news, but he did not stay to confide it to me.'

'He? He's back?' Cadfael was momentarily distracted, even alarmed. 'What can he have found, I wonder? And how wide will he have spread it already?' He shook the speculation away from him. 'Well, that makes my business all the more urgent. Girl dear, it's you I want! Had Hugh been here, I would have begged the loan of you of your lord in a proper civil fashion, but as things are . . . I need you for an hour or two. Will you ride with me in a good cause? We'll need horses – one for you to go and return, and one for me to go further still – one of Hugh's big fellows that can carry two at a pinch. Will you be my advocate, and see me back into good odour if I borrow such a horse? Trust me, the need is urgent.'

'Hugh's stables have always been open to you,' said Aline,

'since ever we got to know you. And I'll lend myself for any enterprise you tell me is urgent. How far have we to go?'

'Not far. Over the western bridge and across Frankwell. I must ask the loan of some of your possessions, too,' said Cadfael.

'Tell me what you want, and then you go and saddle the horses – Jehan is there, tell him you have my leave. And you can tell me what all this means and what I'm needed for on the way.'

Adam Heriet looked up sharply and alertly when the door of his prison was opened at an unexpected hour of the early evening. He drew himself together with composure and caution when he saw who entered. He was practised and prepared in all the questions with which he had so far had to contend, but this promised or threatened something new. The bold oaken face the jeweller's wife had so shrewdly observed served him well. He rose civilly in the presence of his betters, but with a formal stiffness and a blank countenance which suggested that he did not feel himself to be in any way inferior. The door closed behind them, though the key was not turned. There was no need, there would be a guard outside.

'Sit, Adam! We have been showing some interest in your movements in Winchester, at the time you know of,' said Hugh mildly. 'Would you care to add anything to what you've already told us? Or to change anything?'

'No, my lord. I have told you what I did and where I went. There is no more to tell.'

'You memory may be faulty. All men are fallible. Can we not remind you, for instance, of a silversmith's shop in the High Street? Where you sold three small things of value – not your property?'

Adam's face remained stonily stoical, but his eyes flickered briefly from one face to the other. 'I never sold anything in Winchester. If anyone says so, they have mistaken me for some other man.'

'You lie!' said Nicholas, flaring. 'Who else would be carrying these very three things? A necklace of polished stones, an engraved silver bracelet – and *this*!'

The ring lay in his open palm, thrust close under Adam's

nose, its enamels shining with a delicate lustre, a small work of art so singular that there could not be a second like it. And he had known the girl from infancy, and must have been familiar with her trinkets long before that journey south. If he denied this, he proclaimed himself a liar, for there were plenty of others who could swear to it.

He did not deny it. He even stared at it with a well-assumed wonder and surprise, and said at once: 'That is Julian's! Where did you get it?'

'From the silversmith's wife. She kept it for her own, and she remembered very well the man who brought it, and painted as good a picture of him as the law will need to put your name to him. Yes, this is Julian's!' said Nicholas, hoarse with passion. 'That is what you did with her goods. *What did you do with her?*'

'I've told you! I parted from her a mile or more from Wherwell, at her orders, and I never saw her again.'

'You lie in your teeth! You destroyed her.'

Hugh laid a hand on the young man's arm, which started and quivered at the touch, like a pointing hound distracted from his aim.

'Adam, you waste your lying, which is worse. Here is a ring you acknowledge for your mistress's property, sold, according to two good witnesses, on the twentieth of August three years ago, in a Winchester shop, by a man whose description fits you better than your own clothes . . .'

'Then it could fit many a man of my age,' protested Adam stoutly. 'What is there singular about me? The woman has not pointed the finger at *me*, she has not seen me . . . .'

'She will, Adam, she will. We can bring her, and her husband, too, to accuse you to your face. As I accuse you,' said Hugh firmly. 'This is too much to be passed off as a children's tale, or a curious chance. We need no better case against you than this ring and those two witnesses provide – for robbery, if not for murder. Yes, murder! How else did you get possession of her jewellery? And if you did not connive at her death, then where is she now? She never reached Wherwell, nor was she expected there, it was quite safe to put her out of the world, her kin here believing her safe in a nunnery, the nunnery undisturbed by her never arriving, for she had given no forewarning. So where is she, Adam? On the earth or under it?'

'I know no more than I've told you,' said Adam, setting his teeth.

'Ah, but you do! You know how much you got from the silversmith – and how much of it you paid over to your hired assassin, outside the shop. Who was he, Adam?' demanded Hugh softly. 'The woman saw you meet him, pay him, slither away round the corner with him when you saw her standing at the door. Who was he?'

'I know nothing of any such man. It was not I who went there, I tell you.' His voice was still firm, but a shade hurried now, and had risen a tone, and he was beginning to sweat.

'The woman has described him, too. A young fellow about twenty, slender, and kept his capuchon over his head. Give him a name, Adam, and it may somewhat lighten your load. If you know a name for him? Where did you find him? In the market? Or was he bespoken well before for the work?'

'I never entered such a shop. If all this happened, it happened to other men, not to me. I was not there.'

'But Julian's possessions were, Adam! That's certain. And brought by someone who much resembled you. When the woman sees you in the flesh, then I may say, brought by *you*. Better to tell us, Adam. Spare yourself a long uncovering, make your confession of your own will, and be done. Spare the silversmith's wife a long journey. For she *will* point the finger, Adam. This, she will say when she sets eyes on you, *this* is the man.'

'I have nothing to confess. I've done no wrong.'

'Why did you choose that particular shop, Adam?'

'I was never in the shop. I had nothing to sell. I was not there . . . .'

'But this ring was, Adam. How did it get there? And with neckless and bracelet, too? Chance? How far can chance stretch?'

'I left her a mile from Wherwell . . . .'

'Dead, Adam?'

'I parted from her living, I swear it!'

'Yet you told the silversmith that the lady who had owned these gems was dead. Why did you so?'

'I told you, it was not I, I was never in the shop.'

'Some other man, was it? A stranger, and yet he had those

168

ornaments, all three, and he resembled you, and he knew and said that the lady was dead. Here are so many miraculous chances, Adam, how do you account for them?'

The prisoner let his head fall back against the wall. His face was grey. 'I never laid hand on her. I loved her!'

'And this is not her ring?'

'It *is* her ring. Anyone at Lai will tell you so.'

'Yes, they will, Adam, they will! They will tell the court so, when your time comes. But only you can tell us how it came into your possession, unless by murder. Who was the man you paid?'

'There was none. I was not there. It was not I . . . .'

The pace had steadily increased, the questions coming thick as arrows and as deadly. Round and round, over and over the same ground, and the man was tiring at last. If he was breakable at all, he must break soon.

They were so intent, and strung so taut, like overtuned instruments, that they all three started violently when there was a knock at the door of the cell, and a sergeant put his head in, visibly agape with sensational news. 'My lord, pardon, but they thought you should know at once . . . There's word in town that a boat sank today in the storm. Two brothers from the abbey drowned in Severn, they're saying, and Madog's boat smashed to flinders by a tree the lightning fetched down. They're searching downstream for one of the pair . . . .'

Hugh was on his feet, aghast. '*Madog*'s boat? That must be the hiring Cadfael told me of . . . Drowned? Are they sure of their tale? Madog never lost man nor cargo till now.'

'My lord, who can argue with lightning? The tree crashed full on them. Someone in Frankwell saw the bolt fall. The lord abbot may not even know of it yet, but they're all in the same story in the town.'

'I'll come!' said Hugh, and swung hurriedly on Nicholas. 'God knows I'm sorry, Nick, if this is true. Brother Humilis — your Godfrid — had a longing to see his birthplace at Salton again, and set out with Madog this morning, or so he intended — he and Fidelis. Come with me! We'd best go find out the truth of it. Pray God they've made much of little, as usual, and they've come by nothing worse than a ducking . . . Madog can outswim most fish. But let's go and make sure.'

Nicholas had risen with him, startled and slow to take it in. 'My lord? And he so sick? Oh, God, he could not live through such a shock. Yes, I'll come . . . I must know!'

And they were away, abandoning their prisoner. The door closed briskly between, and the key turned in the lock. No one had given another look or thought to Adam Heriet, who sank back slowly on his hard bed, and bowed himself into his cupped hands, a demoralised hulk of a man, worn out and emptied at heart. Gradually slow tears began to seep between his braced fingers and fall upon his pillow, but there was no one there to see and wonder, and no one to interpret.

They took horse in haste through the town, through streets astonishingly drying out already in the gentle warmth after the deluge. It was still broad day and late sunlight, and the roofs and walls and roads steamed, so that the horses waded a shallow, frail sea of vapour. They passed by Hugh's house without halting. As well, for they would have found no Aline there to greet them.

People were emerging into the streets again wherever they passed, gathering in twos and threes, heads together and chins earnestly wagging. The word of tragedy had gone round rapidly, once it was whispered. Nor was it any false alarm this time. Out through the eastern gate and crossing the bridge towards the abbey, Hugh and Nicholas drew rein at sight of a small, melancholy procession crossing ahead of them. Four men carried an improvised litter, an outhouse door taken from its hinges in some Frankwell householder's yard, and draped decently with rugs to carry the corpse of one victim, at least, of the storm. One only, for it was a narrow door, and the four bearers handled it as if the weight was light, though the swathed body lay long and large-boned on its bier.

They fell in reverently behind, as many of the townsfolk afoot were also doing, swelling the solemn progress like a funeral cortège. Nicholas stared and strained ahead, measuring the mute and motionless body. So long and yet so light, fallen away into age before age was due, this could be no other but Godfrid Marescot, the maimed and dwindling flesh at last shed by its immaculate spirit. He stared through a mist, trying impatiently to clear his eyes.

'That is this Madog, that man who leads them?'

Hugh nodded silently, yes. No doubt but Madog had recruited friends from the suburb, part Welsh, as he was wholly Welsh, to help him bring the dead man home. He commanded his helpers decorously, dolorously, with great dignity.

'The other one — Fidelis?' wondered Nicholas, recalling the retiring anonymous figure forever shrinking into shadow, yet instant in service. He felt a pang of self-reproach that he grieved so much for Godfrid, and so little for the young man who had made himself a willing slave to Godfrid's nobility.

Hugh shook his head. There was but one here.

They were across the bridge and moving along the approach to the Foregate, between the Gaye on the left hand and the mill and mill-pool on the right, and so to the gatehouse of the abbey. There the bearers turned in to the right with their burden, under the arch, into the great court, where a silent, solemn assembly had massed to wait for them, and there they set down their charge, and stood in silent attendance.

The news had reached the abbey as the brothers came from Vespers. They gathered in a stunned circle, abbot, prior, obedientiaries, monks and novices, brought thus abruptly to the contemplation of mortality. The townspeople who had followed the procession to its destination hovered within the gate, somewhat apart, and gazed in awed silence.

Madog approached the abbot with the Welshman's unservile readiness to accept all men as equals, and told his story simply. Radulfus acknowledged the will of God and the helplessness of man with an absolving motion of his hand, and stood looking down at the swathed body a long moment, before he stooped and drew back the covering from the face.

Humilis in dying had shed all but his proper years. Death could not restore the lost and fallen flesh, but it had relaxed the sharp, gaunt lines, and smoothed away the engraved hollows of pain. Hugh and Nicholas, standing aloof at the corner of the cloister, caught a brief glimpse of Humilis translated, removed into superhuman serenity and repose, before Radulfus lowered the cloth again, blessed the bier and the bearers, and motioned to his obedientiaries to take up the body and carry it into the mortuary chapel.

171

Only then, when Brother Edmund, reminded of old reticences those two lost brothers had shared, and manifestly deprived of Fidelis, looked round for the one other man who was in the intimate secrets of Humilis's broken body, and failed to find him – only then did Hugh realise that Brother Cadfael was the one man missing from this gathering. He, who of all men should have been ready and dutiful in whatever concerned Humilis, to be elsewhere at this moment! The dereliction stuck fast in Hugh's mind, until he made sense of it later. It was, after all, possible that a dead man should have urgent unfinished business elsewhere, even more dear to him than the last devotions paid to his body.

They extended their respects and condolences to Abbot Radulfus, with the promise that search should be made downstream for the body of Brother Fidelis, as long as any hope remained of finding him, and then they rode back at a walking pace into the town, host and guest together. The dusk was closing gently in, the sky clear, bland, innocent of evil, the air suddenly cool and kind. Aline was waiting with the evening meal ready to be served, and welcomed two men returning as graciously as one. And if there was still a horse missing from the stables, Hugh did not linger to discover it, but left the horses to the grooms, and devoted his own attention to Nicholas.

'You must stay with us,' he said over supper, 'until his burial. I'll send word to Cruce, he'll want to pay the last honours to one who once meant to become his brother by law, and he has a right to know how things stand now with Heriet.'

That caused Aline to prick up her ears. 'And how do things stand now with Heriet? So much has happened today, I seem to have missed at least the half of it. Nicholas did say he brought grim news, but even the downpour couldn't delay him long enough to say more. What has happned?'

They told her, between them, all that had passed, from the dogged search in Winchester to the point where news of Madog's disaster had interrupted the questioning of Adam Heriet, and sent them out in consternation to find out the truth of the report. Aline listened with a slight, anxious frown.

'He burst in crying that two brothers from the abbey were

172

dead, drowned in the river? Named names, did he? There in the cell, in front of your prisoner?'

'I think it was I who named names,' said Hugh. 'It came at the right moment for Heriet, I fancy he was nearing the end of his tether. Now he can draw breath for the next bout, though I doubt if it will save him.'

Aline said no more on that score until Nicholas, short of sleep after his long ride and the shocks of this day, took himself off to his bed. When he was gone, she laid by the embroidery on which she had been working, and went and sat down beside Hugh on the cushioned bench beside the empty hearth, and wound a persuasive arm about his neck.

'Hugh, love – there's something you must hear – and Nicholas must *not* hear, not yet, not until all's over and safe and calm. It might be best if he never does hear it, though perhaps he'll divine at least half of it for himself in the end. But *you* we need now.'

'*We*?' said Hugh, not too greatly surprised, and turned to wind an arm comfortably about her waist and draw her closer to his side.

'Cadfael and I. Who else?'

'So I supposed,' said Hugh, sighing and smiling. 'I did wonder at his abandoning the disastrous end of a venture he himself helped to launch.'

'But he did not abandon it, he's about resolving it this moment. And if you should hear someone about the stables, a little later, no need for alarm, it will only be Cadfael bringing back your horse, and you know he can be trusted to see to his horse's comfort before he gives a thought to his own.'

'I foresee a long story,' said Hugh. 'It had better be interesting.' Her fair hair was soft and sweet against his cheek. He turned to touch his lips to hers, very softly and briefly.

'It is. As any matter of life and death must be. You'll see! And since it was blurted out in front of poor Adam Heriet that two brothers have drowned, you ought to pay him a visit as soon as you can, tomorrow, and tell him he need not fret, that things are not always what they seem.'

'Then tell me,' said Hugh, 'what they really are.'

She settled herself warmly into the circle of his arm, and very gravely told him.

The search for the body of Brother Fidelis was pursued diligently from both banks of the river, at every spot where floating debris commonly came ashore, for more than two days, but all that came to light was one of his sandals, torn from his foot by the river and cast up in the sandy shoals near Atcham. Most bodies that went into the Severn were also put ashore by the Severn, sooner or later. This one never would be. Shrewsbury and the world had seen the last of Brother Fidelis.

FOURTEEN

The burial of Brother Humilis brought together in the abbey
guest-hall representatives of all the small nobility of the shire,
and most of the Benedictine foundations within the region.
Sheriff and town provost would certainly attend and so would
many of the elders and merchants of Shrewsbury, more by
reason of the dramatic and tragic nature of the dead man's
departure than for any real knowledge they had had of him in
his short sojourn in the town. Most had never seen him, but
knew his reputation before he took the cowl, and felt that his
birth and death here in their midst gave them some title in
him. It would be a great occasion, befitting an entombment
within the church itself, a rare honour.

Reginald Cruce came down from Lai a day in advance of the
ceremony, malevolently gratified at all that Nicholas had to
report, and taking vengeful pleasure in having the miscreant
who had dared do violence to a member of the Cruce family
securely in prison and tacitly acknowledged as guilty, even if
trial had to await the legal formalities. Hugh did nothing to
cast doubts on his satisfaction.

Reginald held the enamelled ring in a broad palm, and
studied the intricate decoration with interest. 'Yes, I remember it. Strange it should be this small thing that condemns
him. She had another ring, I recall, that she valued, perhaps
all the more because it was given to her as a child, when her
fingers were far too small to retain it. Marescot sent it to her
when the contract of betrothal was concluded, it was old, one
that had been handed down bride to bride in his family. She
used to wear it on a chain round her neck because it was too
big for her fingers. I'm sure she would not leave that behind.'

'This was the only ring listed in the valuables she took with

175

her,' said Nicholas, taking back the little jewel. 'I'm pledged to return it to the silversmith's wife in Winchester.'

'The list was of the things intended for her dowry. The ring Marescot sent her she probably meant to keep. It was gold, a snake with red eyes making two coils about the finger. Very old, the scales were worn smooth. I wonder,' said Reginald, 'where it is now. There are no more Marescots left, not of that branch, to give it to their brides.'

No more Marescots, thought Nicholas, and no more Julians. A double, grievous loss, for which revenge, now that he seemed to have it securely in his hands, was no compensation at all. 'Should you be mistaken, and she is still living,' the silversmith's wife had said, 'and wants her ring, then give it back to her, and pay me for it whatever you think fair.' If I had more gold than king and empress put together, thought Nicholas, nursing the ache he carried within him, it would not be enough to pay for so inexpressible a blessing.

Brother Cadfael had behaved himself extremely modestly and circumspectly these last days, strict to every scruple of the horarium, prompt in every service, trying, he admitted to himself ruefully, to deserve success, and disarm whatever disapproval the heavens might be harbouring against him. The end in view, he was certain, was not only good but vitally necessary, for the sake of the abbey and the church, and the peace of mind of all those whose fate it was to live on now that Humilis was delivered out of the body, and safe for ever. But the means – he was less certain that the means were above reproach. But what can a man do, or a woman either, but use what comes to hand?

He rose early on the funeral day, to have a little time for his private and vehement prayers before Prime. Much depended on this day, he had good reason to be uneasy, and to turn to Saint Winifred for indulgence, pardon and aid. She had forgiven him, before this, for very irregular means towards desirable ends, and shown him humouring kindness when sterner patrons might have frowned.

But this morning she had another petitioner before him. Someone was crouched almost prostrate on the three steps leading up to her altar. The rigid lines of body and limbs, the convulsive knot of the linked hands contorted on the highest step, spoke of a need at least as extreme as his own. Cadfael drew back silently into shadow, and waited, and after what seemed a long and anguished time the petitioner gathered himself stiffly and slowly, like a man crippled, rose from his knees, and slipped away towards the south door into the cloister. It came as a surprise and a wonder that Brother Urien should be tearing out his heart thus alone in the early morning. Cadfael had never paid, perhaps, sufficient attention to Brother Urien. Who did? Who talked with him, who was familiar with him? The man elected himself into solitude.

Cadfael made his prayers. He had done what seemed best, he had had loyal and ingenious helpers, now he could only plump the whole matter confidingly into Saint Winifred's tolerant Welsh arms, remind her he was her distant kin, and leave the rest to her.

In the morning of a mild, clear day, with all due ceremony and every honour, Brother Humilis, Godfrid Marescot, was buried in the transept of the abbey church of Saint Peter and Saint Paul.

Cadfael had been looking in vain for one particular mourner, and had not found her, but having rested his case with the saint he left the church not greatly troubled. And as the brothers emerged into the great court, Abbot Radulfus leading, there she was, neat and competent and comely as ever, waiting near the gatehouse to advance to meet the concourse, like a lone knight venturing undeterred against an army. She had a gift for timing, she had conjured up for herself a great cloud of witnesses. Let the revelation be public and wonderful.

Sister Magdalen, of the Benedictine cell of Godric's Ford, a few miles distant towards the Welsh border, had been both beautiful and worldly in her youth, a baron's mistress by choice, and honest and loyal to her bargain at that. True to her word and bond then, so she was now in her new vocation. If she had brought as escort some of her devoted army of countrymen from the western forests on this occasion, she had discreetly removed them from sight at this moment. She had the field to herself.

A plump, rosy, middle-aged lady, bright-eyed and brisk, the remnant of her beauty wisely tempered by the austere whiteness of her wimple and blackness of her habit into something homely and comfortable, at least until her indomitable dimple plunged dazzlingly in her cheek, like the twinkling dive of a small golden fish, and again smoothed out as rapidly and demurely as the water of a stream resuming its sunny level. Cadfael had known her for a few years now, and had had occasion to rely on her more than once in complex matters. His trust in her was absolute.

She advanced decorously upon the abbot, glanced aside and veered slightly towards Hugh, and succeeded in halting them both, arresting sacred and secular authority together. All the remaining mourners, monks and laymen, flooded out from the church and stood waiting respectfully for the nobility to disperse unimpeded.

'My lords,' said Sister Magdalen, dividing a reverence between church and state, 'I pray your pardon that I come so late, but the recent rains have flooded some parts of the way, and I did not allow enough time for the delays. *Mea culpa!* I shall make my prayers for our brothers in private, and hope to attend the Mass for them here, to make amends for today's failing.'

'Late or early, sister, you have a welcome assured,' said the abbot. 'You should stay a day or two, until the ways are clear again. And certainly you must be my guest at dinner now you are here.'

'You are very gracious, Father,' she said. 'Having failed of my time, I would not have ventured to trouble you now, but that I am the bearer of a letter, to the lord sheriff.' She turned and looked full at Hugh, very gravely. She had the rolled and sealed parchment leaf in her hand. 'I must tell you how this came to Godric's Ford. Mother Mariana regularly receives letters from the prioress of our mother house at Polesworth. In the most recent, which came only yesterday, this other letter was enclosed, from a lady just arrived with a company of other travellers, and now resting after her journey. It is superscribed to the lord sheriff of Shropshire, and sealed with the seal of Polesworth. I brought it with me at this opportunity, seeing it may be important. With your leave, Father, here I deliver it.'

How it was done remained her secret, but she had a way of holding people so that they felt they might miss some prodigy if they went away from her. No one had moved, no one had slipped into casual talk, all the movement there was in the court was of those still making their way out to join the press, and sidling softly round the periphery to find a place where they might see and hear better. There was only the softest rustling of garments and shuffling of feet as Hugh took the scroll. The seal would be immaculate, for it was also the seal of Polesworth's daughter cell at Godric's Ford.

'Have I your leave, Father? It may well be something of importance.'

'By all means, read,' said the abbot.

Hugh broke the seal and unrolled the leaf. He read with brows drawn close in fixed attention. Round the great court men held their breath, or drew it very softly and cautiously. There was tension in the air, after all that had passed.

'Father,' said Hugh, looking up abruptly, 'there is matter here that concerns more than me. Others here have much more to do in this, and deserve and need to know at once what is set down here. It is a marvel! Of such weight, I should have had to issue its purport as a public proclamation. With your leave I'll do so here and now, before all this company.'

There was no need to raise his voice, every ear was strained to attend on every word as he read clearly:

'"My lord Sheriff,
It is come to my ears, to my great dismay, that in my own shire I am rumoured to be dead, robbed and done to death for gain. Wherefore I send in haste this present witness that I am not so wronged, but declare myself alive and well, here arrived into the hospitality of the house of sisters at Polesworth. I repent me that lives and honours may have been put in peril mistakenly on my account, some, perhaps, who have been good friends and servants to me. And I ask pardon if I have been the means of disruption and distress to any, unknown to me but through my silence. There shall be amends made.

'"As to my living heretofore, I confess with all humility that I came to doubt whether I had the nun's true vocation before ever I reached my goal, and therefore I have been living retired and serviceable, but have taken no vows as a nun. At Sopwell Priory by Saint Albans a devout woman may live a life of holiness and service short of the veil, through the charity of Prior Geoffrey. Now, being advised I am sought as one dead, I desire to show myself to all those who know me, that no one may go any longer in grief or peril because of me.

"'I entreat you, my lord, make this known to my good brother and all my kin, and send some trustworthy man to bring me safe to Shrewsbury, and I shall rest your lordship's grateful debtor.

Julian Cruce.'"

Long before he had reached the end there had begun a stirring, a murmur, an eddy that shook its way like a sudden rising wind through the ranks of the listeners, and then a roused humming like bees in swarm, and suddenly Reginald's stunned silence broke in a bellow of wonder, bewilderment and delight all mingled:

'My sister *living*? She's alive! By God, we have been wildly astray . . .'

'Alive!' echoed Nicholas in a dazed whisper. 'Julian is alive . . . alive and well . . .'

The murmur grew to a throbbing chorus of wonder and excitement, and above it the voice of Abbot Radulfus soared exultantly: 'God's mercies are infinite. Out of the shadow of death he demonstrates his miraculous goodness.'

'We have wronged an honest man!' cried Reginald, as vehement in amends as in accusation. 'He was as truly her man as ever he claimed! Now it comes clear to me – all that he sold he sold for her, surely for her! Only those woman's trinkets that were hers in the world – she had the right to what they would fetch . . .'

'I'll bring her from Polesworth myself, along with you,' said Hugh, 'and Adam Heriet shall be hauled out of his prison a free man, and go along with us. Who has a better right?'

The burial of Brother Humilis had become in a moment the resurrection of Julian Cruce, from a mourning into a celebra-

180

tion, from Good Friday to Easter. 'A life taken from us and a life restored,' said Abbot Radulfus, 'is perfect balance, that we may fear neither living nor dying.'

Brother Rhun came from the refectory with his mind full of a strange blend of pleasure and sorrow, and took them with him into the quietness and solitude of the abbey orchards along the Gaye. There would be no one there at this hour of this season if he left the kitchen garden and the fields behind, and went on to the very edge of abbey ground. Beyond, trees came right down to the waterside, overhanging the river. There he halted, and stood gazing downstream, where Fidelis was gone.

The water was still turgid and dark, but the level had subsided slightly, though it still lay in silvery shallows over hollows in the water-meadows on the far shore. Rhun thought of his friend's body being swept down beneath that opaque surface, lost beyond recovery. The morning had seen a woman supposed dead restored to life, and there was gladness in that, but it did not balance the grief he felt over the loss of Fidelis. He missed him with an aching intensity, though he had said no word of his pain to anyone, nor responded when others found the words he could not find to give expression to sorrow.

He crossed the boundary of abbey land, and threaded a way through the belt of trees, to have a view down the next long reach. And there suddenly he stopped and drew back a pace, for someone else was there before him, some creature even more unhappy than himself. Brother Urien sat huddled in the muddy grass among the bushes at the edge of the water, and stared at the rapid eddies as they coiled and sped by. Downstream from here the dull mirrors of water dappling the far meadows had been fed, since the storm, by two nights of gentler rain, and once filled could not drain away, they could only dry up slowly. Their stillness and tranquillity, reflecting back the pale blue of sky and fleeting white of clouds, made the demonic speed of the main stream seem more than a mere aspect of nature, rather a live, malignant force that gulped down men.

Rhun had made no noise in his approach, yet Urien grew aware that he was not alone, and turned a defensive face, hollow-eyed and hostile.

'You, too?' he said dully. 'Why you? It was I destroyed Fidelis.'

'No, you did no such thing!' protested Rhun, and came out of the bushes to stand beside him. 'You must not say or think it.'

'Fool, you know what I did, why deny it? You know it, you did what you could to undo it,' said Urien bleakly. 'I drove, I threatened – I destroyed Fidelis. If I had the courage I would go after him by the same way, but I have not the courage.'

Rhun sat down beside him in the grass, close but not touching him, and earnestly studied the drawn and embittered face. 'You have not slept,' he said gently.

'How should I sleep, knowing what I know? Not slept, no, nor eaten, either, but it takes a long time to die of not eating. A man can go on water alone for many weeks. And I am neither patient nor brave. There's only one way for me, and that is full confession. Oh, not for absolution, no – for retribution. I have been sitting here preparing for it. Soon I will go and get it over.'

'No!' said Rhun, with sudden, fierce authority. 'That you must not do.' He was not entirely clear himself why this was so urgent a matter, but there was something pricking at his mind, some truth deep within him that he could glimpse only by sidelong flashes, out of the corner of his mind's eye. When he turned to pursue it directly, it vanished. Life and death were both mysteries. A life taken from us and a life restored, Abbot Radulfus had said, is perfect balance. A life taken, and a life restored, almost in the same moment . . .

He had it, then. Light opened brilliantly before him, the load on his heart was lifted away. A perfect balance, yes! He sat entranced, so filled and overfilled with enlightenment that all his senses were turned inward to the glow, like cold hands spread blissfully at a bright fire, and he scarcely heard Urien saying savagely: 'That I must and will do. How can I bear this longer alone?'

Rhun stirred and awakened from his trance of bliss. 'You need not be alone,' he said. 'You are not alone now. I am here. Say what you choose to me, but never to any other. Even the confessional might not be secret enough. Then you would indeed have destroyed all that Fidelis was, all that Fidelis did, fouled and muddied it into a byword, a scandal that would cast a shadow on us all, on the Order, most of all on his memory . . . .' He caught himself up there, smiling. 'See how strong is habit! But I do know – I know now what you could tell, and for the sake of Fidelis it must never be told. Surely you see that, as clearly as I now see it. Do no more harm! Bear what you have to bear, and be as silent as Fidelis was.'

Urien's stony face quivered and melted suddenly like wax. He clenched his arms fiercely over his eyes and bowed himself into the long, wet grass, and shook with a terrible storm of dry and silent sobbing. Rhun leaned down and confidently embraced the heaving shoulders. At the touch a great, soft groan passed through Urien's body and ebbed out of him, leaving him limp and still. Once it had been Urien who touched, and Rhun who looked him mildly in the eyes and filled him with rage and shame. Now Rhun touched Urien, laid an arm about him and let it lie quiet there, and all the rage and shame sighed out of him and left him clean.

'Keep the secret. You must, if you loved him.'

'Yes – yes,' said Urien brokenly out of his sheltering arms.

'For his sake . . . .' This time Rhun turned back, smiling, to set right what he had said. 'For her sake!'

'Yes, yes – to the grave. Stay with me!'

'I'm here. When we go, we'll go together. Who knows? Even the harm already done may not be incurable.'

'Can the dead live again?' demanded Urien bitterly.

'If God pleases!' said Rhun, who had his own good reasons for believing in miracles.

Julian Cruce arrived at the abbey of Saint Peter and Saint Paul just in time to attend the Mass for the souls of Brother Humilis and Brother Fidelis, drowned together in the great storm. It was the second day after the burial of Humilis, a fresh, cool day of soft blue sky and soft green earth, the gloss of summer briefly restored. By that time every soul in and around Shrewsbury had heard the story of the woman come back from the dead, and everyone was curious to witness her return. There was a great crowd in the court to watch her ride in, her brother at her side and Hugh Beringar and Adam Heriet following. Within the gates they dismounted, and the horses were led away. Reginald took his sister by the hand, and brought her between the eager watchers to the church door.

Cadfael had had some qualms about this moment, and had taken his stand close beside Nicholas Harnage, where he could pluck at his sleeve in sharp warning should he be startled into some indiscreet utterance. It might have been better to warn him beforehand, and forestall the danger. But on the other hand, it must be gain if the young man never did make the connection, and it seemed worth taking the risk. If he was never forced to consider how formidable a rival was gone before him, and how indelible must be the memory of a devotion unlikely ever to be matched, there would be less of a barrier to his own courtship. If he approached her in innocence he came with strong advantages, having had the trust and affection of Godfrid Marescot, as well as amply proving his concern for the girl herself. There was every ground for kindness there. If he recognised her, and saw in a moment the whole pattern of events, he might be too discouraged ever to approach her at all, for who could follow Humilis and not be diminished? But he might – it was just possible – he might even be large enough to accept all the disadvantages, hold his tongue, and still put his fortune to the test. There was promise in him. Still, Cadfael stood alerted and anxious, his hand hovering at the young man's elbow.

She came through the crowd on her brother's arm, no great beauty, simply a tall girl in a dark cloak and gown, with a grave oval face austerely framed in a white wimple and a dark blue hood. Sister Magdalen and Aline between them had done well by her. The general mourning forbade bright colours, but Aline had carefully avoided providing anything that could recall the rusty monastic black. They were of much the same build, tall and slender, the gown fitted well. The tonsure would take some time to grow out, but hiding the ring of chestnut hair completely and covering half the lofty brow did much to change the shape of the serious face. She had darkened her lashes, which gave a changed value and an iris shade to the clear grey of her eyes. She held up her head and walked slowly past men who had lived side by side with Brother Fidelis for many weeks now, and they saw no one but Julian Cruce, nothing to do with the abbey of Shrewsbury, simply a nine days' wonder from the outer world, interesting now but soon to be forgotten.

Nicholas watched her draw near, and was filled with deep, glowing gratitude, simply that she was alive. Her life might have no place for him, but at least it was hers, all the years he had thought stolen from her by a cruel crime, while here, it seemed, was no crime at all. He could, he would, make the assay, but not yet. Let her have time to know him, for she knew nothing of him yet, and he had no claim on her, unless, perhaps, Hugh Beringar had told her of his part in the search for her. Even that gave him no rights. Those he would have to earn.

But as she drew level with him she turned her head and looked him in the eyes. An instant only, but it was enough.

Cadfael saw him start and quiver, saw him open his lips, perhaps to cry out in the sheer shock of recognition. But he made no sound, after all. Cadfael had gripped him by the arm, but released him at once, for there had been no need. Nicholas turned on him a face of starry brightness, dazzled and dazzling, and said in a rapid whisper: 'Never fret! I am the dumb one now!'

So quick and agile a mind, thought Cadfael approvingly, would not be put off by difficulties. And the girl was still barely twenty-three. They had time. Why should a girl who had had the devoted company of one fine man therefore fail to appreciate the value of a second? I wonder, he thought, what Humilis said to her at Salton that last day? Did he know, in the end, what and who she was? I hope he did. Certainly he knew the candlesticks and the cross, once Hugh described them to him, for of course she took them with her into Hyde, and with Hyde they must have gone to dust. But then, I think, he was in two minds, half afraid his Fidelis had been mixed up in Julian's death, half wondering . . . By the end, however the light came, surely he knew the truth.

In his chosen stall next to Brother Urien, Rhun leaned close to whisper: 'Look! Look at the lady! This is she who should have been wife to Brother Humilis.'

Urien looked, but with listless eyes that saw only what they

185

expected to see. He shook his head.

'You know her,' said Rhun. 'Look again!'

He looked again, and he knew her. The load of guilt and grief and penitence lifted from him like a lark rising. He ceased to sing, for his throat was constricted and his tongue mute. He stood lost between knowledge and wonder, the inheritor of her silence.

Julian emerged from the church into the temperate sunlight with the blankness of wonder, endurance and loss still in her face. Watching her from the shadow of the cloister, Nicholas abandoned all thought of approaching her yet. Now that he understood at last the magnitude of what she had done, it became impossible to offer her an ordinary marriage and a customary love. Not yet, not for a long while yet. But he could bide his time, keep touch with her brother, make his way to her by delicate degrees, open his heart to her only when hers was reconciled and at peace.

She had halted, looking about her, withdrawing her hand from her brother's as if she sought someone to whom recognition was due. The palest of smiles touched her face. She came towards Nicholas with hand extended. About the middle finger the little golden serpent twined in a double coil, he caught the tiny glitter of its ruby eyes.

'Sir,' said Julian, in a voice pitched almost childishly high, but very soft and sweet, 'the lord sheriff has told me of all the pains you have been spending for me. I am sorry I have caused you and others so much needless trouble and care. Thanks are poor recompense for so much kindness.'

Her hand lay firm and cool in his. Her smile was still faint and remote, acknowledging nothing of any other identity but that of Julian Cruce. He might have thought she was denying her other self, but for the clear, straight gaze of her grey eyes, opened wide to admit him into a shared knowledge where words were unnecessary. Nothing need ever be said where everything was known and understood.

'Madam,' said Nicholas, 'to see you here alive and well is all the recompense I need or want.'

'But I hope you will come soon to visit us at Lai,' she said. 'It would be a kindness. I should like to make better amends.'

And that was all. He kissed the hand he held, and she turned and went away from him. And surely this was nothing more than paying a due of gratitude, as she paid all her dues, to the last scruple of pain, devotion and love. But she had asked, and she was not one of those women who ask without meaning. And he would go to Lai, soon, yes, very soon. To make do with the touch of her hand and her pale smile and the undoubted trust she had just placed in him, until it was fair and honourable to hope for more.

They sat in Cadfael's workshop in the herb-garden, in the after-dinner hush, Sister Magdalen, Hugh Beringar and Cadfael together. It was all over, the curious all gone home, the brothers innocent of all ill except the loss of two of their number, and two who had been with them only a short time, and somewhat withdrawn from the common view, at that. They would soon become but very dim figures, to be remembered by name in prayer while their faces faded from memory.

'There could still be some awkward questions asked,' admitted Cadfael, 'if anyone went to the trouble to probe deeper, but now no one ever will. The Order can breathe again. There'll be no scandal, no aspersions cast on either Hyde or Shrewsbury, no legatine muck-raking, no ballad-makers running off dirty rhymes about monks and their women, and hawking them round the markets, no bishops bearing down on us with damning visitations, no carping white monks fulminating about the laxity and lechery of the Benedictines . . . And no foul blight clinging round that poor girl's name and blackening her for life. Thank God!' he concluded fervently.

He had broached one of his best flasks of wine. He felt they deserved it as much as they needed it.

'Adam was in her confidence throughout,' said Hugh. 'It was he who got her the clothes to turn her into a young man, he who cut her hair, and sold for her the few things she considered her own, to pay her lodging until she presented herself at Hyde. When he said she was dead, he spoke in the bitterness of his heart, for she was indeed dead to the world, by her own choice. And when I brought him from Brigge, he was frantic to get news of her, for he'd given her up for lost after

187

Hyde burned, but when I told him there was a second brother come from Hyde with Godfrid, then he was easy, for he knew who the second must be. He would have died rather than betray her. He knew the ugliness of which men are capable, as well as we.'

'And she, I hope and think,' said Cadfael, 'must know the loyalty and devotion of which one man, at least, was capable. She should, seeing it is the mirror of her own. No, there was no other solution possible but for Fidelis to die and vanish without trace, before Julian could come back to life. But I never thought the chance would come as it did . . . .'

'You took it nimbly enough,' said Hugh.

'It was then or never. It would have come out else. Madog would never have said anything, but she had stopped caring when Humilis died.' He had had her in his arms, herself half-dead, on that ride to Godric's Ford to commit her to Sister Magdalen's care, the russet tonsure wet and draggled on his shoulder, the pale, soiled face stricken into ice, the grey eyes wide open, seeing nothing. 'It was as much as we could do to get him out of her arms. Without Aline we should have been lost. I almost feared we might lose the girl as well as the man. But Sister Magdalen is a powerful physician.'

'That letter I composed for her,' said Sister Magdalen, looking back on it with a critical but satisfied eye, 'was the hardest ever I had to write. And not a lie from start to finish! Not one in the whole of it. A little mild deception, but no lies. That was important, you understand. Do you know why she chose to be mute? Well, there is the matter of her voice, of course, a woman's if ever there was. The face – it's a good face, clear and strong and delicate, one that could as well belong to a boy as to a girl, but not the voice. But beyond that,' said Sister Magdalen, 'she had two good reasons for being dumb. First, she was resolute she would never ask anything of him, never make any woman's appeal, for she held he owed her nothing, no privilege, no consideration. What she got of him she had to earn. And second, she was absolute she would never lie to him. Who cannot speak cannot plead or cajole, and cannot lie.'

'So he owed her nothing, and she owed him all,' said Hugh, shaking his head over the unfathomable strangeness of women.

'Ah, but she also had her due,' said Cadfael. 'What she wanted and held to be hers she took, the whole of it, to the end, to the last moment. His company, the care of him, the secrets of his body, as intimate as ever was marriage – his love, far beyond the common claims of marriage. No use any man telling her she was free, when she *knew* she was a wife. I wonder is she free even now.'

'Not yet, but she will be,' Sister Magdalen assured them. 'She has too much courage to give over living. And if that young man who fancies her has courage enough not to give over loving, he may do very well in the end. He starts with a strong advantage, having loved the same idol. Besides,' she added, viewing a future that held a certain promise even for some who felt just now that they had only a past, 'I doubt if that household of her brother's, with a wife in possession, and three children, not to speak of another on the way – no, I doubt if an unwed sister's part in Lai will have much lasting attraction for a woman like Julian Cruce.'

The half-hour of rest after dinner had passed, the brothers stirred again to their work, and so did Cadfael, parting from his friends at the turn of the box hedge. Sister Magdalen and her two stout woodsmen would be off back to Godric's Ford by the westward track, and Hugh was heading thankfully for home. Cadfael passed through the herb-garden into the small plot where he had a couple of apple trees and a pear tree of his own growing, just old enough to crop. He surveyed the scene with deep content. Everything was greening afresh where it had been pale as straw. The Meole Brook had still a few visible shoals, but was no longer a mere sad, sluggish network of rivulets struggling through pebble and sand. September was again September, mellowed and fruitful after the summer heat and drought. Much of the abundant weight of fruit had fallen unplumped by reason of the dryness, but even so there would still be harvest enough for thanksgiving. After every extreme the seasons righted themselves, and won back the half at least of what was lost. So might the seasons of men right themselves, with a little help by way of rain from heaven.

* * *

O God, who hast consecrated the state of Matrimony to such an excellent mystery . . . Look mercifully upon these thy servants.

from 'The form of Solemnization of Matrimony'
in *The Book of Common Prayer*

All Futura Books are available at your bookshop or
newsagent, or can be ordered from the following address:
Futura Books, Cash Sales Department,
P.O. Box 11, Falmouth, Cornwall TR10 9EN.

Please send cheque or postal order (no currency), and
allow 60p for postage and packing for the first book
plus 25p for the second book and 15p for each additional
book ordered up to a maximum charge of £1.90 in U.K.

B.F.P.O. customers please allow 60p for
the first book, 25p for the second book plus 15p per
copy for the next 7 books, thereafter 9p per book.

Overseas customers, including Eire, please allow £1.25
for postage and packing for the first book, 75p for the
second book and 28p for each subsequent title ordered.

Eight and a half centuries have passed since Brother Cadfael walked the streets of Shrewsbury but you can still follow in his footsteps.

The Abbey of Saint Peter and Saint Paul and Shrewsbury Council have joined together to create a series of walks round this ancient town that will allow you, literally, to stand in the steps of Brother Cadfael. You can see the castle, the Meole Brook, St Giles' Church and many other locations that have survived from mediaeval times.

These walks have been created by the Abbey Restoration Project, which is dedicated to the upkeep of the Abbey of Saint Peter and Saint Paul and the excavation and preservation of the monastery ruins.

If you would like further details, or even to make a contribution to the horrendous cost of preservation, please contact:

> Shrewsbury Abbey Restoration Project,
> Project Office,
> 1 Holy Cross Houses,
> Abbey Foregate,
> Shrewsbury SY2 6BS